REFLECTIONS ON MURDER:
Selected Short Stories of Nedra Tyre

Edited and Introduced by Bill Kelly

Stark House Press • Eureka California

REFLECTIONS ON MURDER:
SELECTED SHORT STORIES OF NEDRA TYRE

Published by Stark House Press
1315 H Street
Eureka, CA 95501, USA
griffinskye3@sbcglobal.net
www.starkhousepress.com

ISBN: 979-8-88601-085-5

Text and cover design by Mark Shepard, shepgraphics.com
Cover art by Christian Schad
Proofreading by Bill Kelly

First Stark House Press Edition: May 2024

REFLECTIONS ON MURDER

Sixteen tales of murder, pre-meditated and unplanned, plotted and accidental, crimes of love, crimes of hate… with weapons as innocent as a box of candy, a darkened stairway, a bottle of sleeping pills, a second helping of cake—used to kill with only the best of intentions. These are stories that sympathize with the murderers, providing understanding and justification for their crimes.

As Bill Kelly writes in his introduction, "the stories in this collection display a wide range of styles and situational settings, pathos as well as humor … Nedra Tyre presents a wide range of murderers and would-be murderers (and victims) and portrays them with subtlety and understanding."

Sixteen stories from the pages of *Alfred Hitchcock's* and *Ellery Queen's Mystery Magazines*… guaranteed to shock, startle and amuse.

"I think the greatest prejudice you will find is against the short detective story. And that's a pity. Because the most precious gems in the field are short stories."—Nedra Tyre

Table of Contents

Acknowledgements

Another Turn of the Screw: *Ellery Queen's Mystery Magazine*, December, 1969
Back for a Funeral: *Ellery Queen's Mystery Magazine*, October, 1978
Carnival Day: *Ellery Queen's Mystery Magazine*, July, 1958
The Disappearance of Mrs. Standwick: *Ellery Queen's Mystery Magazine*, July, 1968
Fear: *Alfred Hitchcock's Mystery Magazine*, November, 1977
The Gentle Miss Bluebeard: *Alfred Hitchcock's Mystery Magazine*, November, 1959
Killed By Kindness: *Alfred Hitchcock's Mystery Magazine*, July, 1963
Laughter Before Dying: *Ellery Queen's Mystery Magazine*, May, 1975
The More the Deadlier: *Alfred Hitchcock's Mystery Magazine*, October, 1978
Murder at the Poe Shrine: *Ellery Queen's Mystery Magazine*, September, 1955
Murder Between Friends: *Alfred Hitchcock's Mystery Magazine*, August, 1963
A Murder is Arranged: *Alfred Hitchcock's Mystery Magazine*, March, 1975
A Nice Place to Stay: *Ellery Queen's Mystery Magazine*, June, 1970
Recipe for a Happy Marriage: *Ellery Queen's Mystery Magazine*, March, 1971
Reflections on Murder: *Sleuth Mystery Magazine*, December, 1958
Tour de Couleur: *Ellery Queen's Mystery Magazine*, August, 1956

Murder and the
Ethical Perspective

by Bill Kelly

Many of the sixteen stories in this collection examine the subtleties, nuances and consequences of murder and its effects on the perpetrators of the crimes, as well as on the victims. One story, "The Disappearance of Mrs. Standwick" features no murder in a literal sense, but a loss that leaves the "victim" as devastated as if she had lost a loved one. Murder, of course, from a purely legal or literal perspective is a punishable crime that in the strictest sense, uses the guidelines established by a codified legal process to exact a proscribed punishment. "Justice" is far harder to define due to its subjective nature: its very definition (just = "reasonable") and whether "justice has been served" are in the end, opinions that lie in the eye of the beholder. Therefore, the reasonableness of justice regarding any particular criminal act will vary based on one's viewpoint—most dramatically the concept of justice as seen through the eyes of the criminal vs. the eyes of the victim. Although legal guidelines and "philosophies" of justice wax and wane through time and are of course mutually influential, the conflict between the application of law and the justice of that application remains a constant source of debate and conflict both at an individual and at a societal level. Ethics, by contrast, is a set of principles used to determine the quality of justice in a much broader sense than a set legal dicta. Such terms as "street justice" and "natural justice" exist because people believe the legal system, in passing judgment, may not or cannot consider all the elements that contribute to a proper understanding of the events that contribute to the commission of an offense against society. Several of the stories is this volume explore the right and wrong of events and their outcomes based upon principles more ethical in nature than purely legal.

Nedra Tyre (1912-1990) wrote the stories in this collection over a period of slightly more than twenty years (1955-1978), but I don't believe that the stories in this collection can be labeled as "dated". Indeed, except for obvious background and cultural elements, they could have been written yesterday. Another factor contributing to their universality is that Tyre grinds no axes. Neither characters nor situations are pretexts for promoting specific hot-button social issues or rigid ideologies. The stories contain no underlying or "hidden" contexts. Plot is mostly character driven and most of the good and evil acts and their consequences derive from human nature, an eternal factor not to be ignored. Several of the stories do feature the "ills of society" as perpetrated by established systems, and of course are influential on character behavior, but Tyre maintains her focus on what these characters do in response to the conditions they find themselves in, rather than painting anguished portraits of the hapless, hopeless and helpless being buried by the system and its culture.

Nedra Tyre also wrote six mystery novels and a collection of monologues taken from her social services clients, *Red Wine First* (1947). Stark House press has reprinted four of her mystery novels in two two-fer volumes, both with introductions by Curtis Evans that provide detail on her life and career as a writer.

The story from which this volume takes its title, "Reflections on Murder", opens with the narrator discussing her enthusiasm for the mystery genre. She briefly opines on various sub-genres of the form and reveals that she has compiled a "commonplace book on murder", but more specifically reveals:

> I have wanted to read of the guilt that the murderer feels.

> … not many writers choose the philosophical aspects of murder; with most of them it is simply a matter of crime and punishment or the tracking down of a criminal.

> … what murder would create good?

The narrator has been pursuing an intellectual and ethical analysis of the subject and has focused on "the nice person" murder (the nice person being either victim and/or murderer), contemplating situations where motivations for murder may be far from malevolent and the perpetrator's moral guilt problematic. In the narrator's own life, being a satisfied and successful person, but possessing "neither talents nor gifts and very little competitive spirit", she encounters a situation that brings some of her musings on the topic of murder literally to her doorstep. An apartment dweller, for whom "intimate personal relationships are impossible", she nevertheless engages in a prolonged and tentative feeling-out process with a reticent neighbor whom she eventually befriends. The neighbor very subtly draws her into a conspiracy that will answer some of her questions on the nature of murder, including "Does the victim choose the killer even more than the killer chooses the victim?"

Several stories in this collection are studies of "the sympathetic murderer", a description that is of course a loaded one, as sympathy for a particular person and their plight relies, to a certain extent at least, on the author's skill for both plotting and characterization. The perversion of this concept, of course, is the amoral or "sociopathic" murderer whose sympathies lie only with themselves. Although perhaps ill, these characters are not excused by Tyre, but the depth to which she explores their motivations elevate them above being merely regarded as a mere type.

Tyre's most anthologized story is "A Nice Place to Stay", the sad and often horrifying tale of a young woman unable to settle into a situation for very long that affords her the most basic of life's requirements. This story shows society at its cruelest, but Tyre's portrait of the protagonist shows her to be devoid of self-pity, totally forthcoming regarding her defects and amazingly resilient throughout all her difficulties. She can even be philosophical regarding the poor cards fate has dealt her:

> ... then I got to thinking: well, I didn't steal Mrs. Crowe's box but I had stolen other things and it was the mills of God grinding exceeding fine, as I once heard a preacher say, and I was being made to pay for the transgressions that had caught up with me.

The young woman does however have a breaking point and the tragedy of her fate lies in the extreme nature of the solution to her lifelong problem, this solution being the only path left open that will enable her to fulfill her goal of finding that nice place to stay.

"Killed by Kindness" and "A Murder Is Arranged" both feature spouse pairs with murder on their minds, but the stories vary sharply in perspective.

In "Killed by Kindness", John wants to kill Mary, rather than divorce her:

No, he wasn't going to humiliate her by asking for a divorce. She deserved something better from him than that.

Both Mary and John are being pressured by their respective lovers to end their marriage. Mary feels somewhat sorry for herself blaming her fate on John's insistence on continuing to breathe and maintain a pulse:

> Why couldn't her darling John just drop dead? It would simplify everything.

If she merely leaves him, John would be leading a life of shame and embarrassment:

> Poor, miserable John was what everyone would call him. He'd be better off dead, they'd say.

John, in turn, feels he owes Mary a debt for the qualities she has shown during their twenty-year marriage:

> It seemed a pity that he would have to kill her. But he certainly wasn't going to shame her by telling her he was leaving her; not when they'd just celebrated their twentieth anniversary two months before and had congratulated each other on being the happiest married couple in the whole world.... After all that John couldn't just toss Mary aside. Such a trick would be the action of a cad.

Both of course get their comeuppance in this satiric account of two people whose selfishness is rationalized by them as "kindness".

"A Murder is Arranged" provides a more serious perspective as the John and Mary of this tale have deeply loved each other until John's sudden inexplicable change in his behavior toward Mary forces a showdown. Mary resolves to kill John for what she perceives as a betrayal of his love, but like several other characters in these stories, she wonders just how a respectable person goes about murdering someone. And getting away with it. John has a much different problem; he is terminally ill and would commit suicide, but:

> John might have taken his own life, but that would have been cowardly. It would have been an affront to Mary, who had made him completely happy—the life she had given him was more than happy, it had been blissful. To the world his

suicide would have negated their perfect years together, and it would have placed upon Mary a terrible, unendurable burden of guilt.

How they resolve their respective problems provides an in-depth look at some of the issues considered by the narrator of "Reflections on Murder", but also furnishes an intriguing variation on what could be regarded as an act of love.

Although the narrator of "Reflections on Murder" looks somewhat askance at detective stories, Nedra Tyre does full justice to the sub-genre with three of the stories in this collection: "The Disappearance of Mrs. Standwick", "Tour de Couleur" and "Murder at the Poe Shrine". In addition, a fourth story, "Another Turn of the Screw" is basically a send-up of "amateur detective" stories.

"The Disappearance of Mrs. Standwick" finds Ellen Williams using the techniques she has read about in mystery stories to locate a woman she has met, but who has now disappeared. Williams possesses a rarified sense of duty and obligation, so endures some harrowing experiences in pursuit of uncovering what she believes to be a sinister ending for Mrs. Standwick. In the process, what has started as piqued curiosity becomes an instrument for Williams to become forever bonded to someone who was originally a casual acquaintance. Williams solves the mystery, but experiences something other than the sense of triumph experienced by detectives, amateur or professional, before her.

Miss Wilson is curator of the Poe shrine in Richmond, Virginia, the city where Tyre spent much of her life. "Murder at the Poe Shrine" is a typical classic detective story with an added dimension: Miss Wilson is guided in her investigation by employing the techniques she has studied in Poe's own works. Wilson possesses considerable gifts of her own however, and her "channeling" of Poe is more a centering device when she becomes confused or frustrated. Part of the charm of this story is Wilson coming into her own, her reliance on Poe's principles revealing itself to be a useful tool, but not the sole reason for her success, although in the end, she gives Poe full credit, which is consistent with Tyre's characterization of Miss Wilson. Contributing additional warmth to the story is Lieutenant Williams of the police force, at first skeptical, but quickly respecting Wilson's diligence and deductive acuity. They work together to uncover the murderer, but the core of the story is Wilson's love and respect for the deeply troubled Poe and her devotion and loyalty to the deduction principles created by one of the originators of detective mystery fiction.

Mystical or quasi-mystical elements appear in several of Tyre's stories, but are perhaps most pronounced in "Tour de Couleur", which poses a seemingly absurd question—can color be used as a weapon to commit murder? Intrigued by his studies of the effects of color on human psychology, reporter John Anderson investigates the case of a young woman who the police believe died of natural causes after entering her newly redecorated home. The woman's husband and the interior decorator, present at the time of her death, provoke Anderson's suspicions, as does the home in which she died:

> … he was possessed by a macabre feeling that somehow color had been used beyond the borders of art and in a way that approached diabolism.

Anderson has no proof of a crime so is forced to confront the complexity and likely impossibility of obtaining justice for the woman he believes has been murdered. At this point Tyre makes a clever stylistic choice and rather than offer an unlikely solution to a puzzle than cannot be solved by logical investigation, and eschewing a supernatural solution to the supernatural puzzle posed by Anderson, she offers a straightforward narrative demonstrating how the woman actually died and by doing so answers the question posed by Anderson. Tyre adds to the disorientation element caused by both the situation and its seemingly impossible resolution by structuring the story in five parts with the first part labeled as "Part Four", followed by parts 2, 3, 1 and 5. The numbers indicate the chronological order of events in the story, but by placing the events out of sequence, she causes no confusion for the reader, but rather uses this stylistic choice as a reinforcement of the story's disorientation motif.

With "Another Turn of the Screw", Nedra Tyre uses her social services career as fodder for delivering natural justice to the familiar authoritarian figure using power through position to crush the spirits of the unfortunates held in bondage. Rather than write a bitter comeuppance piece, Tyre turns several mystery fiction conventions on their heads as the object of authority's tyranny refuses to have her spirit crushed and instead triumphs through the application of experience, sharp observational skills and basic logic. The social worker bees, in discussing the likely crushing of an honest conscientious worker, Miss Prentice, by archetype evil boss Mrs. Rugby, see stormy weather ahead as one of the downtrodden intones:

"I have a horrible foreboding that it will all end in blood and violence."

There is blood and violence, but the victims are three residents of a senior home serviced by Mrs. Prentice and slain in baffling fashion. Mrs. Rugby, who has accused Miss Prentice of incompetence, as payback for Miss Prentice having the spine to stand up to her, can only look on as Miss Prentice proceeds to solve the mystery in a whirlwind, but ho-hum fashion to the amazement of all, including the initially skeptical police. The story uses a mock-heroic style throughout and lampoons, among other things, the classic mystery solution where good triumphs over evil and a lone figure of justice puts all to right and collects the reward given by an amazed and grateful society.

Several other stories in this collection use the technique of humor leavening tragedy, but as always, Tyre has a serious theme to develop. The narrator of "Reflections on Murder" regrets the decline of "nice people murders" in contemporary mystery fiction, meaning, at least sometimes, "nice people" who murder. This is of course an appearance-based gloss label, so Tyre explores the rationalizations employed by such people while doing their deeds. "Recipe for a Happy Marriage", "The Gentle Miss Bluebeard" and "Murder Between Friends" all feature protagonists who are viewed by those who know them as beneficent harmless folk, the classic "But he was such a good boy". All the malefactors view their acts as justifiable, logical extensions of dealing with life's inherent injustices. They conduct their mayhem or intended mayhem in matter-of-fact near blissful fashion. But they too must pay the piper.

"Recipe for a Happy Marriage" tells the story of Lucy, serial husband murderer who, through luck and the good fortune to have the town coroner in love with her, has managed to dispose of several spouses, though she seems to bear neither grief nor guilt, but rather is the unfortunate one:

> I had them one at a time, a husband at a time, and perfectly legally. They all just died on me. I couldn't stay the hand of fate. I was always a sod widow—there weren't any grass widows in our family.

A grass widow is an old-fashioned term for a wife or "mistress" abandoned by her lover/husband. But Lucy never needs cheering after one her losses and indeed has trouble remembering the sequence and/or circumstances of their deaths, but in any case she remains undisturbed:

> ... after all the losses I've sustained, I've become philosophical.

> and:

> Poor man [Luther, the only teetotaler she married]. He was run over by a beer truck. ... The irony of it, Mama said. There's a lesson in it for us all.

This story is mostly pure entertainment as Lucy describes what has happened to her "unlucky" spouses, but Lucy will meet her fate, and as befitting a convinced innocent, will meet it in the same blissed-out manner by which she has lived.

"The Gentle Miss Bluebeard" is the story of retiree who has taken up murder as a hobby, out of boredom "to fill the hours", but with the added element of pre-destiny as a motivating factor. Recalling a childhood trauma, she states:

> The name Bluebeard had hurt as it had been meant to hurt, yet she had forgotten it until the time of her first murder. Her talent for murder had been dormant all those years and it might very well have been that the little boy— what was his name?—something simple—she had no head for names—had been gifted with unusual intuition and had divined her true nature.

Motivated by only the highest motives and with great pride for the efficiency and quality of her work, Miss Bluebeard dispatches only those she believes are in need of mercy:

> And so it went, murder only slightly premeditated—one after the other, with no malice, and no such maudlin emotion as regret; murder in these instances seemed required and Miss Beard did not flinch; she felt no sorrow for what she had done and the persons she murdered benefited from her action.

As we know, the idea of mercy killing has long been a hotly debated issue, but in this story I believe, as always, Tyre is exploring not only the psyche of someone who would commit such an act, but also the factors society may contribute to the development of such a person. Miss Bluebeard is not insane and is seemingly a product of various external factors contributing to her warped perceptions; she is always fully conscious of her surroundings and the effects of her acts beyond the murders themselves, e. g. what the police must be thinking and doing—and she worries about getting caught, not that when it happens, she won't be content.

Tyre riffs on the popular evil landlord vs. victim tenants scenario in "Murder Between Friends". Elderly women plotting to dispose of someone is a familiar story in mystery fiction, but as usual Tyre offers a different plot twist and an uncommon moral resolution to the proceedings. Matilda and Mary Sue have had it with the abuse and neglect heaped upon them by their landlord, Mr. Shafer. Notable is the calm calculated reasoning that goes into their day-to-day planning sessions, devising just the right means of disposing of Mr. Shafer and not getting caught doing it. The two have fully bonded and have complete trust in each other's resolve. But they lack a key element to make their plan a success:

> They longed for nerve enough to murder Mr. Shafer, but
> really they couldn't say boo to a goose.

The desired resolution to their Mr. Shafer problem is attained, but the solution results in a punishment of a different sort for Matilda and Mary Sue, as retribution for their bad intentions toward Mr. Shafer leads to a dramatic change in the nature of their friendship.

Both "Fear" and "Back for a Funeral" employ the theme of redemption to examine how characters confront the darker aspects of their natures. "Fear" is a taut suspense thriller (evocative of Poe's work) as we see a woman struggle with an inner demon whose origin she cannot fully account for:

> Fear was a vicious mongrel and she was a small terrified
> animal being tracked by it, about to be snapped in its jaws
> at any moment.

Ellen Anderson believes the crippling fear under which she labors every day is irrational and she fights its dominance of her life, struggling to determine its source: she is recently and happily married, loves her job and her employer and has recently come into a large inheritance. This "I know there is something wrong, but I don't know what it is" story possesses the suspense one would expect from of story of this type, but Tyre supplies an ending that threatens Ellen's triumph over fear: at the point she rejoices the conquering of her demons, it is revealed to her that her fear was not wholly imaginary.

"Back for a Funeral" is the ironic tale of a man, John Whyte, seeking to atone for the long-ago abandonment of his one true love, a betrayal he committed long ago by submitting to the wishes of his parents, who disapproved of his choice. Throughout his life he has quietly mourned:

> Though he had visited Lucy for only a few months while he was a student at the university, the happiness he had known with her had sustained him all his life. Lucy had been the lodestar, the *sine qua non* of his life.

Many years after forsaking his dream, John returns to his hometown and is inexorably drawn to the site of the now deceased Lucy's former home:

> He couldn't even remember the color of Lucy's eyes or of her hair or how tall she was. He could only remember what she had meant to him, the absolute joy of being with her, and he thought again of the outrageous statements made by his parents and uncle.

When John had spoken of his desire to marry Lucy, his mother went as far as saying that Lucy would be the death of him. Although mourning his loss and haunted by his decision throughout his life, John knows that however irrationally motivated, the compulsion drawing him to Lucy's former house must be obeyed. In an ironic Hitchcock-like kicker ending, we learn the final price he is forced to pay for both his sentimental pilgrimage and his long-ago choice of choosing family obedience over love.

"Laughter Before Dying" and "The More the Deadlier" are near-farcical tales of murder, one with a wholly unexpected comeuppance ending and the other forcing the reader to ask—can there be an ending to this madness? It is often not easy to be a murderer in a Nedra Tyre story. The process required to achieve satisfaction may be quite convoluted as we see in "Laughter Before Dying", where poisoned chocolates make the rounds of a circle of friends and acquaintances, only one of whom knows their lethal potential. There is an old expression that says, "Good intentions can be the death of you" and that is certainly true here, as the chocolates are passed from well-wisher to well-wisher, each of whom finds a reason to pass them on to the next recipient, but eventually the chocolates claim a victim. Tyre employs a "tag you're it" type scenario, in which each character gets their own moment on the spot, until an ironically blind justice triumphs at last.

"The More the Deadlier" is also a playful mystery featuring a common type of murderer in these stories, a person who has absolutely no qualms that they are doing the right thing by taking a life. Angelina is married to Parry, but has grown tired of both him and the isolated life they lead in the country.

> This ideal life was suffocating Angelina. Damn fate for getting her into this fix.

She comes to an inevitable conclusion worthy of a sociopathic murderer:

> It was his own fault that she had to murder him.

Angelina lacks experience as a murderer, but her tortured machinations and complex schemes seem to finally bear fruit and she is overjoyed:

> Angelina waited for an appropriate reaction of guilt to overwhelm her, but she had only a sense of freedom and well-being.

Angelina is almost a parody of the self-justifying murderer, and unfortunately for her, Parry does not stay dead and seems to possess the ability to resurrect himself after each "murder." She becomes increasingly frustrated with Parry (a character less and less sympathetic as the story develops), and at one point utters, "What a bother" when confronted by yet another complication to be resolved while hatching yet another murder plot. She exclaims, "Any other man would have died decently and finally the first time." But no quitter is Angelina and she resolves to soldier on. Parry's "resurrections" are the core of the mystery, but much of the suspense is derived from wondering whether Angelina will ever be successful in her quest to do away with her seemingly unkillable husband.

Easily the most poignant story in this collection is "Carnival Day" as it portrays the trauma a child experiences during a broken marriage. Eleven-year-old Betty's parents are separated and she misses her father, who lives apart, but has promised to take her to the yearly carnival, a promise her mother tells her he will probably not keep. He does cancel and Betty resolves to go alone, but before she leaves the father shows up at their home and a row between the parents ensues:

He and her mother were talking now, then shouting; the deadly barrage of their voices was wounding each other. Betty did not matter at such a time, not even on carnival day. She didn't belong to them when they were like that. She was alone.

Betty uses a series of coping mechanisms, including imagining that the "ghost" of her father is accompanying her to the carnival. She has several exciting adventures on her own once there, but the experience is bitter sweet:

> Nothing was the same without her father; she had done all the things they did together. He wasn't there and it would serve him right if she saw things they hadn't seen together.

At one point, Betty encounters a fortuneteller, Dr. Vision, who after attempting the usual ploys and getting little response, asks Betty to look into a crystal ball and tell it what she wants:

> Let everything be like it was, let everything be like it was, let everything be like it was.

She remembers her favorite carnival activity when she was with her father, the merry-go-round. She begins to ride it and then spots her father in the crowd and he joins her. Tyre employs an empathetic touch at the ending of this story as the child is spared the horrific knowledge that the reader possesses regarding the outcome and fate that awaits her.

The stories in this collection, I believe, display a wide range of styles and situational settings, pathos as well as humor, as they all are subtle studies of those who encounter murder or personal loss in or out of the justice system. For the most part, the usual players present in crime fiction—police, private detectives, lawyers, gangsters, judges—are absent or relegated to non-factor roles. Tyre chooses, mainly, to look at "the little people" and more often than not, those in the lower income brackets. This is not surprising based on Tyre's career in social work; these were the people she perhaps knew best and had the most sympathy for. Being "common" of course, has never excluded the desire and will to murder, nor the impulse to seek justice, perhaps for a perfect stranger. Let other writers portray the rich, glamorous and powerful; Tyre is more interested in you and me.

One component of the appeal Tyre's writing holds is her understanding and—when warranted—empathy, for all those involved in an act of murder. The juxtaposition of good and evil in murder mysteries often reveals that those who are murdered are far less deserving of sympathy than the person who has made the world a better place by dispatching them. Such an attitude is abhorrent and, in any case, irrelevant in a legal sense and this unyielding position is supported by those who prefer a strict application of the letter of the law, period. Therefore, the challenge for the author attempting to reach as many people as possible (should this be a goal) is to portray an event as completely as possible using characters who are more than simply victim and perpetrator cutouts. In both these stories and her novels, Nedra Tyre presents a wide range of murderers and would-be murderers (and victims) and portrays them with subtlety and understanding, providing an ethical perspective of events that replaces the cut and dried legal interpretation of murder with a more penetrating and humane vision.

—Mesa, AZ
January, 2024

Bill Kelly has proofread many Stark House releases since 2017 and recently has contributed introductions to several volumes, including the recently released *The Deadly Pay-Off* by William H. Duhart, as well as having edited short story collections by Helen Nielsen and Lorenz Heller. Kelly received a B.A. in English from Columbia University and was a technical writer and illustrator for several corporations. His first exposure to crime fiction was the works of Raymond Chandler, Penguin UK editions, purchased in Singapore.

REFLECTIONS ON MURDER:

Selected Short Stories of Nedra Tyre

Reflections on Murder

Since you are reading this it is not unlikely that murder interests you. It fascinates me, I confess, and although I can no longer trace the origin of my predilection for death in print it may have begun when I first confronted *The Murder of Roger Ackroyd*. Do you remember the first time that detective fiction held you in thrall and that you realized forever after you would follow it down its labyrinthine ways?

How I wish we might sit facing each other, perhaps in front of a fire and over a glass of wine, and talk of murder as literature and figuratively smack our guilty lips over the classics of the genre and stop to disagree or even to spar over preferences.

All addicts of fanatical proportions—and I am one of them—have their heresies and I would parade mine and, even in this curious and arid predicament in which I find myself, welcome your ripostes however prejudiced I might secretly find them. Would this statement shake you? If you share most of the conventional opinions about detective fiction it may, so brace yourself. I have always found *Trent's Last Case* a bore. While I have no taste for Heard's *A Taste for Honey* I do not think that his *The Black Fox* has ever received its due; to me it is one of the unmistakable masterpieces. As for Josephine Tey, I consider her *The Daughter of Time* unsurpassed, but the rest of her work, except for *Miss Pym Disposes*, I find, in spite of critical raves, no better than the good average that is maintained by most mystery writers.

Are you one of the apostates who denigrate *The Moonstone* and say it is no detective story at all? Then may the briars and thorns of Sergeant Cuff's roses prick and scratch you!

In recent years I have deplored the decline of the nice person murder and have grown concerned over the ascendancy of the private eye, but then you may agree with a reviewer with whose opinion I usually concur and always respect who says that the private eye of detective fiction has become the folk hero of our present-day culture. Puzzles have piqued my interest but have not ever satisfied it, so on the whole I do not care for this type of mystery. And instead of police procedure in its minutiae which now floods the field, I have wanted to read of the guilt that the murderer feels. It is his reactions I hunger after rather than his pursuit by detectives.

All of this is opinionated, I admit, and if only you were here to talk with me your exchange might help me to modify my ideas on murder, but I do not think that I would ever alter them to any considerable extent.

I have often wondered over the appeal of fiction dealing with death by violence. A certain school of analysts may be correct in its hypothesis that it is our guilt that is catered to and our sadistic tendencies that are fed and momentarily satiated. I think there may be other reasons. We are all threatened by disaster. Death may approach us at any time—a flight of steps, a street crossing, even the bath is filled with hazard. Illness or ruin may confront us at any moment. This sense of doom can haunt us. Detective fiction, on the other hand, gives us a feeling of peril which has form and shape to it; its peril has cause and effect, it is not the blind, idiotic, unnamed anxiety that stalks us in everyday living. Or something like that.

Yes, I wish someone with a passion like mine for this art form of the detective story could be with me to recite the names that are music and that I can scan as if they were meters of a poem: Collins, Iles, Christie, Sayers, Queen, Chandler, Innes, Crispin, Daly, Poe, Hammett, all these and dozens more.

And—like you, I'm sure—I've often thought after reading a mediocre piece of mystery fiction that I could write one just as good with one or both hands tied behind my back. So I began one, only to find that even the least of them required more than was apparent to the reading eye.

And of course in my unconscious as in everyone's there is down some unlit corridor in some dark and secret room the thought of actual murder; it is undoubtedly a remnant of our childhood, of the megalomania of the infantile mind in which lurks the wish of death for everyone that stands in its way. Perhaps it is a refinement of those early feral impulses that is in a calm contemplation of potential murder and of a dispassionate speculation on such a question as: what murder would create good? The death of what public figure would have the most felicitous result? Or since many of us are not of a political turn, this question can center on the death of which person of our acquaintance would be most fortunate—perhaps a nagging wife, but the more logical of us would counter that no one has to put up with a nagging wife, a man has chosen such a wife out of some valid need for her. Surely a fit object of murder would be a possessive mother who will not release her child to marriage, but a child in his torturous progress toward adulthood must have effected his own release or he could not use the freedom provided by a fortunate murder. What then? Who then? Perhaps a person hopelessly ill suffering the continuous torment of pain. Call it humane or inhumane, as your conscience prescribes, but I have found the thought untenable that a person doomed to invalidism and to constant pain should have an indeterminate stay on this earth.

All these random thoughts and more I jotted down in what I call my commonplace book on murder. It has been a pleasant exercise of the mind to consider and reconsider such reflections, to argue with myself, or to put aside the suspense or detective novel I had in my hand and parry the point of view presented, not that many writers choose the philosophical aspects of murder; with most of them it is simply a matter of crime and punishment or the tracking down of a criminal.

I would like to keep my reflections on murder general, but they must now become specific. I must present myself to you, but I should like to do so without reference to my name or my age or my profession. I may even try to keep my sex out of it, and if I am successful I might make a feeble joke about this being one of the rare modern instances where sex in murder is minimized. Well, to begin: I am, or I was, a reasonably satisfied person, and though I have neither talents nor gifts and very little competitive spirit, I have considerable application and conscientiousness and I have had a fair share of what is called success.

I should mention that my profession requires a great deal of traveling so that I am out of town much of the time. My work is such that I have had few friends. No one can count on me for a fourth at bridge because too often I have to go away unexpectedly, and I have left too many last-minute gaps in seating arrangements to be a welcome dinner guest. Almost two years ago my headquarters were moved to this city and I have not formed anything resembling a friendship, though I am glad to say that my job, which is one of responsibility, presupposes that I can establish immediate rapport with persons of all classes and positions.

The place where I live is for persons of fairly substantial means or at least for those who for one reason or another can afford rather steep rents. In my particular section of the building there are only two apartments, both of identical size, but for a while I knew nothing at all about my neighbor. I had not ever had even an accidental contact, such as being on the elevator at the same time, or happening to answer the door just when he or she entered or left.

This interpolation is necessary: A fondness for flowers is another passion with me, perhaps not so marked as my attachment for detective fiction, but keen and intense. I would like to have a garden but my life being what it is I cannot, and since I am away from my apartment so much of the time even pot flowers are beyond me. For a while I tried to keep them and entrusted their care in my long absences to the elevator boy and the janitor or the assistant superintendent, but I would return only to find the flowers drowned or parched, killed by too much or too little attention. Since I was in no position then to indulge my taste for flowers I was delighted with the remarkable arrangements on a long low table in the hall which I shared with the tenant about whom I had no knowledge. I had thought at first that the flowers were supplied by the management and were a recompense for the high rental we paid and I commented once on their beauty to the elevator operator; he shrugged and told me that she did it, and he pointed to the apartment across from mine.

Talent and care and thought invariably went into the arrangements; sometimes they were pot flowers, sometimes they were leaves, and very often they were cut flowers and these were not allowed to stay beyond their first beauty.

Shortly before Christmas there appeared an especially attractive display; this consisted of one of those interesting wooden figures, a primitive carving, Mexican I believe, some two feet high, painted in rich dark colors, and beside it there was a huge brass container filled with cedar boughs. My description is shamefully inadequate and does not in any way suggest the taste and artistry that went into the piece.

At Christmas time I count my blessings and my obligations, and I thought how during the four months I had so far lived in the apartment house the flowers had been a constant joy to me, and I did not know at all how to show my appreciation of them. I realized that it was not usual for people living on the same floor to make calls on a newcomer, or even necessarily to know when there was a newcomer, but I felt that if any advance were made it should issue from the person already there when a new tenant arrived. So it appeared obvious to me that whoever lived across the hall wanted to be left alone. Still I was most eager to show my gratitude. At last I thought that a gift of a bottle of wine at the door might be acceptable, but then I had misgivings that the tenant might be abstemious, in which case she would resent my offering. Then I decided on brandy instead of wine and that I would write a brief ambiguous greeting that the brandy might be used for cooking or fruit, so that my neighbor if a teetotaler would not think I was plying her with spirits. Somehow this idea confused me even more and I decided that I would do nothing, that however much I enjoyed the flowers they were of the tenant's doing and had no connection with me. But again I felt like an ingrate not to do something, especially just after I entered or left the hall and my eyes were delighted by the centerpiece; so my dilemma grew more painful.

Here I am reliving my uncertainty on that first Christmas, and it is well that I do because if I had done nothing I might not now have occasion to make some of these reflections on murder.

It was sherry that I settled on after all, an expensive cream sherry. Around the bottle's neck I attached a ribbon and a note. My note was not overly cordial and I purposely said nothing about wishing to thank personally the one who was so generous with her flowers. I remember the message as rather warm but on the whole formal.

On Christmas Eve I placed the wine at the door.

Days went by and there was no acknowledgement at all; not that I wanted or even expected one; I simply hoped the recipient understood my gratitude.

The winter days passed pleasantly, my job was demanding but most rewarding and at night I indulged myself in my usual delight of reading detective fiction. Occasionally I would stop reading and write an observation or so in my commonplace book on murder. I do not now remember the title of the book which I put aside for an instant to write: *The Murder of An Absolute Stranger. Would not the true connoisseur of murder take the most satisfaction in causing the death of someone he did not know, with whom he had no ties at all? No one could ever assign the murder to him, and because he was in no way connected with his victim he could not know great remorse. Is this perhaps what happens in war? Men who kill in war cannot feel guilt for the unknown persons who are their victims.*

So the months went on and I was satisfied; my job gave me pleasure and my reading of murder and speculations about the subject made as happy a life as one could ever expect when intimate personal relationships are impossible.

The exquisite flower arrangements continued.

There is only one flower to which I am allergic, or rather I should say which I dislike. The lily. It is beautiful but its odor is pervasive and obnoxious to me and I do not care for it. For that reason I was somehow dreading Easter and what might appear in the hall; but when Easter came there was one gigantic pot of white hyacinths in a white wrapping and around it clustered a number of small pots of white and pink and blue hyacinths. My sense of beauty was so satisfied and captivated that again I wanted to do something to show appreciation and once more, but this time with no note of any kind, I set a bottle of sherry at the door.

Again there was no acknowledgment and I wanted none; so spring left and summer came and went and fall blustered in with that suddenness that eternally confounds me.

It was the first of October and I remember being grateful that the heat had been turned on. I did not plan to read that night but intended to devote some time to my fall clothes—pulling them out of mothproof bags, deciding what was usable and what had to be discarded, for no matter how satisfactory clothes may look when they are put away they somehow acquire a shabbiness.

I had just ripped a dangling button from a jacket when I heard a frantic knock at the door. I was expecting no one and in my lonely existence I had few callers. I was somewhat disheveled from working with my clothes, but the knock was so doom-laden that I did not take the time to tidy myself.

A woman stood at my door. I knew at once that she was my neighbor. She was in a dressing gown, there was true elegance about her; the gown was black satin, her hair was white and beautifully kept, and her eyes were the only violet ones I have ever seen; her face wore a mask of concern and though it was distorted by worry and consternation I saw that age had only increased its beauty. Voices are apt to be affected by tension and when she spoke hers was, but even in that high, unnatural range her voice had a resonance of remarkable loveliness.

In my early days in statistics and research when I made door to door canvasses I was confronted by extraordinarily varied receptions, and I have found that however inwardly I may be concerned or even shocked I can maintain a certain external complacency. I was shocked by her appearance on my threshold and concerned by her obvious distress.

"Good evening," I said. "Won't you come in?"

There was a wariness about her, she took a step forward but stopped as if she could not pass beneath the lintel and I thought fleetingly of witches who cannot cross water or passages that have nails embedded in them.

She turned and went to her own door and then she said: "If you will, please come in here."

I followed her across the hall into a place of matchless taste. My eyes did not have time to particularize the furnishings, I only knew that I was in one of the most gracious series of rooms I had ever entered. She motioned to me to sit beside her on a small sofa upholstered in deep green velvet and I glanced at a Manet and a Berthe Morisot before I concentrated on the woman who was my hostess.

"I've a most unusual request to make of you," she said. "I've no one else to appeal to. You've been so understanding. I couldn't have asked for a more considerate neighbor."

This is what she wanted of me, and she instructed me in deadly earnest. At nine-fifteen I was to ring her doorbell, there would be guests with her, I was to act ill at ease as if I hadn't known she had company, she would insist that I come in and I would agree after some hesitation. I was to mention casually a few times that she had dined with me and refer to several games of bridge she had played with me and some other friends, and I was to leave with the reminder that she had promised to play cards in my apartment on the following Friday and she was not to disappoint me as I was inviting two dear friends who wanted most especially to meet her.

She made no explanation of her request and gave no reason for the need for such fabrications on my part. There was a shyness about her and an absolute goodness. I knew intuitively that my lies would be for an innocent purpose.

It was then eight-thirty. I had a brief rehearsal which quite satisfied her and then I went back to my apartment. I sat down at my commonplace book and I wrote easily and without thought as if it were automatic writing: *Does the victim choose the killer even more than the killer chooses the victim?* I found my question so provocative that I thought of it until nine-fifteen.

When I rang her bell I heard her voice cry out to me to enter. Three persons were present beside herself. I could tell that a conversation of extreme urgency had been interrupted and it took very little acting on my part to offer apologies and try to withdraw, but she insisted that I join them. I was somehow flattered to see that the sherry I had given her was on the table in front of her though I would have thought with the lovely decanter on the sideboard she would have emptied the wine into it; no matter, I began my speech about the dinners and the hands of bridge; she had assigned names to some of the persons supposedly my guests and she said wasn't Charles wonderfully witty and that Frank was a superb bridge player; she thanked me for my kindness in sending her more of the sherry that I knew she liked so well and wouldn't I have a glass; I declined with some reference to claret being the only wine I enjoyed, and then I mentioned the forthcoming bridge game and made my adieux. I was so intent on our dialogue that I did not pay much attention to the other persons there, but it seemed to me that there was a resemblance, not necessarily of the nature of close relatives, but perhaps of cousins; she might even have been the aunt of the two younger men. Their interest in our brief conversation was what I can only term profound and intense.

Since we had been conspirators I thought that when her guests left she might sneak across the hall to smile over our performance and to explain the reason for it, but nothing of the sort happened. Anyway, I hoped the charade in which we acted out a history of social contact was convincing. I did not speculate to any extent as to its purpose. Long since I have taken as a tenet for my conduct this quotation from Henry James: *Remember that every life is a special problem which is not yours but another's, and content yourself with the terrible algebra of your own.* I had no intention whatever of probing or delving into the woman's affairs.

Again time passed and the flowers in their beauty and their variety continued to appear, but there was no word from the tenant across the hall.

Another spring had almost progressed into summer when there was another knock on my door. It was she; this time she wore a blue robe and this time there was nothing at all distressful about her appearance; the third time I saw her I realized that she had beauty of remarkable proportions and not even youth had been kinder to her looks than age was, not that I could judge her age, she might have been in her middle forties, she could even have been sixty, and though she smiled I sensed a sadness and a wistfulness about her.

"I didn't think it would work," she said, "but it has. All these months. My dear, I have no right to drag you into matters that don't concern you. Those people whom you saw are my relatives. I feel no real affection for them—nothing but the goodwill I try to feel toward all human beings. But they were trying to manipulate me. Their behavior was monstrous. I can't give you the details of my life—I've been fortunate in many ways and unfortunate in others. I came to mistrust people, to mistrust the world, and all I want is to be let alone, to stay by myself in quietness. But they insisted that I move out in the world. They even wanted me to come live with them. They said my withdrawal was a sign of a breakdown. I thought if they couldn't understand my point of view, then—well, our little hoax—if they could be made to think that I did go out occasionally and that I had friends. I can't thank you enough for what you did. I can't tell you how grateful I am. If I'm made to leave here for any reason, I'll die or I'll go into a madness that is worse than death."

Though I found her words melodramatic she spoke quietly. She made no further elaborations and I did not ask any questions; I only know that her thank you to me when she left my living room was the most genuine statement ever directed to me.

Then some weeks later there was the morning when the flowers looked rather wilted and that had not ever happened in our corridor; she did not allow the slightest taint of wilt to touch them, they were removed at the very peak of their beauty. The next day the crisp brownness of death had laid its blight on the flowers and withered petals were strewn on the table. That evening when I returned late from dinner the dead flowers were a desecration to the time of their loveliness and I removed them.

I was concerned over my neighbor but I did not venture to make an inquiry; I remembered her desperate need to be left alone, or I thought that perhaps the dead flowers had left their own message and she had finally been persuaded by her relatives to move in with them. The hall table remained bare and I grew nostalgic for its former beauty.

One night after a particularly trying day at the office I took too long over my after-dinner coffee and I was startled to see that I had only moments to pack and to get a plane. I was frantically jerking clothes from the closet and out of drawers when someone knocked on my door.

A woman in a nurse's uniform stood there. I saw that beyond the frame of my door in which she stood the door across the hall had swung open. Even as the nurse spoke she was pulling on a coat. "I must go," she said. "My husband is downstairs waiting for me. The other nurse is late. My patient said perhaps you wouldn't mind coming in for a moment. She belongs in a hospital, and no matter how she objects they're going to put her in one tomorrow."

I did not protest my own lateness for the plane, but went at once to the apartment.

My neighbor looked small on the tremendous tester bed; she was ravaged, it seemed to me, not so much by illness as by hopelessness, and beauty that had stayed with her so long was still faithful, it had not deserted her even in this nadir of despair. I looked at her as through bars of a cage, she was of a particular and rare loveliness and deserved nothing so little as the trap in which she obviously found herself, she could exist only in an atmosphere of her own choosing, she could not survive removal from this beautiful retreat. I have wished for many things in my life but I know they were idle wishes with no real intent behind them in comparison with the passionate desire I then had to do something to relieve her suffering and her predicament. We looked at each other and I do not know what there was in the stare that we exchanged, we had lived as neighbors for almost two years in that house and we had seen each other only three times before and those times were moments only, but in those moments she had revealed herself and she had fathomed my nature.

"In the living room, in the top drawer," she said to me in her exquisite voice. I went where her lovely, pathetic gesture indicated. Various objects were there in the secretary but I had not the slightest hesitation when I saw the box. There was no need for words. I knew what she wanted. I knew what she meant. I did not need to read the label or the dosage or the warning. Neither of us faltered as I helped her to a sitting position and handed her the box and a glass of water. Yes, I knew very well what I had done, what we had done together, and then she said: "Please go. I feel I can rest now. I am forever grateful to you."

I saw then that only four minutes had passed since the nurse had summoned me and if I hurried and if I were lucky I could still get my plane. I snatched my suitcase and buzzed continuously for the elevator and shouted down the shaft for service, something I had not ever done before, and I begged the operator to hurry when he made his casual appearance. He later testified as to my hysteria, my frantic and distressed air as I tried to escape from the terrible deed of murder.

We want to question you about the circumstances surrounding the death of so-and-so, and you should be warned that anything you say may be taken down as evidence against you. I had read those words a hundred times in detective fiction; I did not know their import until the police in the city where I had flown on the business trip told me that the authorities in the town where I lived wanted to question me in connection with the death of Miss Teresa Covington, and they did not believe me when I said I was not acquainted with any person by that name; you see we had not introduced ourselves, there was no nameplate at her door, and since there was a desk at which we received our mail I had not even seen her name on a box.

The police had found my commonplace book on murder before I returned, they were interested in my various observations, and when I protested that I had not known the dead woman long enough or intimately enough to kill her they produced my speculations about the perfect murder, the murder that could not be solved, that of a stranger. But my protestation that I did not know her well was contradicted by the relatives who testified against me; they had seen me in her apartment and we had exchanged conversation which confirmed many meetings. They described me as fawning, ingratiating. But even now I think that nothing would have come of it if Miss Covington had not left me a small fortune, at least it was a fortune in my estimation. It was not that she disinherited her relatives in my favor, they received handsome bequests, as did many charitable organizations, but a legacy of fifty thousand dollars was enough to convince the most lenient jury that I had motive and to spare for murder.

Yes, yes, yes, I was the instrument of her death. I admit it, as I later admitted in testimony. She selected me as her murderer and it was exactly as I had written: does the victim choose the killer even more than the killer chooses the victim? And the answer was yes.

I at last came to that awful, that fateful moment when sentence was pronounced and I almost forgot the despair in her eyes and their terrible pleading for death, and I wished then that she were alive and suffering; I was overcome by the profound intimation that every moment of being, under whatever conditions, is a prize and a premium.

Time that has so often stumbled and stood still is now galloping and my final night is almost gone. I must be detached about what will happen to me early tomorrow and I will turn even now for comfort to what has so often buoyed me. Not even this last predicament can altogether deaden it, though my taste for murder fiction did falter and leave me for a while when the feeling of numbness and puzzlement and bewilderment engulfed me. It is back now, almost as strong as ever, and in the few hours that remain I am wondering what I will ask for to sustain me. My mind has considered many choices; those possibilities have narrowed however; and at the moment I cannot decide between "The Hands of Mr. Ottermole" and "The Two Bottles of Relish".

Carnival Day

Betty wanted to lie in bed a little longer and look at the lowered shade that held out the sunlight except for a bright streak of it nosing through at the bottom. Then she could think about the nice things that might happen. Except that they might not.

Her mother was in the hall cleaning, doing the brisk morning work of Saturday. Betty listened to the rub of the mop, the whispering of the dust cloth. She pulled the Teddy bear from his crumpled position on the floor and placed him on the pillow beside her. His hanging button of a left eye seemed to leer; his fur was worn and in spots was missing, as if he had mange. She took his right paw that was jerked toward his forehead in a kind of salute and rubbed it against her face so that he caressed her.

Outside the mop made its way down the hall—the only sound in the house. Then the ringing of the telephone tore open the silence—first the ringing downstairs, then the echoing ring of the extension upstairs. Her mother would answer it, just outside Betty's door.

Betty knocked the Teddy bear so that he made a somersault and landed face down on the floor. She knew the telephone call would be the sign she had been waiting for to tell her what kind of day it would be, and she was not quite ready to learn. She grabbed her pillow and burrowed beneath it, pressing the sides tight against her ears. The feathers, the ticking, the pillow case, nothing kept the noise out. She had heard the words before they were spoken, she had dreamed them all through the night.

Her father had said weeks ago when the first signs were pasted on the billboards, the placards set up in the drugstore windows, the shoe shop, the beauty parlors—that of course they must go to the carnival together. Hadn't they gone for years? But she couldn't really believe him because everything had been so different these last months. He understood her fear, her uncertainty, and weeks ago had given her five crisp dollar bills to hide away in her desk. The money was there for her to spend at the carnival, even if he didn't get to go with her.

Betty heard her mother's voice; if her mother had been at the North Pole her voice couldn't have been colder, and yet it was so nice, so distinct, every syllable of every word sounded.

"I tried to tell Betty not to count on you. She'll be hurt. But then you seem to take pleasure in hurting us."

It wasn't fair of her mother to talk to him like that; he'd left the money; he'd made his apologies, he'd said something might come up so that he couldn't take her; and now her mother talked to him as if he had broken a solemn promise.

Her mother didn't say goodbye but Betty heard the little latching click the telephone made as it slid back into place.

The autumn wind puffed the shade so that it slapped the sill. Betty reached down for the Teddy bear and threw him across the room.

Outside there were the sounds of her mother putting away the mop in the utility cabinet, then a knock on the door.

"Good morning," her mother said, and filled the room with her briskness. "It's time you were up."

Betty kicked the sheet and made a wad of it at the foot of the bed.

"Your father telephoned to say he can't go to the carnival after all. I know how disappointed you are. But you can go with some of the other children on the street." She stooped over the Teddy bear and picked him up, regimenting him so that his legs were straight and his arms were close to his sides. "It's silly the way you hang on to this old thing. You're nearly twelve—much too old for Teddy bears. He ought to be thrown in the trash."

She was picking up clothes, straightening shoes—her mother was always, always picking up, straightening up now; she didn't use to be that way.

"Here's your robe. Go on downstairs and eat your breakfast. You'll find a glass of orange juice in the refrigerator. Take your milk from the bottle nearest the freezing unit. I'll be down in a minute to cook your egg."

"I don't want an egg," Betty said. Betty tried to stamp as she walked down the stairs; she wanted to have the house filled with the jolting sounds of heavy footsteps and to have her mother tell her to stop, but the soft soles of her bedroom shoes sounded quieter than tiptoes.

She stood in the kitchen door looking at the neat rows of cabinets with everything stacked precisely in them, the white sink scrubbed spotless, the chairs lined up tight against the walls like shy children at a party. On the second shelf of the refrigerator she found the glass of orange juice. She held it in both hands and rubbed her nose against the film outside until she I made a wobbly circle; then she started to drink the juice—but it wouldn't go down; it held back because this was the day of the carnival and her father wasn't going with her.

Her mother was coming downstairs. Betty heard her precise heels strike the steps. She wanted to gulp the orange juice but the first taste of it made her sick. Betty looked at the full glass in her hands; she couldn't listen to a lecture, not today, on the way thousands of children in foreign countries would give anything for this delicious orange juice. There just might be time to get rid of it. She ran to the sink and poured the juice down the drain.

"You must drink some milk now," her mother said, as she entered the kitchen and saw the empty glass in Betty's hand.

"I don't want any milk," Betty said, waiting for the threat to come, waiting for her mother to say she couldn't leave the house until she had drunk some milk.

"I suppose it won't hurt you to go without it this once. Anyway, you'll eat enough junk at the carnival to fill you up. Run on upstairs and bathe."

Her mother said the words but she wasn't paying attention even to herself; her mother's mind seemed to be deep inside her, digging away at other thoughts. In the bathroom Betty played the lovely forbidden game. If her mother downstairs buzzing with the vacuum cleaner on the dining room rug knew, she'd be mad. Betty brushed her teeth and punched the brush hard on the back of her tongue so that she gagged and the little bit of orange juice that she had swallowed came up. Next she stood in the middle of the floor holding a glass of water in her hand and spit water into the basin, spitting like old man Robinson who could stand in a store door and hit the middle of the street, making a cascade over the sidewalk. She filled the tub half full, then stuck only her toes in the water and rubbed herself hard with the towel as if she had taken a bath all over.

She dressed and was trying to sneak out of the house without last minute admonitions from her mother. But there was no need to try to sneak out. While Betty had dawdled over dressing, her father had left his office and come home. He and her mother were talking now, then shouting; the deadly barrage of their voices was wounding each other. Betty did not matter at such a time, not even on carnival day. She didn't belong to them when they were like that. She was alone. She wasn't even born. She darted down the hall onto the porch and jumped across the front steps.

At the corner she heard a high scream and then a noise that she had never heard before, but she did not dare stop to listen to it.

Long before she got to the huge vacant lot across the railroad tracks, the sounds of the carnival came to her, the voices jabbering, pleading, cajoling, then the music all scrambled up so there was no tune, like children yelling at each other, nothing making sense. And then she was there. It felt good to walk in the sawdust, to have it slow her down like walking in water, to have it creep inside her shoes. She made the rounds to see what she wanted to do; she might do everything; first, though, she must look things over, be cautious, the way you were careful about a new child or a new teacher or a new book before you accepted them.

Betty thought she had remembered it all, yet she hadn't; her memory had changed the carnival, but now it all came back, like a movie she was seeing for the second time—all the small booths with shelves, almost like the vegetable stalls at the Farmers' Market, but instead of vegetables they were strewn with dolls and animals and blankets and lamps and clocks.

The shooting gallery was just ahead. She stopped, remembering last year her father had stood right there, shooting as hard as he could, yet all the ducks marched past ignoring him and his shots until he had popped off a tail. This was the first place they had gone; she closed her eyes trying to make her memory bring it all back, trying to recall what her father had worn, what she had worn; but nothing came—nothing except the emptiness of her father's absence. A man picked up a rifle and squinted, then shot, and Betty walked past him.

Above all the invitations to step this way folks, try your skill for valuable prizes, she heard someone say, "You, young lady with the pigtails, you look like someone who could win. Toss the ring on the numbered pegs and if they add up to an odd number you can pick out what you want." His smile slashed his face and he waggled his hand at her. Betty pulled the envelope her father had given her out of her skirt pocket. The five new dollars made crackling sounds as she fingered them to be sure she gave the man only one.

The man's fingers reached greedily for the dollar; they lingered in his change box. "Naturally you want more than one chance," he said. "One for a quarter or three for fifty cents."

"One," Betty said firmly.

She bumped hard against the counter as she made her first throw. The twine ring fell to the ground before it reached the target. The next one flew past the target and thumped against the thin wall of the booth; the third one looped a peg from which dangled a little placard with 16 painted on it.

"Too bad," the man said. "Sixteen is not a lucky number. But you made a good try. I'm sure you could win the next time."

"No, thank you," Betty said. The man's smile dwindled; he erased her from his consciousness, the way Miss Collins erased the arithmetic lesson in one swoop from the blackboard so that nothing was left, and was calling out, "You, young man in the corduroy jacket, come this way and try your luck at this interesting game of chance and skill."

"One, please," Betty said and tiptoed to shove her money through the mouse trap of an opening in a ticket booth before a tent splashed with signs reading *Thrill to the Death Defying Riders. Crashes. Spills.*

The roar of the motorcycles frightened her; she leaned down and watched them make rushing-spluttering circles; a man fell off, she screamed, wanting to grab her father, to dig her hands into his arms, the way she did when they had watched the riders in the years before. The helmeted men roared past, goggled men stooping, spread over the motorcycles like frogs.

Nothing was the same without her father; she had done all the things they did together. He wasn't there and it would serve him right if she saw things they hadn't seen together. He hadn't exactly steered her away from them; he had mentioned shows and rides he thought they might enjoy more. Now she walked up to the platform where the girls stood in their costumes, wearing robes, then one girl unloosened her robe and showed her costume. The men near Betty grinned; two whistled. The man on the platform winked and said, "Plenty more of the same on the inside."

Betty bought a ticket and sat down in a chair on the outer circle. The ground was uneven and her chair rocked back and forth. The lights went off; six girls came out on the stage and threw kisses at the audience; then a man came out and said something; hoots followed what the man said. Next to Betty a man placed his hand on the knee of a woman sitting on his right and the man and woman smiled at each other. Hoots came again from the audience—hoots full of a special and secret knowledge, shutting out everyone who didn't understand and share the knowledge; Betty looked at the upturned faces of the men sitting near her, their eyes catching strange lights from the stage; and all around, the sun sprinkled through holes in the tent and sifted through in bright dots to the ground. A woman sang a song while some girls in back of her danced, none of them doing the steps quite like any other or at the same time; then the curtain slapped to in gigantic relief that the show was over. The men around Betty got up and reached for cigarettes and they all walked out into the sunlight.

After that Betty went to the Jungle of Snakes; she looked over the canvas sides of an enclosure down to the waving bodies, the snakes writhing-twisting-squirming like all the nightmares of her life, and in the middle of their weaving a woman sat caressing them, letting them climb around her body, small ones making bracelets around her arms and anklets around her ankles; one large one twisted three times around her waist; heads darted back and forth, back and forth, their tongues licking like flames in and out of their flattened heads; then the woman picked up one from the canvas floor and held it to her, fondling it as if it were a baby, kissing it as if it were sweet. To escape her the snake wiggled down, moving in the shape of an *s*, then lost himself among the other twists and whorls. Fear like fire swept over Betty and she rushed out of the tent.

She stood shivering and her teeth were clamped hard together as if she were playing in snow on the coldest morning in the year, though the midday sun felt like hot August heat on her shoulders. Twice she made the circuit of the booths and shows, trying to decide which one to see next. A sign beckoned to her. *Consult Dr. Vision the Visionary, the Mystic, the Clairvoyant. He Sees All. He Knows All. Come In and Discuss Your Problems.*

Her father didn't approve of fortunetellers; he said it was much nicer to wait and see what the future brought. But her father wasn't there. Betty stood half in and half out of the tent opening, the way she did in the dentist's reception room, waiting to push the buzzer to let the dentist's assistant know she had come. There was movement within a tent and a man said, "Do you wish to seek the advice of Dr. Vision?" He wore a green satin suit, with a gold sash, and his head held up the huge burden of a turban from which a limp feather drooped like a coxcomb. His mustache was drawn on in a thin black line and his eyebrows almost filled his forehead.

She nodded. It was still like being at the dentist's, not able to deny having an appointment.

"You are speaking to Dr. Vision," the man said, pointing to a chair. She sat at a table across from him; his turbaned head seemed to sit on the crystal ball that separated them.

"The fee is one dollar," he said. Betty's hand rummaged in her pocket for money. Fifty cents bounced to the ground. Dr. Vision sat still with his hands pressed against his forehead and Betty fell to the ground hunting for the money, beating against a small rug that seemed to float on the grass and rubble beneath it. She found the money near Dr. Vision's feet and was surprised to see that he wore unlaced tennis shoes and no socks. She scrambled back to her chair and gave him an apologetic look, as if she had had to excuse herself from the table to be sick. He paid no attention and said in a voice that was a strange kind of whisper, "Do you have some special problem?"

She answered him in the same kind of whisper. "Yes, my mother—" And then she could go no further. What she was about to say had been betrayal, spreading the dark misery in her house before him, undressing her mother's hurt and her father's hurt before a stranger.

Dr. Vision looked into the crystal.

"I see," he said. "Your mother. Yes. She's been ill. She'll be all right. Don't worry about her. Is there anything else?"

Betty looked at her fingernails. There was one, just one that wasn't chewed; she had tried to leave at least one; one whole nail showed that she had some control; she held her hand tightly but the finger sprang to her mouth and she started biting the nail.

"Maybe your schoolwork is bothering you. Is that it?"

School. Miss Smith saying, until this year you did good work. What's the matter now? It's not that you aren't capable. Don't you like your teachers? Are you getting lazy? What is it?

She couldn't answer Dr. Vision any more than she could answer Miss Smith; the words stopped in her throat.

He smiled, his mustache curling around in his smile like a cat's whiskers. "It's a little early but maybe you want advice about love."

"No," she shouted. Her voice startled them both, so that she dropped it back to the whisper they were using and said, "No, no."

"Then there's just one thing left. A career. You want advice about your career. Well, finish school first, then decide what you want to do. I predict a successful career for you."

Betty stood up and the chair fell behind her. She expected a banging, jolting noise but the grass caught the chair like a net and hushed the sound of its fall. She started to run.

"Just a minute," Dr. Vision said. "You are permitted to communicate with the Secret Powers of the Universe and ask a secret question or make a secret request. They will send you an answer, and only you will know their answer. Look closely into the crystal and repeat your request or your question to yourself three times." Betty walked toward the crystal and bent over it. She made her request silently, as reverently as she said her prayers, her hands folded and her eyes closed: Let everything be like it was, let everything be like it was, let everything be like it was.

There was no noise—the whole carnival seemed quiet and still. Then Dr. Vision said words that she didn't understand and all the time he made huge gestures in the air. His hand moved under the table and his thumb reached around his little finger and he held a paper there. "This is your answer. The Powers have spoken," he said and made a bow as if he were waiting for applause. Betty snatched the paper from him and ran, grabbing at the slit in the tent, feeling herself almost smothered by the curtain as she rushed out. She couldn't look at the paper—she didn't dare look; she had the feeling she had had one Christmas when she had been sure that she wouldn't get anything, when she hadn't dared go to the Christmas tree in the living room. Only this wasn't quite like that; this was more—this wasn't being frightened over not getting presents, this was asking for what had to be. The small piece of paper was her destiny and she wadded it in the desperate knot of her fist.

Ahead of her was the largest cluster of people she'd seen all day. Above them on a platform a man took off his coat and swept his brow; as he raised his hand a huge circle of sweat showed underneath his arm on the yellow silk of his shirt. He had the voice of all the men standing on platforms, a chant that came from the back of his nose. "Ladies and gentlemen, you have seen many remarkable things today but you have seen nothing to equal the phenomenon we are presenting. The half man, half woman. This phenomenon can be legally married in any state of our great and beloved America to either a man or woman. You will hear a scientific lecture, absolutely clean, explaining this sexual phenomenon. I urge you to buy your ticket at once. For this performance only the cost is thirty-five cents, the usual price of admission is seventy-five cents, you will be paying less than half the usual charge. Only adults allowed. No one under sixteen admitted."

People moved against Betty, crushing her, pushing her toward the tall box where a man sold tickets. She tried to move away from them, but the man kept looking down at her and saying thirty-five cents please, thirty-five cents, and the ones behind her were saying go on, what's holding us up, and she was trying to tell the man she was only twelve.

The crowd pushed Betty, shoved her, thrust her closer to the man. She felt that she was being suffocated.

"No," she cried out. "No. I don't want to see." She threw back the rocks of their bodies and squirmed through.

She sobbed and plunged through the sawdust, her feet kicked up little storms of it; then her sorrow told her what she was searching for, longing for, what she loved most of all about the carnival. The merry-go-round. That was all she wanted now. She ran toward it and its piping tune embraced her and she saw the stiff ponies with their arched tails and prancing legs making their rounds far away. She dashed toward the merry-go-round, remembering how her father used to let her ride it for hours; how he rode a pony alongside her, and his long legs dangled, striking the floor when his pony descended; how sometimes he doubled up his legs in the stirrup so that he looked like a jockey; how sometimes they got off their ponies and sat together in a chariot. Her father would get tired at last and stand outside the merry-go-round's circle waving to her as she rode by; their waving lasted so long that one wave was not over before she was back again, passing him, waving to him again. She reached for money to buy tickets and the paper with her destiny on it dropped to the ground. She did not even notice.

"Five," she shouted above the magic piping. "I want five tickets for the merry-go-round."

She folded the tickets and waited on the outside for the merry-go-round to slow down. Some boys leaped off before it stopped, and the younger children squatted down to jump flatfooted to the ground.

Betty found a red pony and climbed on it.

The music started, the merry-go-round began to revolve, while all the booths and shows were lined up outside, not able to touch the enchanted circle of the merry-go-round; voices were saying what they had been saying all day, but now the music blotted them out so that Betty had to strain to hear—hot dogs ten cents, hamburgers made of the finest beef twenty cents, souvenirs you'll value the rest of your life, canary birds two dollars, pennants of your favorite college fifty cents, see the half man half woman, take a chance at this interesting game of skill … hurry, hurry, hurry.

And then she did not hear them at all; she would not let her ears hear and she closed her eyes; she was holding on to her pony and listening only to the music, safe from everything, safe from her mother's eternal cleaning and the sad things that went on at home, the harsh voices and the harsher silences.

The merry-go-round slowed and Betty opened her eyes.

He was there.

Her father was just outside the circle of parents waiting for their children. And Betty's day was saved. She should have known her father would not disappoint her.

He waved at her and she saw that he was not alone. It was funny. She knew the man he was with. It was Mr. Williams the policeman— everybody in town knew Mr. Williams. They must have met each other accidentally at the carnival. Maybe Mr. Williams was waiting for someone he knew to get off the merry-go-round. Her father seemed to be pleading with him, as if he were asking permission, and Mr. Williams finally nodded.

The music was beginning again, the merry-go-round started its slow turning, the children scrambled on and her father leaped on and came toward her. His arms grabbed for her and his mouth seemed to have words that could not be spoken. Then the man taking the tickets came round and Betty handed him two, one for herself and one for father. The merry-go-round was going faster and her pony started to rise; the lifting took her from her father's embrace, but his hand reached wildly for her hand and their grip was as strong as their love. The carnival around them was not yet the blur it would be when they went at full speed and Betty could still see Mr. Williams watching them, watching most of all her father, and the policeman's face was very sad.

Murder Between Friends

Over their midmorning coffee Mrs. Harrison and Mrs. Franklin settled down to discuss how they were going to murder their landlord, Mr. Shafer. The day before, they had decided that murdering him was the only sane thing to do.

"I believe I'll have a little more sugar for my coffee, please, Matilda," Mrs. Franklin said. At this late date, she was seventy-six, there was nothing she could do about her sweet tooth. "These are the best cheese straws I've ever put in my mouth. You've got to be a born cook to have them turn out this way. Time and again I've followed your recipe exactly, but mine aren't anything like these."

Mrs. Harrison beamed. It was a pleasure to give a little treat to such an amiable person as Mary Sue Franklin, a friend ever since the second grade.

They ate cheese straws and sipped coffee, then wiped their mouths daintily and got down to the business of Mr. Shafer's murder.

"Well, we can't do it with a gun, that's for sure," Mrs. Harrison said. "A gun scares me to death just to look at it. I couldn't bring myself to pull the trigger. Besides, where on earth would we get one? You have to have a permit to buy one and a license to shoot it."

"No, a gun is out," Mrs. Franklin agreed. Then she sighed. "You read a lot about murder, but when you come right down to it, it's hard to plan one."

Even as they talked they could hear Mr. Shafer thundering like a minotaur up and down the halls looking for his next victim.

"I'll take another cheese straw, Matilda, and then I've got to go to the store. Can I get anything for you? I'll be glad to."

"No, thank you, Mary Sue. But tomorrow we've got to get down to brass tacks. Mr. Shafer gets meaner every day."

They finished their coffee. Mrs. Franklin offered to wash up, but Mrs. Harrison wouldn't hear of it. So Mrs. Franklin went back down the hall to her own tiny room and kitchenette to get her shopping bag. She bumped right into Mr. Shafer, who was coming up the back stairway.

"What you old biddies been yakking about today?" he boomed out at her. "Are you planning to overthrow the government?"

Mrs. Franklin liked banter. A woman never got too old to do a bit of discreet, ladylike flirting. But no light exchange was possible with Mr. Shafer. She smiled her sweetest smile and gave a little bow. "No, my dear," she said in the most genteel conversational tone, "we've been trying to decide how to murder you."

Mr. Shafer paid no attention. He never did pay any attention to what anyone said. "Damned old biddies," he muttered, and stalked on past. "Why is the world so cluttered up with old women?"

He turned out the little glowworm of a light in that part of the hall. He slammed a door somewhere. Even the house shuddered; and he had no business being there at all. The place had belonged to his wife and when she had died it had been willed to their daughter, but Mr. Shafer made the daughter so miserable that she'd left after one of his scenes. Then he had taken over everything.

The next morning the old friends talked again about murdering Mr. Shafer.

Mrs. Franklin asked, as usual, for more sugar for her coffee. She told Mrs. Harrison that was the best apple pie she'd ever eaten.

"It's the cinnamon that makes the difference, that's all," Mrs. Harrison said modestly, "and a little lemon juice."

They finished their snack. They wiped their mouths delicately.

"Well, we can't poison Mr. Shafer," Mrs. Harrison said. "What do we know about poison?"

"We could learn," Mrs. Franklin answered.

"How could we learn, Mary Sue? If we go to the library and ask for books on poison, they're sure to remember us. I know all the staff there. Anyway, when you buy poison the clerk keeps a record of it. The police could trace it straight to us."

Over their chocolate cake the next day, Mrs. Franklin said, "We certainly can't drown him." She was so enmeshed in the cake that she wore a chocolate mustache and for the first time since they'd talked of murder she looked a bit sinister.

"No, I guess we can't drown him. There's no deep water anywhere but in the lake at the city park, and how could we get Mr. Shafer there?"

"He wouldn't go with us. He hates women."

"He hates everybody."

On Thursday when they had finished their pineapple upside-down cake neither of them had any suggestion about how to kill Mr. Shafer.

"I feel so inept and inane, Mary Sue. We've got heads on our shoulders. It looks like we ought to be able to figure out something."

"Maybe we can tomorrow." Mrs. Franklin sounded optimistic.

"What about an axe?" Mrs. Harrison said the next day when they'd eaten every crumb of their cheese cake. "I woke up last night and it came to me as plain as day. Why not an axe?" Her eyes brightened.

"Too messy," Mrs. Franklin said. "We'd ruin our clothes and even if we burned them the police would find the buttons and know they belonged to us."

"I don't mean chop him up," Mrs. Harrison said in alarm that her old friend had thought her capable of such an atrocity. "I just mean hit him on the head with it."

"But we don't have an axe, and if we bought one at the hardware store they'd be sure to remember and report it to the police."

"Now listen, Mary Sue, we've got to put on our thinking caps. We've got to figure out something soon. Mr. Shafer put poor Mrs. Grove out day before yesterday because she wouldn't get rid of her cat, and last night he made Mr. Floyd leave because he said he wheezed too much with his asthma."

"Well, have you thought of a way, Matilda?"

"No, I haven't, Mary Sue. But we will. I just know we will. While we're stuck about a method, there're still lots of other things we could be working on. We've got to figure out when the best time to do it will be. In a rooming house full of people we'll have to draw up some kind of time scheme so no one will be around to see us."

They spent a week devising a time schedule, snooping on the coming and going of the other tenants.

They didn't seem to doubt that they would succeed in their plan. They talked as if their murder was over and done with.

"It's sort of sad," Mrs. Harrison said. "Not a soul in this world will mourn Mr. Shafer."

"Not a tear will be shed for him," Mrs. Franklin said.

"Do you think we ought to send flowers to the funeral?"

"Good gracious, Matilda, I never once thought of that. I just don't know."

"Why not chip in together and send a potted lily? A big floral offering might look like gloating."

"Of course we've got to go to the service."

"Yes, we'll have to or the rest of the people in the house might get suspicious. But don't you think it would look better if we sat more toward the back of the church than the front?"

"I believe about midway would be the best."

"I've thought of it, Matilda," Mrs. Franklin said when she was on her second piece of pecan pie. "It's simple. I'm surprised we haven't thought of it before. Can't you guess?"

"Surely it's not any of the ways we've already talked about."

"Of course not. We couldn't use any of them. We'd be caught red-handed."

"Well, I just don't know. I hate to seem stupid, but I can't even make a good guess."

"A push."

"A push?"

"Yes, just shove Mr. Shafer down the stairs. The basement steps are steep and dark and he goes down there like clockwork every day at eleven. We could take him by surprise. Reach for the small of his back, or use a broom or a mop and give him a shove. The world would be rid of one of the meanest men who ever drew breath."

"Any day at eleven will do?"

"Yes, any day except Sunday, of course. We go to church at eleven then. We couldn't do it on Sunday. I've no intention of missing church just to do away with Mr. Shafer." Mrs. Franklin was flushed over having found their solution. It made her prettier than ever, almost childlike in appearance. No one would have believed that she had been seventy-six on January ninth.

"I've just thought of something, Mary Sue. That man, Mr. Allen, who moved in last week. He never leaves the place. He'd be here at eleven."

"He's no threat," Mrs. Franklin said. "He's hard of hearing. Besides, he's so engrossed in painting that nothing could budge him out of his room except an earthquake."

"Well, then, we'd better get it over with as soon as we can."

"The sooner the better," Mrs. Franklin said.

Of course, they didn't mean it.

Or did they?

They longed for nerve enough to murder Mr. Shafer, but really they couldn't say boo to a goose. Mr. Shafer was mean, he was surly, he made them miserable, exactly as he made everyone else miserable. They wished they could just move out and be rid of him that way, but they'd looked and looked and couldn't find anything for what they could pay; anyhow, they liked living where they were, near stores, near their church, near their doctor's office. They loved the old neighborhood, though it had deteriorated from family dwellings to rooming houses. If only they could get rid of Mr. Shafer and his cruelty. But they couldn't. They had just been whistling in the dark with all their talk of murder. They had just been playing with their imagination. It was their game, as if they were two bettors talking about winning a fortune when they didn't have a dollar between them to place on a horse.

Spring came the very next morning after Mrs. Franklin and Mrs. Harrison had decided that a push was the proper way to murder Mr. Shafer. They couldn't ignore the first warm day of spring. They postponed their usual morning coffee until afternoon. Mrs. Harrison said that she was heading for town to see what the new hats looked like, not that she could buy one. Mrs. Franklin sauntered off to see the daffodils and crocuses in the park.

Mr. Shafer heard them leave. "Darned old harpies," he said. "Maybe I can draw a deep breath with them out of the way for a little while."

The only other person in the house then was Lawrence Allen, who lived in the room next to Mrs. Franklin. But he didn't hear the women go out even though the walls were thin. He couldn't hear very well. He didn't mind that he was growing deaf and that people had to shout at him. Nothing mattered so long as he kept his sight and could lift his right hand to paint. He had waited all his life to paint. He had refused to be a Sunday painter or an after-working-hours painter. Dabbling hadn't been for him. He had to be a dedicated painter every waking moment. Now that his youth and middle age and all their responsibilities were over he could try to be a painter. He had supported his parents, then his own family; his wife was dead and his two sons were grown and with almost-grown children of their own. After a lifetime of meeting obligations, Allen owed nothing to anyone but himself. All he needed was a place to paint and painting material. He could get by on one meal a day. Nothing was going to stop him from painting, and after months of looking for a place with a proper light, and one that he could afford on his social security, he had found it. Life in one small room with one scanty meal was paradise.

He had just stretched a canvas and had picked up a brush when the door to his room flew open. Mr. Shafer filled the doorway.

"What in hell's going on in here? What's that stink?" Even Allen's defective ears were outraged by Shafer's bellow.

"Get that muck out of here. This is a bedroom, not a workshop. I won't have it. I tell you I won't have it. It smells like a pigsty. It looks like a garbage dump. I had no idea this was going on. Get this damned junk out of here at once."

He stalked out of the room and walked down the hall. Allen dropped his brush. His hands jerked, his throat grew dry. He ran after Shafer.

"But you can't do this to me, Mr. Shafer. I've waited all my life to paint. I looked all over town for a room with a good light. You can't make me give it up. I won't go." His voice was a shriek. The dark, empty halls boomed with his shouted despair.

Shafer lumbered down the rear stairway. He shouted back to Allen, "I've told you once and for all. You and that damned muck have got to get out of here."

Allen pursued him, entreating him to change his mind. Allen was distraught. He was possessed. He had to convince the man. He couldn't be put out. He couldn't. He wouldn't be. He babbled. He yelled. "Listen to me, Mr. Shafer. You've got to listen."

The emotion in Allen's voice made Shafer turn around. "Get your muck out of here or I'll—" He didn't finish his threat. What he saw on Allen's face terrified him. He ran toward the back porch and, when he had reached it, he slammed the back door in Allen's face. He charged toward the steep basement stairs. It was exactly eleven o'clock—the time that Mrs. Franklin and Mrs. Harrison had decided would be the safest in which to murder him—when he rushed to descend the stairs, but fear over what he had seen on Allen's face made him falter. His foot missed the first step. He stumbled and sprawled.

Lawrence Allen didn't hear the fall. He was weak with rage and numb from the violence he had felt toward Shafer. But the slammed door had brought his sanity back. Thank God, he was in control of himself now. There was no telling what he might have done if Shafer hadn't shut the door. Allen walked back upstairs. He picked his brush up from the floor and began to paint. It steadied him, brought back his purpose and his optimism. Somehow or other he believed he would find a way to keep his room.

After Mr. Shafer's death, Mrs. Harrison and Mrs. Franklin didn't have much to talk about to each other. It was as if they'd talked themselves out in planning Mr. Shafer's murder. Mr. Shafer's pleasant daughter came back and took over the house. It was a happy place then. Mrs. Grove and her cat returned, and Mr. Floyd and his asthma. Mr. Shafer's daughter didn't mind Mr. Allen's painting. In fact, she encouraged him, even sat for him. It wasn't any time before he had two pictures accepted for the Annual State Exhibit.

Mary Sue Franklin and Matilda Harrison were still devoted friends, but a bit miffed with each other. Sometimes Mrs. Harrison's blood boiled a little. Accidental death, her foot, let the poor benighted police think that if they chose. But, of course, Mary Sue Franklin had done it. Mary Sue's lie didn't fool Mrs. Harrison at all—she hadn't gone to the park that day. She'd sneaked back the moment Mrs. Harrison had turned her back and she'd shoved Mr. Shafer down the stairs at eleven o'clock, just the way they'd planned.

As for Mrs. Franklin, she was put out because the method of the murder had been something she'd worked out all by herself, with no help from Matilda Harrison, yet Matilda had gone ahead with it all by herself, as if it had been her own idea. Mrs. Franklin had thought Mrs. Harrison was shy. She was surprised that Matilda had turned out to be the pushy type—not that she meant to make a pun. Well, that just proved that you never could tell about anyone, not even your best friend. Imagine, saying she was going to town to look at new hats, when all the time she had been hiding in the back hall waiting to shove Mr. Shafer to Kingdom Come.

The old friends kept on having their morning coffee together, but they were careful not to turn their backs on each other, and when they looked straight into each other's eyes, each was dead sure she saw a murderer.

Killed by Kindness

John Johnson knew that he must murder his wife. He had to. It was the only decent thing he could do. He owed her that much consideration.

Divorce was out of the question. He had no grounds. Mary was kind and pretty and pleasant company and hadn't ever glanced at another man. Not once in their marriage had she nagged him. She was a marvelous cook and an excellent bridge player. No hostess in town was more popular.

It seemed a pity that he would have to kill her. But he certainly wasn't going to shame her by telling her he was leaving her; not when they'd just celebrated their twentieth anniversary two months before and had congratulated each other on being the happiest married couple in the whole world. With pink champagne, and in front of dozens of admiring friends, they had pledged undying love. They had said they hoped fate would be kind and would allow them to die together. After all that John couldn't just toss Mary aside. Such a trick would be the action of a cad.

Without him Mary would have no life at all. Of course she would have her shop which had done well since she had opened it, but she wasn't a real career woman. Opening the shop had been a kind of lark when the Greer house, next door to them in a row of townhouses, had been put up for sale. No renovation or remodeling had been done except to knock down part of a wall so that the two houses could be connected by a door. The furniture shop was only something to occupy her time, Mary said, while her sweet husband worked. It didn't mean anything to her, though she had a good business sense. John seldom went in the shop. Come to think of it, it was a jumble. It made him a little uneasy; everything in it seemed so crowded and precarious. Yes, Mary's interest was in him; it wasn't in the shop. She'd have to have something besides the shop to have any meaningful existence. If he divorced her she'd have no one to take her to concerts and plays. Dinner parties, her favorite recreation, would be out. None of their friends would invite her to come without him. Alone and divorced, she would be shunted into the miserable category of spinsters and widows who had to be invited to lunch instead of dinner.

He couldn't relegate Mary to such a life, though he felt sure that if he asked her for a divorce she'd give him one. She was so acquiescent and accommodating.

No, he wasn't going to humiliate her by asking for a divorce. She deserved something better from him than that.

If only he hadn't met Lettice on that business trip to Lexington. But how could he regret such a miracle? He had come alive only in the six weeks since he'd known Lettice. Life with Mary was ashes in comparison. Since he'd met Lettice he felt like a blind man who had been given sight. He might have been deaf all his life and was hearing for the first time. And the marvel was that Lettice loved him and was eager to marry him, and free to marry him.

And waiting.

And insisting.

He must concentrate on putting Mary out of the way. Surely a little accident could be arranged without too much trouble. The shop ought to be an ideal place, there in all that crowded junk. Among those heavy marble busts and chandeliers and andirons something from above or below could be used to dispatch his dear Mary to her celestial reward.

"Darling, you must tell your wife," Lettice urged when they next met at their favorite hotel in Lexington. "You've got to arrange for a divorce. You have to. You've got to tell her about us." Lettice's voice was so low and musical that John felt hypnotized.

But how could he tell Mary about Lettice?

John couldn't even rationalize Lettice's appeal to himself. Instead of Mary's graciousness, Lettice had elegance. Lettice wasn't as pretty or as charming as Mary. But he couldn't resist her. In her presence he was an ardent, masterful lover; in Mary's presence he was a thoughtful, complaisant husband. With Lettice life would always be lived at the highest peak; nothing in his long years with Mary could approach the wonder he had known during his few meetings with Lettice. Lettice was earth, air, fire and water, the four elements; Mary was—no, he couldn't compare them. Anyway, what good was it to set their attractions off against each other?

Then, just as he was about to suggest to Lettice that they go to the bar, he saw Chet Fleming enter the hotel and walk across the lobby toward the desk. What was Chet Fleming doing in Lexington? But then anyone could be anywhere. That was the humiliating risk illicit lovers faced. They might be discovered anywhere, anytime. No place was secure for them. But Chet Fleming was the one person he wanted least to see, and the one who would make the most of encountering

John with another woman. That blabbermouth would tell his wife and friends, his doctor, his grocer, his banker, his lawyer. Word would get back to Mary. Her heart would be broken. She deserved better than that.

John cowered beside Lettice. Chet dawdled at the desk. John couldn't be exposed like that any longer, a single glance around and Chet would see him and Lettice. John made an incoherent excuse, then sidled over to the newsstand where he hid behind a magazine until Chet had registered and had taken an elevator upstairs. Anyway, they had escaped, but only barely.

John couldn't risk cheapening their attachment. He had to do something to make it permanent right away, but at the same time he didn't want to hurt Mary. Thousands of people in the United States had gotten up that morning who would be dead before nightfall. Why couldn't his dear Mary be among them? Why couldn't she die without having to be murdered?

When John rejoined Lettice and tried to explain his panic, she was composed but concerned and emphatic.

"Darling, this incident only proves what I've been insisting. I said you'd have to tell your wife at once. We can't go on like this. Surely you understand."

"Yes, dear, you're quite right. I'll do something as soon as I can."

"You must do something immediately, darling."

Oddly enough, Mary Johnson was in the same predicament as John Johnson. She had had no intention of falling in love. In fact, she thought she was in love with her husband. How naive she'd been before Kenneth came into her shop that morning asking whether she had a bust of Mozart. Of course she had a bust of Mozart; she had several busts of Mozart, not to mention Bach, Beethoven, Victor Hugo, Balzac, Shakespeare, George Washington and Goethe, in assorted sizes.

He had introduced himself. Customers didn't ordinarily introduce themselves, and she gave him her name in return, and then realized that he was the outstanding interior designer in town.

"Quite frankly," he said, "I wouldn't be caught dead with this bust of Mozart and it will ruin the room, but my client insists on having it. Do you mind if I see what else you have?"

She showed him all over the shop then. Later she tried to recall the exact moment when they had fallen in love. He had spent all that first morning there; toward noon he seemed especially attracted to a small backroom cluttered and crowded with chests of drawers. He reached for a drawer pull that came off in his hands, then he reached for her.

"What do you think you're doing?" she said. "Goodness, suppose some customers come in."

"Let them browse," he said.

She couldn't believe that it had happened, but it had. Afterward, instead of being lonely when John went out of town on occasional business trips, she yearned for the time when he gave her his antiseptic peck of a kiss and told her he would be gone overnight. The small backroom jammed with the chests of drawers became Mary's and Kenneth's discreet rendezvous. They added a chaise longue.

One day a voice reached them there. They had been too engrossed to notice that anyone had approached.

"Mrs. Johnson, where are you? I'd like some service, please."

Mary stumbled out from the dark to greet the customer. Mary tried to smooth her mussed hair. She knew that her lipstick was smeared.

The customer was Mrs. Bryan, the most accomplished gossip in town. Mrs. Bryan would get word around that Mary Johnson was carrying on scandalously in her shop. John was sure to find out now.

Fortunately, Mrs. Bryan was preoccupied. She was in a Pennsylvania Dutch mood and wanted to see butter molds and dower chests.

It was a lucky escape, as Mary later told Kenneth. Kenneth refused to be reassured.

"I love you deeply," he said. "And honorably. I've reason to know you love me, too. I'm damned tired of sneaking around. I'm not going to put up with it any longer. Do you understand? We've got to get married. Tell your husband you want a divorce." Kenneth kept talking about a divorce, as if a divorce was nothing at all—no harder to arrange than a dental appointment. How could she divorce a man who had been affectionate and kind and faithful for twenty years? How could she snatch happiness from him?

If only John would die. Why couldn't he have a heart attack? Every day thousands of men died from heart attacks. Why couldn't her darling John just drop dead? It would simplify everything.

Even the ringing of the telephone sounded angry, and when Mary answered it Kenneth, at the other end of the line, was in a rage.

"Damn it, Mary, this afternoon was ridiculous. It was insulting. I'm not skulking anymore. I'm not hiding behind doors while you grapple around for butter molds to show customers. We've got to be married right away."

"Yes, darling. Do be patient."

"I've already been too patient. I'm not waiting any longer."

She knew that he meant it. If she lost Kenneth life would end for her. She hadn't ever felt this way about John.

Dear John. How could she toss him aside? He was in the prime of life; he could live decades longer. All his existence was centered on her. He lived to give her pleasure. They had no friends except other married people. John would have to lead a solitary life if she left him. He'd be odd man out without her; their friends would invite him to their homes because they were sorry for him. Poor, miserable John was what everyone would call him. He'd be better off dead, they'd say. He would neglect himself; he wouldn't eat regularly; he would have to live alone in some wretched furnished apartment. No, she mustn't condemn him to an existence like that.

Why had this madness with Kenneth started? Why had that foolish woman insisted on having a bust of Mozart in her music room? Why had Kenneth come to her shop in search of it when busts of Mozart were in every secondhand store on Broad Street and at much cheaper prices?

Yet she wouldn't have changed anything. Seconds with Kenneth were worth lifetimes with John. Only one end was possible. She would have to think of a nice, quick, efficient, unmessy way to get rid of John. And soon.

John had never seen Mary look as lovely as she did that night when he got home from his business trip. For one flicker of a second, life with her seemed enough. Then he thought of Lettice, and the thought stunned him into the belief that no act that brought them together could be criminal. He must get on with what he had to do. He must murder Mary in as gentlemanly a way as possible, and he must do it that very night. Meantime he would enjoy the wonderful dinner Mary had prepared for him. Common politeness demanded it, and anyhow he was ravenous.

Yes, he must get on with the murder just as soon as he finished eating. It seemed a little heartless to be contriving a woman's death even as he ate her cheese cake, but he certainly didn't mean to be callous.

He didn't know just how he would murder Mary. Perhaps if he could get her into her shop, there in that corner where all the statuary was, he could manage something.

Mary smiled at him and handed him a cup of coffee.

"I thought you'd need lots of coffee, darling, after such a long drive."

"Yes, dear, I do. Thank you." Just as he began to sip from his cup he glanced across the table at Mary. Her face had a peculiar expression. John was puzzled by it. They had been so close for so many years that she must be reading his mind. She must know what he was planning. Then she smiled; it was the glorious smile she had bestowed on him ever since their honeymoon. Everything was all right.

"Darling, excuse me for a minute," she said. "I just remembered something in the shop that I must see to. I'll be right back."

She walked quickly out of the dining room and across the hall into the shop.

But she didn't come back right away as she'd promised. If she didn't return soon John's coffee would be cold. He took a sip or two, then decided to go to the shop to see what had delayed Mary.

She didn't hear him enter. He found her in the middle room where the chandeliers were blazing. Her back was turned toward him and she was sitting on an Empire sofa close to the statues on their stands. She was ambushed by the statues.

Good lord, it was as he had suspected. She had been reading his thoughts. Her shoulders heaved. She was sobbing. She knew that their life together was ending. Then he decided that she might be laughing. Her shoulders would be shaking like that if she were laughing to herself. Whatever she was doing, whether she sobbed or laughed, it was no time for him to speculate on her mood. This was too good a chance to miss. With her head bent over she would be directly in the path of the bust of Victor Hugo or Benjamin Franklin or whoever it was towering above her. John would have to topple it only slightly and it would hit her skull. It needed only the gentlest shove.

He shoved.

It was so simple.

Poor darling girl. Poor Mary. But it was all for the best and he wouldn't ever blame himself for what he'd done. Still, he was startled that it had been so easy, and it had taken no time at all. He would have tried it weeks before if he had known that it could be done with so little trouble.

John was quite composed. He took one last affectionate glance at Mary and then went back to the dining room. He would drink his coffee and then telephone the doctor. No doubt the doctor would offer to notify the police since it was an accidental death. John wouldn't need to lie about anything except for one slight detail. He would have to say that some movement of Mary's must have caused the bust to fall.

His coffee was still warm. He drank it unhurriedly. He thought of

Lettice. He ached for the luxury of telephoning her that their life together was now assured and that after a discreet interval they could be married. But he decided he had better not take any chances. He would delay calling Lettice.

He felt joyful yet calm. He couldn't remember having felt so relaxed. No doubt it came from the relief of having done what had to be done. He was even sleepy. He was sleepier than he had ever been. He must lie down on the living room couch. That was more urgent even than telephoning the doctor. But he couldn't wait to get to the couch. He laid his head on the dining table. His arms dangled.

None of Mary's and John's friends had any doubt about how the double tragedy had occurred. When they came to think of it, the shop had always been a booby trap, and that night Mary had tripped or stumbled and had toppled the statue onto her head. Then John had found her and grief had overwhelmed him. He realized he couldn't live without Mary, and his desperate sense of loss had driven him to dissolve enough sleeping tablets in his coffee to kill himself.

They all remembered so well how, in the middle of their last anniversary celebration, Mary and John had said they hoped they could die together. They really were the most devoted couple any of them had ever known. You could get sentimental just thinking about Mary and John, and to see them together was an inspiration. In a world of insecurity nothing was so heartening as their deep, steadfast love. It was sweet and touching that they had died on the same night, and exactly as they both had wanted.

Fear

Where did the terror come from?

Why did she feel that every step led to her annihilation?

It was just an early morning walk that took Ellen Anderson from her cherished husband to her cherished employer.

Many women rose from the beds they shared with their husbands, dressed themselves and went to work, exactly as she did.

Her situation was commonplace. Then why did her walk to work fill her with dread?

Fear stalked her the moment she left the apartment house. Fear was a vicious mongrel and she was a small terrified animal being tracked by it, about to be snapped in its jaws at any moment.

Her walk was rather long, about three miles, beginning two blocks from the edge of the university campus where she and her husband Victor lived. Her route was west, past substantial townhouses, then south through slums, then all the way across a vast park and into a suburban area of large estates, one of which was her destination.

The first morning she had tried to reach Dr. Arnold's house by using the city transit system. But that required two transfers and long waits between connecting buses so that she didn't arrive until after nine. Dr. Arnold was an early riser and began work at seven-thirty. It pleased him that she was willing to report at seven-thirty. The early hour didn't bother her. She rose at seven, had a quick shower, dressed and had a glass of orange juice, then walked from her apartment to Dr. Arnold's office on the university campus in five minutes. But that was before Dr. Arnold's illness. Now he no longer came to the campus and Ellen walked to his house in the suburbs. She got up at six instead of seven.

She could have taken a taxi; but the taxi service in Kingborough was notoriously erratic and even more notoriously expensive, and it seemed a vast waste of money. Not that money was of any concern to her, at least if her Aunt Martha's lawyer knew what he was talking about. As a matter of fact, money wasn't of concern to her in any case since she earned as much as an associate professor in her job as executive assistant to Dr. Arnold, the president of the university.

She could have asked Victor to take her and he would have done so gladly. But he didn't go to his office until nine, and he often worked very late at night and needed his rest in the morning. Besides, it would be tactless of her to ask him to take her to Dr. Arnold's. She had given Victor her car after they were married, insisting she didn't need it at all. It had been convenient to have when she drove up on weekends to stay with her Aunt Martha in Concord, but after her aunt had died Ellen had seldom driven the car. Everything was at hand in the university complex—movies, newsstands, book shops, concert halls, supermarkets, liquor stores, dress shops, flower stalls. Victor was more than welcome to her car. Anyway, she had her two legs, and walking was good for one. You couldn't pick up a magazine or a paper without being admonished to exercise, and walking was said to be the best exercise of all.

Perhaps if she had had to walk both ways, she might have felt imposed upon, but there were convenient bus connections in the late afternoon.

At first she hadn't felt any fear at all. On the contrary, the long walk had been stimulating. It was interesting to be out so early and to saunter past the attractive townhouses.

The street lamps illuminated her progress enough so that she was warned of steep curbs or an uneven sidewalk, and every now and then she passed a paperboy flinging papers toward the dark houses or the driver of a milk truck sprinted in front of her to set containers on a porch.

Past the handsome townhouses, the slums were like open wounds. Everything was laid bare. Unhinged doors gaped onto endless dark halls. There were broken windows and sagging blinds and yards blemished by trash and discarded toys, smashed liquor bottles; and buckled beer cans.

When the derelict houses were behind Ellen, she entered the park—at a vulnerable and unprotected time. Used to crowds of people, designed for the pleasure of many, it had an aloofness, even arrogance, when it was trespassed by a person all alone. And yet Ellen was sure it could never be more beautiful. She walked along the paths that led past the two lakes. The empty park held magic. As the sharp wind struck her, she felt as if she were a child again, living in the fantasy of a fairy story. She was Red Riding Hood on the way to visit her grandmother, she was Goldilocks about to arrive at the house of the three bears, or perhaps the woods and briars would close in upon her and she would be Sleeping Beauty dreaming away the decades until the prince came to wake her.

From the cinder and stone walks of the park she crossed over to the solid squares of pavement leading past houses that seemed as vacant and forbidding as mansions in gothic romances, but must be lived in by ordinary people to exhibit such well-trimmed lawns and symmetrical hedges.

And as she became more accustomed to her route, the distance seemed shorter. Sometimes she hurried the last quarter mile in her eagerness to reach Dr. Arnold and begin work. She rang the bell to the side entrance. Mrs. Greene, Dr. Arnold's housekeeper, admitted her. The two women had coffee together and after they had rinsed their cups in the sink, Ellen went upstairs to Dr. Arnold's study. Though she had been away from him for only a short time, it shocked her to look at him. The night had robbed him of whatever frail strength he had. His will power was keeping him alive so that he could finish his history of the university, and he was depending on her help. She must not disappoint him....

What was best about her walks in the brisk biting cold was the welcome time they gave her to assimilate the astonishing events that had so recently changed her life.

First her beloved Aunt Martha had died. Ellen's parents had died when she was fifteen, and afterward Ellen and her aunt had been very close. But Aunt Martha had a talent for closeness. It sometimes seemed to Ellen when she visited her aunt's house in Concord that Aunt Martha was close to everyone in the town and county. Her house buzzed with guests and callers. There were no secrets between the two women and Ellen knew that her aunt had very little money with which to dispense her hospitality, but she loved entertaining people and had a knack for stretching food and drink. No one ever left her house unsatisfied.

"Darling," she often said to Ellen, "if only I had something to leave you besides this big barn of a place and all these worthless acres."

And she had contrived to make Ellen an heiress. A few days before her sudden death from a heart attack, Aunt Martha had disposed of her property. The house and its surrounding land were to be made into a suburban shopping center and the area around the lake would be converted into a resort. But for all Ellen knew, the settlement might require years.

Dr. Arnold had told Ellen to take all the time she needed when her aunt died, and when she returned to Kingborough she learned that he was in the hospital. She rushed to see him and he appeared forlorn and stranded on his tall, narrow bed surrounded by stiff, formal bouquets and screens and walls plastered with get-well cards.

She had cried when he told her he had terminal cancer. Her tears made him angry. He had never been angry with her before. "Damn it, Ellen, you shame me with your sentimentality. I've had a wonderful life. I've had everything I wanted. I've been president of the university my forebears founded, and I've got a fine son to carry on after me. I've just one last wish and with your help I can make it come true. I want to finish my history of the university."

Her tears increased from a discreet trickle to uncontrolled splashes.

"A man has to die of something," he said sternly.

Once he was out of the hospital, he moved from the president's house on the campus to his suburban estate, and Ellen left his suite of offices in the Administration Building to work with him in his upstairs study. They were astonished at how well the history went when away from the constant telephone calls and faculty meetings, campus crises and continuous visitors.

Before fear snatched her quiet contemplation during her morning walks, Ellen had thought even more of Victor than of her aunt and Dr. Arnold. How little she knew Victor in comparison with them. Yet her commitment to him was deeper and stronger. She wanted to learn everything about him from his first memory as a child to the day of their marriage. At the moment nothing mattered except that she was in love with him.

Their meeting had been commonplace enough. It had occurred while Dr. Arnold was still in the hospital. Victor had telephoned to say how sorry he was to learn about her Aunt Martha, whom he'd known when he was a law student in Concord and later when he worked there for a development concern. He wondered if she remembered that they had met at her aunt's. He'd recently found a job as associate with a law firm in Kingborough.

He invited Ellen to dinner. She didn't remember having met him in Concord but it would have been rude to say so. He was pleasant, and quite tall and handsome—the only thing that irked her was that he carried a cane with a silver handle, which she felt made him appear a bit of an Edwardian dandy. Then she saw that he limped and that the cane must be necessary to his balance, and she was ashamed of having been annoyed by it. But Victor never referred to his disability—even after they were married. Often in the morning the bedclothes were pulled away from his feet and she was appalled at how crippled his left foot was. At first glance, his shoes appeared to be of standard make, but on closer inspection she saw a difference in the left one and she realized that a miracle of shoemaking had gone into contriving such an artful support for such a mangled foot.

One night she asked him about it. His answer was matter-of-fact. He had been driving back to law school after an emergency visit home to attend his father's funeral. He had dozed and was startled awake when his car smashed into a tree. "I'm lucky to be alive," he said. "It delayed me a year in finishing my law degree. But it gave me time to decide what I wanted out of life and how to get it."

She was lucky. She was the most fortunate woman in the world to divide her days between two such remarkable men as Dr. Arnold and Victor.

Victor was truly ambitious. It was a pity he was a lawyer with Kingborough so overpopulated with them, but thank God he had settled in Kingborough or they wouldn't be married. Perhaps rather than discourage him, the number of lawyers acted as a challenge. He had the same glint in his eye she had noticed in certain students and professors and politicians and directors who frequented the campus. That glint spelled success. Raw ambition was distasteful to her. But Victor was different. There was nothing about him that didn't please and delight her.

The fear had such an innocent origin.

At least as far as Ellen could trace its beginning, it came from Mrs. Greene's concern for her safety.

That morning, as usual, Ellen had eased from bed so as not to disturb Victor. After her glass of orange juice, she had set out food to make it easy for Victor to prepare his breakfast. She split an English muffin and put the two pieces in the toaster. She measured coffee for the percolator and placed two eggs on the counter. She had written a note to Victor—"Enjoy your breakfast, darling. I love you." Leaning the note against the jar of strawberry preserves, she had put on her coat, gathered up her tote bag, and walked out into the dark.

By the time she reached the park, a mean penetrating rain began to fall. She grappled for the flimsy rainhat in her bag and put it on, but it was no shield against such a downpour. By the time she reached Dr. Arnold's she was drenched.

"You look like a drowned rat," Mrs. Greene said when she let Ellen in.

She took Ellen's sodden coat and hung it up. She gave Ellen a towel for her hair and some slippers, and then she served the customary coffee. "I don't see how you could get so wet just walking from the bus stop."

"I walked all the way. I walk every morning."

Her news stunned Mrs. Greene.

"That's the craziest thing I've ever heard of. Don't you know it's dangerous? You could be mugged or murdered or raped."

"It's dark. Nobody can see me. It's barely daylight by the time I reach the park. Nobody is out so early."

"The time doesn't have a thing to do with it. There's no time, day or night, when it's safe to be alone on the streets of Kingborough. Don't you read the papers? Good lord, haven't you got eyes in your head?"

After her drenching, Ellen put a folding umbrella and boots in her tote bag to protect herself against unpredicted rain. But a strange fear began to possess her during her morning walk, and the distance between her apartment house and Dr. Arnold's estate seemed to stretch itself. The park was endless and its pathways became sinister curves and turnings that led nowhere. The length she covered became a treadmill and no matter how fast she walked the space between her and Dr. Arnold's increased. When she finally arrived, she had to collect herself before she rang the bell.

Mrs. Greene seemed equally apprehensive. "Thank God you're here," she said.

The house in which Ellen and Victor lived was neatly kept. No trash littered the halls and the mailboxes glistened from regular polishing. Morning papers outside the apartment doors were comforting proof of ordinary domesticity and the wide lobby was bright and innocent of intruders. But when she opened the front door and went down the short walkway to the sidewalk she found herself stopping. She couldn't make herself go farther. She wanted to rush back to Victor.

But Dr. Arnold needed her. Whatever the cost, she must reach him.

During her morning walks, she no longer thought about the loss of her aunt or of the approaching death of Dr. Arnold or of her love for Victor. Her anxiety killed the composure she needed to think of them.

Her fear made her feel that she was walking in quicksand. Sometimes she was sure that her heart would burst from the extreme effort of putting one foot in front of the other. Yet she must go on.

Once she saw the shadow of her pursuer, and then realized it was her own shadow changing shape as she walked from one street lamp to the next.

Or there were footsteps behind her—someone was about to grab her throat. Somehow she dared to turn around to see a paperboy throwing a paper on a stoop.

During those sieges of terror she longed to die. She had read of persons who were so terrified of death that they killed themselves, and she had been astonished, but it surprised her no longer.

Mrs. Greene's warning had aroused in her a morbid interest. Previously she had barely skimmed newspaper accounts of crime. Now she tracked down every reference to murder, assault, and robbery in Kingborough, taking particular note of where the crimes had occurred and learning that the route she walked was the scene of many offenses. But she learned that she had been right to insist to Mrs. Greene that no one dangerous was about as early in the morning as she. Her route was a no man's land for criminals at that hour. Their violence occurred later in the day or in the dark of night. In conforming to Dr. Arnold's working hours, she had chanced upon the magic time when Kingborough was safest.

Even so, her fear didn't lessen. Instead, her apprehension convinced her that her luck couldn't last, and she was most terrified in a place where no crime had ever been committed, and that was in the area at the edge of the park, just before she crossed to the sidewalks that led past the large old estates.

There was one morning when she faltered at the edge of the park, and she could not make herself take the few steps necessary to reach the safety of the sidewalk that would lead her to Dr. Arnold's. She looked around her and was surprised to see that crocuses were beginning to bloom. They were especially profuse in the spot that threatened her, and their unexpected beauty helped to ease her terror.

That afternoon, when Dr. Arnold and Ellen assembled the various sections of the history, they realized it was all but finished. Some minor revisions were necessary, and the index and acknowledgments must be written, and the final selection of photographs and engravings had to be made, but it was work anyone could do.

Dr. Arnold embraced Ellen and called down to Mrs. Greene to bring up a bottle of champagne. They all toasted each other, and Dr. Arnold said he couldn't have managed without either Ellen or Mrs. Greene.

The next morning Ellen had entered the park before she realized that she hadn't felt any fear at all during her walk. It astonished her. Perhaps the end to fear was like the end to pain, so unaccountable that one wasn't aware of the exact moment of relief. She saw with pleasure that there were more crocuses. She hoped it would be an early spring and that before she returned to work on campus, the violets and azaleas for which the park was famous would bloom.

She felt buoyant. What had lifted her fear? Had she been afraid that something might happen to her before Dr. Arnold finished the history and now that it was finished she need no longer be concerned?

All that day she and Dr. Arnold worked hard and joyously and her exhilaration hadn't ebbed when she arrived home and checked the mailbox. There was only one letter. It was from her Aunt Martha's lawyer and his message was brief. Final settlement had been made of her aunt's property and the cash was available. The lawyer suggested that Ellen would want to confer with her own attorney and/or financial adviser about investment and disposition.

Ellen had never needed an attorney before. How nice that she had married one. She hoped Victor would be pleased about the money. She was sure he would be stern and spartan and say he would never touch a penny of it. She wondered if it might dampen his ambition if he learned how large the legacy was. Maybe she shouldn't mention it. But there really wasn't any choice. She couldn't keep a secret of such an amount of money.

Ellen read the letter again. It was a shame that all those serene acres that had belonged to Aunt Martha and many generations of the family were now to be converted. The rambling and gracious house would be destroyed by persons unknown. Well, they were hardly unknown—their name was right in the letter. The Martin Development Company. She had heard of them before. Were they benefactors of the university? Her mind was a jumble of names now that she had begun the index to Dr. Arnold's history.

She didn't have to say anything to Victor. She could just hand him the lawyer's letter to read.

She mustn't have a secret from her husband.

But she had had a secret from Victor. She hadn't mentioned her fear all those mornings when she had left him asleep and had gone out into the dark. She ought to have shared her distress with him. There should be no secrets between lovers.

She would tell him about her fear and the legacy that very night. First, she would tell him about her fear.

Victor telephoned that he had to work late on a case and insisted she go ahead with her meal, but then the work had gone faster than he anticipated and Ellen was just finishing her dessert when he arrived. He was starving and ate the casserole without letting Ellen reheat it.

It pleased her to see how he relished it. They sat for a long time over coffee and Ellen brought out the brandy. She had so much to tell him. "I've been terrified, darling," she began. "I'm not any longer. I can talk about it now."

He listened. His attentiveness encouraged her to go into detail. He held her close and it was as if he were accompanying her on her walk and she was taking him past the townhouses and through the slums and into the park and lingering at the place on the edge of the park where she had been most afraid.

In their deep embrace, she could feel Victor's heart beating and he pulled her closer to him and kissed her. A few minutes later he was the tenderest, most satisfying lover he had ever been.

He was asleep the next morning when she arose, his crippled foot thrust outside the cover.

Her walk was peaceful. Her fear had truly left her and her attention moved easily from observation to reflection on her life and good fortune. She glanced happily at a yard where a camellia bush was in bloom. She began to look for other early blossoms and thought with pleasure of the crocuses at the far boundary of the park.

She thought of the previous night with Victor and the relief she had felt in telling him about her fear. She had planned to tell him about Aunt Martha's money, but that would have intruded in their need to make love.

Anyway, Victor probably knew about her aunt's fortune. Of course he must. When she had read the letter from her aunt's lawyer, the name of the development company had seemed familiar and now she remembered why. It was the company Victor had worked for in Concord. No doubt he had known all along of their interest in the property. So there was no secret to tell him, except that everything had been concluded and the money was theirs to do with as they pleased.

By then she was approaching the boundary of the park, and she was surprised to see someone standing there. Perhaps it was one of the nearby residents out walking his dog, though she hadn't ever encountered anyone there. But the mornings were lighter now and no doubt there would soon be joggers and people riding bikes.

The person's back was to her and he didn't move at all. She wondered if he could hear her footsteps. She didn't want to startle him. The path was narrow there and he would have to step aside to let her pass. They were very close and she said good morning, but he did not answer her. Then he turned slowly to face her.

But he had no face.

She wanted Victor. She needed him. She called his name.

She might have spoken a magic word. The stranger in front of her stumbled as if the name was obscene. She had read with fascination of the disguises thieves and attackers wore. The most cautious were masked and wore gloves. The face of the man in front of her was masked and flattened by a stocking. He wore mittens that made his hands look like hand puppets, and the puppets moved toward her throat.

All the fears and terrors of the dark morning walks had prophesied this last terrible moment, but the grip around her throat was harsher and more cruel than she had ever imagined.

In the instant before she fell dead on the ground where the crocuses were beginning to bloom, she caught a glimpse of that miracle of shoemaker's art that camouflaged Victor's crippled foot.

Laughter Before Dying

Samantha Atkins

Samantha Atkins was dead. Her death didn't surprise anybody as she had been at death's door for two weeks. She had even had an earlier warning six months before when she had suffered her first serious, almost fatal heart attack. She had recovered. A little of the fire had gone out of her, but none of the spirit.

Then two weeks ago she had collapsed in her lawyer's office and had been in critical condition ever since. She was spending her last days in Atkins Hospital, a memorial to her husband, in what amounted to a presidential suite.

No visitors were allowed.

People were just waiting for the word that she had died.

There were a few skeptics who doubted that she was grievously ill. They said they would believe she was dead when they saw her in her coffin. More than one insisted they wouldn't be surprised if Samantha weren't playing possum. Some insisted that even if she was sick she would recover completely. If Samantha makes up her mind to live, she'll live, was the way they put it.

The optimists were wrong. Samantha did die, but her heart condition wasn't the cause. She had been poisoned.

But no one would believe it. There had to be a mistake. The hospital was giving out a false report. Who on earth would have poisoned Samantha? What need was there to poison someone who was already on her deathbed? If you wanted to state it crudely, poisoning Samantha was as foolish and wasteful as shooting a person who was mounting the gallows to be hanged.

The strangest, most mysterious thing about it all was that the nurses who saw Samantha through her last moments said that they had never heard such hearty laughter. At first they hadn't realized what it was. They hadn't been actually in the room when they had heard the rollicking sound—since Samantha hated to have anybody with her they had been hovering in the hall and adjacent rooms.

But when they saw and heard that thunderous laughter coming

from her they couldn't believe their eyes and ears. It was, one of them said later, as if Samantha had been tickled to death. They were all practiced in observing people *in extremis*, but no nurse—and no doctor, for that matter—ever remembered anybody laughing until she died.

Not much in the world had amused Samantha, unless it was having her way about everything and she wasn't given to laughing even then. She considered it her due to have everyone dance to her tune. But something had certainly titillated her when she was dying.

Poisoned!

It was too hard to believe. How?

But, above all, by whom?

Sally Spenser

Sally Spenser had asked at the desk for Samantha's room number. The half-opened door had a *No Visitors* sign on it, but there was no one to stop Sally and all she planned to do was to leave the candy on the bedside table.

Samantha dominated the room as she had dominated life. No doubt Samantha had told death exactly when she would allow it to approach and on what terms.

"I brought you some chocolates, Samantha. Maple-nut creams. I know they're your favorite."

Samantha didn't answer. Perhaps she was asleep. More likely she was being her usual rude self. Samantha had always interested Sally, and Sally was fond of her. Of course Samantha's manners and ruthlessness were deplorable, but they were predictable. There was no question as to what to expect from her. No one escaped her machinations. Well, Samantha had prospered, if having money was everything, and most people seemed to think it was.

There was no use in standing there looking at Samantha. It was an invasion of privacy, really, and Sally turned to leave. All of a sudden Samantha reached out for the box of candy. Her head still lay on the pillows but her hands were as busy and greedy as those of a child shucking off wrappings from a Christmas parcel. Then Samantha's mouth parted almost as wide as if she were in a dentist's chair and she began to pop maple-nut creams onto her outstretched tongue.

Sally Spenser smiled and left.

The next night she had a most unexpected caller. When the doorbell rang her soufflé was almost ready. It needed steady watching and of course somebody *would* ring the bell. Her supper would be ruined if she went to the door. Whenever she made hardboiled eggs nobody showed up, but let her make a soufflé and she could count on someone arriving at the crucial moment when the Pyrex dish was about ready to be pulled from the oven.

She mustn't be rude and keep the caller waiting. She turned off the oven and left the soufflé to its sad fate.

Ted Rankin of the Police Department stood at her front door.

"Mrs. Spenser?"

He knew good and well who she was. In a town that size everybody knew everybody. "I want to ask you a few questions about your visit to Mrs. Atkins."

And when, Sally wanted to say, is visiting the sick a crime? As well as she remembered, visiting the sick was among the cardinal virtues or was she thinking of burying the dead?

She didn't say anything and Ted Rankin stood first on one foot and then on the other. He seemed to be groping for words.

"Well, nobody identified you for sure, but one of the nurses thought it was you she saw going down the hall."

"When are the police supposed to track down visitors to the sick?"

"It's not that exactly. You see, somebody gave Mrs. Atkins a box of candy that was poisoned."

If Ted Rankin had announced the end of the world she couldn't have been more surprised. "That is preposterous," Sally Spenser said and advanced toward him in indignation.

He shuffled backward to keep his distance from her and knocked a pot of begonias off the ledge; then he apologized and said he meant no harm in asking her about the candy, he was only trying to do his job, and then he looked sheepish and muttered goodbye.

Of course the nurse had been right. Sally had visited Samantha and there was no denying that she had brought a box of candy. And at what a sacrifice! Her mouth watered even then when she thought of those beautiful plump nuggets of maple-nut creams in their little paper nests. She had wanted them for herself, but Samantha was as crazy as Sally was about maple-nut creams, and even though Samantha was desperately ill Sally was positive it would cheer her up to have the candy.

Then Sally Spenser reeled.

Those creams had been meant to poison her! It was only by the grace of God or the irony of the devil that Sally wasn't dead instead of Samantha. Just suppose Sally were in her coffin that very minute as she had every right to be. She saw herself lying there surrounded by that pink taffeta that the Jones Funeral Home lined their caskets with. She gazed at herself with folded hands and closed eyes. Oh, she hoped that Julius Jones hadn't painted her cheeks in that garish way that was supposed to represent lifelike flesh tones. She must leave specific instructions not to be painted. She would insist on having a closed casket. No one was to see her after she was dead.

Sally reprimanded herself for behaving in such a befuddled, self-centered manner. What foolishness had prompted her to act as if she could see her own self in a coffin? And what did it matter what happened after she was dead? But she wasn't dead, thank heaven, even though she was supposed to be.

Josephine Foster had given Sally that candy. And Josephine Foster must account for her action. Sally must have it out with Josephine.

What would she say? How could she word her accusation? When your supposed best friend had tried to murder you, how did you proceed? The human heart was truly unfathomable. Here she and Josephine Foster had in a manner of speaking been living out of each other's pockets. They exchanged recipes, had lunch together several times a week, barged in and out of each other's house, mostly by the back door without so much as knocking. Yet somehow or other Sally had so aroused Josephine's hate that death by poison was to be her fate.

How could Josephine have done such a thing? Why, Josephine's mother on her deathbed wouldn't take medicine from anyone but Sally. She refused the nurses and doctors and Josephine herself and had turned to Sally. Suppose that Sally, in spite of her innocence, was found guilty of murdering Samantha? What did they do with murderers now?

Capital punishment had been abandoned, she thought, but there had been such a hue and cry lately about restoring it that it would probably be put back on the books by the time she was sentenced.

Sally was too heartbroken to confront Josephine face to face and accuse her. She would telephone.

"That candy you gave me was poisoned, Josephine," she said, and then she hung up. She'd never in her life hung up a telephone in anyone's ear, but she did then. Sally wanted to cry. She had a right to cry. When the person she thought the most of in the world had tried to poison her she had every reason to cry her eyes out. She waited for the tears to come, but there wasn't so much as a drop in either eye. There were things in this world too deep for tears.

She went to the kitchen and scraped the soufflé from the Pyrex dish into the garbage and then she went to the porch and picked up the shattered pot of begonias. She must report it, but she didn't have the heart to do anything just then.

Josephine Foster

Josephine Foster was too stunned to answer Sally Spenser. Of course she had given Sally the candy, but it was some that had been given to her.

Josephine had felt that Jill Harrison, her son's fiancée, didn't like her. But giving Josephine a box of poisoned candy was taking things a bit too far.

Josephine had been as cordial as she had known how in welcoming Jill as a potential daughter-in-law, and she had tried to steer herself away from the pitfalls of being the widowed mother of an only child, and a son at that. Through the years she had done her best not to be possessive and she had seen to it that Alan had male companionship and father figures. Her brothers, though they lived out of the state, had included Alan in their families' plans—Alan had camped in summer with his first cousins, had skied with them in winter, backpacked with them in spring, and had taken several trips abroad with them.

Then she had worried when Alan came home after graduating from the university law school and had settled happily into his old bedroom and had opened an office on Main Street. He had pooh-poohed her suggestion that he take an apartment of his own. "Mama," he said, "I'd shame you. What would people say if I moved out on you? Besides, I like your cooking. Anyway, I'll be leaving soon enough. I'm looking for a wife."

It had taken him two years to find Jill Harrison, a young teacher who did special work with children, something to do with remedial reading or the use of language. Josephine wasn't exactly sure what Jill's title and training were. Alan was on all kinds of committees and had met Jill at a meeting of some sort. One day he brought Jill home and introduced her as his fiancée, and Josephine and Jill had exchanged very large smiles but, for all that, they didn't take to each other.

Why couldn't Josephine like Jill? Even the way Jill talked somehow annoyed Josephine. The girl was from somewhere in the Middle West where the people prolonged their r's and pushed their voices through their noses. Not that Jill talked much. In fact, she seldom talked in Josephine's presence. Josephine was used to conversationalists who jousted to keep the ball rolling, even though the exchange was nothing but chitchat. But Jill barely nodded after Josephine had rattled on and on in pursuit of some topic of conversation, and with that terse action had killed once and for all Josephine's chatter.

Josephine even found fault with Jill's name. Jill. What kind of name was that? A name from a nursery rhyme. What sort of parents did she have who would name a girl Jill?

Things had improved greatly last week because of the dinner at which Jill had been hostess to Alan and Josephine. The evening had been delightful. Jill had reserved a table in a pleasant, uncrowded restaurant. She had ordered a delicious meal and had the most beautiful flowers for a centerpiece. When dinner was over she had insisted that Josephine take the flowers home with her. That was more than enough, but then she had given Josephine a box of candy.

The flowers were exquisite but the candy looked—well, it looked sort of secondhand; the box was slightly crumpled and smeared with fingerprints, and yet what was so strange was that Jill had pressed it on her as if she were giving Josephine the crown jewels. She thrust the box toward Josephine in the way a child gives its mother something she has made and is so proud of that she's about to burst.

No wonder Jill had seemed so animated or agitated in handing over the chocolates. It would have taken the arrogance of a Borgia to present them with any degree of composure. And she very carefully waited to give Josephine the candy as they were leaving the restaurant. Otherwise Josephine would have opened the candy and passed it around, but it would have been too awkward to do that as they walked along the crowded street to Alan's car. Alan didn't eat sweets, as Jill very well knew, so there was no danger that her darling husband-to-be would be a victim. It was all cleverly planned so that Josephine alone would eat the candy.

Well, Jill Harrrrrrison wasn't going to get away with it.

Josephine would tell Jill that she knew she had tried to poison her.

Jill answered the telephone immediately. "Jill Harrison speaking," she said.

Even the way Jill answered the telephone annoyed Josephine. Why couldn't she just say hello like ordinary mortals? And Jill's tongue trilled both r's in Harrison for the longest, most irritating time that Josephine had so far heard. Josephine identified herself but thought of no introductory remark. She couldn't ask how Jill was, and it was hardly the time to comment on the weather.

"Jill, I'm very upset. I've just learned that the candy you gave me was poisoned."

There was no reply. No denial. No apology. Just another of those long silences Josephine had invariably suffered in Jill's presence.

The wait was painful and awkward, but Josephine intended to have an admission of guilt or at least a remark of some sort from Jill. But none came.

Josephine hung up.

She had never before hung up on anybody in her life.

Josephine had wanted to put the candy in the garbage as soon as she got home from dinner with Jill and Alan. If only she had given in to that impulse, but nothing should be wasted, especially not candy when Sally Spenser was so crazy about it. Sally must have Jill's present, though something would have to be done about the mutilated box.

Josephine had gone to a cupboard in the pantry where she kept odds and ends and found a beautiful tole box that she had bought to keep gloves in, then had decided it was so pretty it must be used sometime as a special gift box. She was happy to see that the candy fitted perfectly into the tole box. Sally would be delighted. How nice to have a special little treat to pass along to such a darling friend.

And now Sally thought that Josephine had tried to poison her.

But what had actually happened was that Jill Harrison had tried to poison Josephine.

Jill Harrison

Jill Harrison hung up the telephone and returned to the stacks of students' papers on the battered card table that listed on spindly, unsteady legs. All the furniture was makeshift in the small furnished apartment she rented by the week. What a contrast there was between the shabby ill-matched pieces around her and the graceful antiques in Josephine Foster's Greek Revival house.

Another unbridgeable gap between her and Alan's mother was that Jill couldn't cook. She could barely open a can without mutilating herself. Thank God for TV dinners and convenience foods. Even if she could have cooked she didn't have the time to prepare proper meals— her students demanded every possible moment and she gave it gladly. It hadn't seemed likely that her life could have had enough room for love, but there was more than enough room for Alan and his love for her and her love for him.

It was his mother who made Jill feel uneasy.

After all the awkward dinners with the Fosters in their elegant home, Jill had ventured to invite them to be her guests in a restaurant, and the evening had gone beautifully. Jill had been proud of the way she looked in her new dress. She was always neat but her clothes were serviceable instead of chic, and it was nice to know that she had a knack for fashion.

That night she had worn the engagement ring that Alan had given her. It had belonged to his grandmother. Alan didn't seem to mind that she didn't wear it habitually, but it was a bit showy to flaunt at work and was a monster in snagging stockings and pantyhose and in getting hung in loose threads of her sweaters.

She had felt very sentimental that night as she was about to leave for the restaurant. She admired Mrs. Foster for her beauty and the way she dressed and ran a household. She had done an admirable job in raising Alan—with all that money and his being the only child he could have been absolutely ruined. Jill admired Mrs. Foster. What she wanted was to love her. How could she not love Alan's mother? What choice did she have but to love the person who had nurtured such a fine person as Alan? And then in that exaggerated moment of sentiment Jill decided to give Mrs. Foster the present Jill loved most in the world—the box of candy Robert had given her earlier that day.

Of course she shouldn't have accepted the present. Teachers were absolutely forbidden to take gifts from their students. But how could she refuse Robert? He had been so intense, so happy, so excited to give her a present that he had clung to it as if someone might tear it from him. The imprints of his moist, nervous hands were on the box and he had crushed the cardboard a little in holding it so tight and so close.

Jill looked with rage at the telephone as if to blame it for having conveyed the information that the candy was poisoned. She began to cry.

She felt there was no consolation for her anywhere. Why had she hypnotized herself into thinking that she had helped Robert and he had given her his trust?

When she had first taken him as a special student he had impressed her as being as near autistic as any child she had ever taught. For long weeks there was no response from him—only a blank mask. Nothing would induce him read or talk. Neither shame nor encouragement would elicit an answer from him. He took her accusations with the same lack of emotion that he took her blandishments and compliments. Nothing flickered behind his dead eyes.

"You must learn to read, Robert," she told him over and over. "You must. There's magic in words. Life can never be dull when you learn to like to read. Language is the greatest gift we've ever been given. You can't refuse to accept it and use it."

At last there was to be victory.

After all her long patient hours and all her wheedling and bullying there was a reward. Robert began to read, hesitantly at first, then quickly. He wrote slowly at first, then so rapidly that the words were illegible.

She was proud of him and he knew it. And he had seemed to be proud of himself, but not at all cocky, and then one day there had been the unexpected gift of candy.

But what she had thought was pride in himself must have been arrogance. He was just waiting to be able to express his hatred and hostility. He wanted to show her his contempt for what they had accomplished together.

And evil came from evil. The evil from Robert which she had mistaken for affection she had passed on to Mrs. Foster. She had given that candy to Mrs. Foster with such pride and even with a sense of sacrifice at parting with what pleased Jill most.

Jill's tears had wet the top papers that she had planned to read and correct. She must be sensible and get on with her work, and then she must put one of the chicken pot pies in the oven for her supper, and then try to decide how to confront Robert.

The night was a torment of sleeplessness and a sense of having been betrayed.

Thank goodness she had Robert in the first class. She could not have postponed talking with him, and she asked to see him privately as soon as the period was over. She had decided not to accuse him. She would make a simple statement and wait for him to answer. "Robert, the candy you gave me was poisoned."

He had been smiling as he stood waiting for her to talk to him, but when she had spoken his face changed back to the mask he had worn all those long dead months when he had refused to read or write or talk.

Robert shrugged, turned around, and walked slowly out of the classroom.

Bessie Green

Robert's rage shocked his mother, Bessie Green. What was that foolishness about the candy being poisoned? He had begged her for the candy and she had told him she wanted to enjoy the candy herself, and he grabbed it from her and she grabbed it back. That wasn't like Robert. He wasn't one to show his feelings. Then she told him all right he could have the candy.

She knew she'd been unfair to Robert. But life had been so hard. She hadn't wanted Robert. He'd come along to surprise her when her hands were too full already. He minded her from the beginning. He didn't give her any of the trouble the older boys did. Never mind that her love was for them. She had to follow her heart. Those older boys had run her a hard race. Everything was up to her. Their father came when he liked and went when he liked and then died the year Robert was born.

That Sonny was a handful. Reform school. Later, trouble with the police. Then escape from jail. No telling where he was now. Every letter in the mailbox had her heart leaping that it might be some word from him.

For a while it had looked as if Joe would follow in his older brother's footsteps, but somewhere along the way that boy took hold of himself. She didn't have anything to do with it. She was too busy keeping a roof over their heads to have much time for child raising. She'd never forget that time the principal came to see her. Oh, Lord, she had thought, here we go again.

First Sonny, now Joe. But not at all. The man wanted her to know she had an exceptional boy in Joe. He ought to go to college. There were lots of scholarships. And somehow Joe had made it. He had to work, of course, because there wasn't a scholarship that covered everything and there was precious little she could give him. He would come in off a job and not so much as take a drink of water before he turned to his books and studied all night. She had thought she worked long hours. Well, she had no cause to complain when she saw what Joe did.

Bessie's one consolation had been Mrs. Litton. When Sonny got into scrapes it was Mrs. Litton who paid for the lawyer. When Sonny needed bail it was Mrs. Litton whom Bessie went to. When Bessie was worried out of her mind and went to see Sonny in jail it was Mrs. Litton who paid her no matter that she didn't work that day. That last year when Joe had to have more time to study it was Mrs. Litton whom Bessie asked for part of the tuition and the books and lunch money and carfare for Joe.

But then when the great day came and Joe was graduated, his name was called twice during the exercises for honors in history and third highest grades in the whole class, she hadn't been able to mention her problem to Mrs. Litton. Joe had to have a present and he had a chance to go on a charter air trip with his classmates to Spain and Portugal. He'd never had a vacation. Who in the family had ever had a vacation, for that matter? Joe just had to have this. He had to. She could go to Mrs. Litton for bail money and lawyer money for Sonny and for school expenses for Joe, but for something special like a graduation trip for Joe she didn't have the face to ask.

So she sinned against God and Mrs. Litton and she sinned gladly by taking silver from the top shelf—it didn't do anybody any good at all, it hadn't been used for years—and pawning it. There was so much silver left it didn't even leave an empty space. Well, Joe had got his trip. And Mrs. Litton had given him $100 for a graduation present— nobody else Bessie worked for so much as sent him a card. And Bessie was a thief. No, she wasn't a thief. She'd just been pushed too far. But she felt guilty because she *was* guilty and she'd die if Mrs. Litton ever found out.

Robert was sitting in the corner glowering at her. Poor child. He never had laughed or cried. In plenty of families the youngest was the favorite. But nobody had ever paid any attention to Robert. He didn't do well in school but they promoted him anyhow. Always changing their tune at schools. If poor Sonny hadn't been bullied by teachers things might have been different, if they had passed him along; but they held him back, made him ashamed of being so big and still in the third grade.

This last year there had been a change of some kind in Robert. Maybe he was trying to imitate his big brother Joe. Anyway, Robert began to study. But he was still too tight-lipped to tell her what might be interesting him. She kept him clean and she fed him and if he wanted to be sullen she didn't have any jokes to tell him to cheer him up.

Now he was beating his fists on the table. He was in such a rage she didn't know what to expect.

"That candy you gave me was poisoned."

He was starting up again about the candy.

"Son, I didn't know that. I'm sorry." She never had called Robert son before. He wasn't even called Bob or Bobby.

Then Bessie Green understood the significance of what Robert had said.

Mrs. Litton had given her that candy. Bessie had thought all the time she had worked for her that Mrs. Litton was too good to be true. It was hard to believe that anybody could be so kind and generous. She had a heart as big as all outdoors, and though she owned one of the prettiest and largest houses in the best section of town she wasn't what you'd call rich. She'd let the gardener go and for two years she'd been doing her own cooking, and the trim on the brick house hadn't been painted for six years.

But there must be a mean streak in her. Mrs. Litton was getting back at Bessie for taking the silver. She had known all along that Bessie had stolen it. Maybe she'd even sneaked up behind her and watched her take it down from the shelf, and she had just bided her time to punish Bessie.

Angela Litton

Angela Litton had never seen Bessie sulk before. Instead of going about her duties in her usual competent way she seemed to attack the house. The blinds rattled, the pans crashed like the timpani of an orchestra, doors slammed, dust billowed from carpets, the clotheslines chattered when Bessie flung the laundry on them. "Bessie, dear, do you feel all right?"

Bessie echoed to herself, "Bessie, dear, do you feel all right?"

"I feel all right considering," Bessie said. For all Mrs. Litton knew Bessie might be in the last throes of death by poisoning.

"What's wrong?"

"Nothing's wrong. But it could be. My, but it could be. That poor child so proud to be taking his teacher a present and what do you know, it was poisoned."

"What poor child?"

"Robert."

"Who is Robert?"

"Robert's my youngest boy."

"Bessie, you've never mentioned Robert to me. I didn't know you had a child named Robert."

"Well, I have. That poor child has had to fend for himself. Nobody to take up for him. Me worried out of my head over Sonny and Joe and finally Robert learns to read and begins to like school and he takes his teacher a present that's poisoned."

"Bessie, that's most distressing."

And Bessie muttered to herself, "Bessie, that's most distressing." Then she said, "Mrs. Litton, I owe you a lot. My boys and I owe you a lot," and the thought of the silver struck her. "We owe you a lot more than I can ever thank you for but that doesn't mean you can do what you did. I'm a human being the same as anybody."

"Bessie, dear, I don't know what you mean."

And Bessie whispered to herself, "Bessie, dear, I don't know what you mean." Then she said aloud, "That candy you gave me was poisoned.

I'd have eaten it and been in my grave if my little boy hadn't grabbed it to give to his teacher."

There was more than time for that to sink in and still Mrs. Litton said nothing. They were in the same room and stood near each other, but when Mrs. Litton spoke her voice seemed to come from as far off as a grave in Moreton cemetery over by the river.

"Bessie, please stop what you're doing and make me a pot of tea."

Bessie propped the vacuum against a closet door. She should have told Mrs. Litton to make her own tea. She should have told her to look her longest because that was the last she was going to see of Bessie. But she couldn't help falling into her old habits. Nothing was too good for Mrs. Litton.

Bessie made the tea and poured it into the prettiest teapot, though with so many to choose from who could say which was the prettiest? Bessie selected the one she knew Mrs. Litton favored. Mrs. Litton was crazy about blue and white china, and God help Bessie she went to the rosebush just outside the kitchen door and cut two buds to set in a little Waterford vase with the other things on the tea tray.

"Bessie, will you have a cup with me?"

"I don't care for hot tea. Ice tea is all right in the summertime with lots of lemon and sugar and a sprig of mint."

"Then make yourself some coffee."

"I've got my work to do."

Mrs. Litton poured a cup of tea, and then she set the cup at a distance as if she didn't intend to drink it after all.

"Bessie, I didn't know the candy was poisoned. It was given to me by someone from whom I didn't want to accept a favor, not even the gift of a box of chocolates. I thought you might enjoy it. It's come as a great shock that you would think I'd try to poison you. And it's an equal shock to learn that someone wanted to poison me."

Bessie wanted to cry. She wanted to cry her eyeballs out the way she did that first time Sonny went to jail. "I'm sorry, Mrs. Litton."

The cup of tea grew tepid. Angela Litton didn't want it. But she needed it. She raised the cup to her lips, then set it down without sipping from it.

She had planned to go to Samantha Atkins' funeral that afternoon and she supposed she would go after all. But Samantha hadn't planned for Angela to be alive to attend her funeral, whenever it might be. She had taken particular pains to keep Angela away.

When had Samantha visited Angela? It had to be before her second heart attack when she had gone back to the hospital. For years

Samantha had tried to feud with Angela, but Angela would have none of it. Samantha would sweep past her at parties or meetings or gatherings and Angela would nevertheless greet her. Over the years she had been snubbed and vilified by Samantha.

Then out of the blue Samantha had appeared at Angela's door saying she had come to end their grudge. Angela assumed that Samantha's first heart attack had changed her, that having been so near death and realizing that it could overtake her at any moment she saw how foolish her imagined enmity had been.

There was no factual basis for the feud. Archibald, Samantha's son, was an alcoholic before he was out of his teens, and he had shown some slight interest in Angela's daughter Susan. But Susan didn't care for him; besides she was engaged to her childhood sweetheart. Later, after Susan had married and moved away, Archibald had gone to Italy and had shot himself. But no one except Samantha had seen any connection between those events. Long before Susan had married, Archibald had courted half a dozen other girls, but they and their parents were as little eager to encourage his attention as Susan and Angela had been.

In some strange warped way Samantha held Angela responsible for Archibald's suicide and insisted that if only Angela had given Archibald's love for Susan half a chance and not forbidden them to see each other, Archibald would be alive that very minute. Samantha had sworn she would get even with Angela if it took her the rest of her life.

Samantha Atkins

Samantha Atkins had not been known to have a sense of humor or even a sense of the ridiculous, though she was adept at laughing at other people's embarrassments and quick to laugh at anyone in an awkward situation. And irony was beyond her.

But even Samantha, entirely lacking in humor and lightness, had been amused to the extent of laughing uproariously on her deathbed at the way fate had contrived to get her to gobble the poisoned chocolates she had delighted in preparing for her old enemy Angela Litton.

A Nice Place to Stay

All my life I've wanted a nice place to stay. I don't mean anything grand, just a small room with the walls freshly painted and a few neat pieces of furniture and a window to catch the sun so that two or three potted plants could grow. That's what I've always dreamed of. I didn't yearn for love or money or nice clothes, though I was a pretty enough girl and pretty clothes would have made me prettier—not that I mean to brag.

Things fell on my shoulders when I was fifteen. That was when Mama took sick, and keeping house and looking after Papa and my two older brothers—and of course nursing Mama—became my responsibility. Not long after that Papa lost the farm and we moved to town. I don't like to think of the house we lived in near the C & R railroad tracks, though I guess we were lucky to have a roof over our heads—it was the worst days of the Depression and a lot of people didn't even have a roof, even one that leaked, plink, plonk; in a heavy rain there weren't enough pots and pans and vegetable bowls to set around to catch all the water.

Mama was the sick one but it was Papa who died first—living in town didn't suit him. By then my brothers had married and Mama and I moved into two backrooms that looked onto an alley and everybody's garbage cans and dump heaps. My brothers pitched in and gave me enough every month for Mama's and my barest expenses even though their wives complained.

I tried to make Mama comfortable. I catered to her every whim and fancy. I loved her. All the same I had another reason to keep her alive as long as possible. While she breathed I knew I had a place to stay. I was terrified of what would happen to me when Mama died. I had no high school diploma and no experience at outside work and I knew my sisters-in-law wouldn't take me in or let my brothers support me once Mama was gone.

Then Mama drew her last breath with a smile of thanks on her face for what I had done.

Sure enough, Norine and Thelma, my brothers' wives, put their feet down. I was on my own from then on. So that scared feeling of wondering where I could lay my head took over in my mind and never left me.

I had some respite when Mr. Williams, a widower twenty-four years older than me, asked me to marry him. I took my vows seriously. I meant to cherish him and I did. But that house we lived in! Those walls couldn't have been dirtier if they'd been smeared with soot and the plumbing was stubborn as a mule. My left foot stayed sore from having to kick the pipe underneath the kitchen sink to get the water to run through.

Then Mr. Williams got sick and had to give up his shoe repair shop that he ran all by himself. He had a small savings account and a few of those twenty-five-dollar government bonds and drew some disability insurance until the policy ran out in something like six months.

I did everything I could to make him comfortable and keep him cheerful. Though I did all the laundry I gave him clean sheets and clean pajamas every third day and I think it was by my will power alone that I made a begonia bloom in that dark backroom Mr. Williams stayed in. I even pestered his two daughters and told them they ought to send their father some get-well cards and they did once or twice. Every now and then when there were a few pennies extra I'd buy cards and scrawl signatures nobody could have read and mailed them to Mr. Williams to make him think some of his former customers were remembering him and wishing him well.

Of course when Mr. Williams died his daughters were johnny-on-the-spot to see that they got their share of the little bit that tumbledown house brought. I didn't begrudge them—I'm not one to argue with human nature.

I hate to think about all those hardships I had after Mr. Williams died. The worst of it was finding somewhere to sleep; it all boiled down to having a place to stay. Because somehow you can manage not to starve. There are garbage cans to dip into—you'd be surprised how wasteful some people are and how much good food they throw away. Or if it was right after the garbage trucks had made their collections and the cans were empty I'd go into a supermarket and pick, say, at the cherries pretending I was selecting some to buy. I didn't slip their best ones into my mouth. I'd take either those so ripe that they should have been thrown away or those that weren't ripe enough and shouldn't have been put out for people to buy. I might snitch a withered cabbage leaf or a few pieces of watercress or a few of those small round tomatoes about the size of hickory nuts—I never can remember their right name. I wouldn't make a pig of myself, just eat enough to ease my hunger. So

I managed. As I say, you don't have to starve.

The only work I could get hardly ever paid me anything beyond room and board. I wasn't a practical nurse, though I knew how to take care of sick folks, and the people hiring me would say that since I didn't have the training and qualifications I couldn't expect much. All they really wanted was for someone to spend the night with Aunt Myrtle or Cousin Kate or Mama or Daddy; no actual duties were demanded of me, they said, and they really didn't think my help was worth anything except meals and a place to sleep. The arrangements were pretty makeshift. Half the time I wouldn't have a place to keep my things, not that I had any clothes to speak of, and sometimes I'd sleep on a cot in the hall outside the patient's room or on some sort of contrived bed in the patient's room.

I cherished every one of those sick people, just as I had cherished Mama and Mr. Williams. I didn't want them to die. I did everything I knew to let them know I was interested in their welfare—first for their sakes, and then for mine, so I wouldn't have to go out and find another place to stay.

Well, now, I've made out my case for the defense, a term I never thought I'd have to use personally, so now I'll make out the case for the prosecution.

I stole.

I don't like to say it, but I was a thief.

I'm not light-fingered. I didn't want a thing that belonged to anybody else. But there came a time when I felt forced to steal. I had to have some things. My shoes fell apart. I needed some stockings and underclothes. And when I'd ask a son or a daughter or a cousin or a niece for a little money for those necessities they acted as if I was trying to blackmail them. They reminded me that I wasn't qualified as a practical nurse, that I might even get into trouble with the authorities if they found I was palming myself off as a practical nurse—which I wasn't and they knew it. Anyway, they said that their terms were only bed and board.

So I began to take things—small things that had been pushed into the backs of drawers or stored high on shelves in boxes—things that hadn't been used or worn for years and probably would never be used again. I made my biggest haul at Mrs. Bick's where there was an attic full of trunks stuffed with clothes and doodads from the twenties all the way back to the nineties—uniforms, ostrich fans, Spanish shawls, beaded bags. I sneaked out a few of these at a time and every so often sold them to a place called Way Out, Hippie Clothiers.

I tried to work out the exact amount I got for selling something. Not, I know, that you can make up for theft. But, say, I got a dollar for a feather boa belonging to Mrs. Bick: well, then I'd come back and work at a job that the cleaning woman kept putting off, like waxing the hall upstairs or polishing the andirons or getting the linen closet in order.

All the same I *was* stealing—not everywhere I stayed, not even in most places, but when I had to I stole. I admit it.

But I didn't steal that silver box.

I was as innocent as a baby where that box was concerned. So when that policeman came toward me grabbing at the box I stepped aside, and maybe I even gave him the push that sent him to his death. He had no business acting like that when that box was mine, whatever Mrs. Crowe's niece argued.

Fifty thousand nieces couldn't have made it not mine.

Anyway, the policeman was dead and though I hadn't wanted him dead I certainly hadn't wished him well. And then I got to thinking: well, I didn't steal Mrs. Crowe's box but I had stolen other things and it was the mills of God grinding exceeding fine, as I once heard a preacher say, and I was being made to pay for the transgressions that had caught up with me.

Surely I can make a little more sense out of what happened than that, though I never was exactly clear in my own mind about everything that happened.

Mrs. Crowe was the most appreciative person I ever worked for. She was bedridden and could barely move. I don't think the registered nurse on daytime duty considered it part of her job to massage Mrs. Crowe. So at night I would massage her, and that pleased and soothed her. She thanked me for every small thing I did—when I fluffed her pillow, when I'd put a few drops of perfume on her earlobes, when I'd straighten the wrinkled bedcovers.

I had a little joke. I'd pretend I could tell fortunes and I'd take Mrs. Crowe's hand and tell her she was going to have a wonderful day but she must beware of a handsome blond stranger—or some such foolishness that would make her laugh. She didn't sleep well and it seemed to give her pleasure to talk to me most of the night about her childhood or her dead husband.

She kept getting weaker and weaker and two nights before she died she said she wished she could do something for me but that when she became an invalid she had signed over everything to her niece. Anyway, Mrs. Crowe hoped I'd take her silver box. I thanked her. It pleased me that she liked me well enough to give me the box. I didn't have any real use for it. It would have made a nice trinket box, but I didn't have any trinkets. The box seemed to be Mrs. Crowe's fondest possession. She kept it on the table beside her and her eyes lighted up every time she looked at it. She might have been a little girl first seeing a brand-new baby doll early on a Christmas morning.

So when Mrs. Crowe died and the niece on whom I set eyes for the first time dismissed me, I gathered up what little I had and took the box and left. I didn't go to Mrs. Crowe's funeral. The paper said it was private and I wasn't invited. Anyway, I wouldn't have had anything suitable to wear.

I still had a few dollars left over from those things I'd sold to the hippie place called Way Out, so I paid a week's rent for a room that was the worst I'd ever stayed in.

It was freezing cold and no heat came up to the third floor where I was. In that room with falling plaster and buckling floorboards and darting roaches, I sat wearing every stitch I owned, with a sleazy blanket and a faded quilt draped around me waiting for the heat to rise, when in swept Mrs. Crowe's niece in a fur coat and a fur hat and shiny leather boots up to her knees. Her face was beet-red from anger when she started telling me that she had traced me through a private detective and I was to give her back the heirloom I had stolen.

Her statement made me forget the precious little bit I knew of the English language. I couldn't say a word, and she kept on screaming that if I returned the box immediately no criminal charge would be made against me. Then I got back my voice and I said that box was mine and that Mrs. Crowe had wanted me to have it, and she asked if I had any proof or if there were any witnesses to the gift, and I told her that when I was given a present I said thank you, that I didn't ask for proof and witnesses, and that nothing could make me part with Mrs. Crowe's box.

The niece stood there breathing hard, in and out, almost counting her breaths like somebody doing an exercise.

"You'll see," she yelled, and then she left.

The room was colder than ever and my teeth chattered.

Not long afterward I heard heavy steps clumping up the stairway. I realized that the niece had carried out her threat and that the police were after me.

I was panic-stricken. I chased around the room like a rat with a cat after it. Then I thought that if the police searched my room and couldn't find the box it might give me time to decide what to do. I grabbed the box out of the top dresser drawer and scurried down the back hall. I snatched the back door open. I think what I intended to do was run down the back steps and hide the box somewhere, underneath a bush or maybe in a garbage can.

Those back steps were steep and rose almost straight up for three stories and they were flimsy and covered with ice.

I started down. My right foot slipped. The handrail saved me. I clung to it with one hand and to the silver box with the other hand and picked and chose my way across the patches of ice.

When I was midway I heard my name shrieked. I looked around to see a big man leaping down the steps after me. I never saw such anger on a person's face. Then he was directly behind me and reached out to snatch the box.

I swerved to escape his grasp and he cursed me. Maybe I pushed him. I'm not sure—not really.

Anyway, he slipped and fell down and down and down, and then after all that falling he was absolutely still. The bottom step was beneath his head like a pillow and the rest of his body was spreadeagled on the brick walk.

Then almost like a pet that wants to follow its master, the silver box jumped from my hand and bounced down the steps to land beside the man's left ear.

My brain was numb. I felt paralyzed. Then I screamed.

Tenants from that house and the houses next door and across the alley pushed windows open and flung doors open to see what the commotion was about, and then some of them began to run toward the back yard. The policeman who was the dead man's partner—I guess you'd call him that—ordered them to keep away.

After a while more police came and they took the dead man's body and drove me to the station where I was locked up.

From the very beginning I didn't take to that young lawyer they assigned to me. There wasn't anything exactly that I could put my finger on. I just felt uneasy with him. His last name was Stanton. He had a first name of course, but he didn't tell me what it was; he said he wanted me to call him Bat like all his friends did.

He was always smiling and reassuring me when there wasn't anything to smile or be reassured about, and he ought to have known it all along instead of filling me with false hope.

All I could think was that I was thankful Mama and Papa and Mr. Williams were dead and that my shame wouldn't bring shame on them.

"It's going to be all right," the lawyer kept saying right up to the end, and then he claimed to be indignant when I was found guilty of resisting arrest and of manslaughter and theft or robbery—there was the biggest hullabaloo as to whether I was guilty of theft or robbery. Not that I was guilty of either, at least in this particular instance, but no one would believe me.

You would have thought it was the lawyer being sentenced instead of me, the way he carried on. He called it a terrible miscarriage of justice and said we might as well be back in the eighteenth century when they hanged children.

Well, that was an exaggeration, if ever there was one; nobody was being hung and nobody was a child. That policeman had died and I had had a part in it. Maybe I had pushed him. I couldn't be sure. In my heart I really hadn't meant him any harm. I was just scared. But he was dead all the same. And as far as stealing went, I hadn't stolen the box but I had stolen other things.

And then it happened. It was a miracle. All my life I'd dreamed of a nice room of my own, a comfortable place to stay. And that's exactly what I got.

The room was on the small side but it had everything I needed in it, even a wash basin with hot and cold running water, and the walls were freshly painted, and they let me choose whether I wanted a wing chair with a chintz slipcover or a modern Danish armchair. I even got to decide what color bedspread I preferred. The window looked out on a beautiful lawn edged with shrubbery, and the matron said I'd be allowed to go to the greenhouse and select some potted plants to keep in my room. The next day I picked out a white gloxinia and some russet chrysanthemums.

I didn't mind the bars at the windows at all. Why, this day and age some of the finest mansions have barred windows to keep burglars out.

The meals—I simply couldn't believe there was such delicious food in the world. The woman who supervised their preparation had embezzled the funds of one of the largest catering companies in the state after working herself up from cook to treasurer.

The other inmates were very friendly and most of them had led the most interesting lives. Some of the ladies occasionally used words that you usually see written only on fences or printed on sidewalks before the cement dries, but when they were scolded they apologized. Every now and then somebody would get angry with someone and there would be a little scratching or hair pulling, but it never got too bad. There was a choir—I can't sing but I love music—and they gave a concert every Tuesday morning at chapel, and Thursday night was movie night. There wasn't any admission charge. All you did was go in and sit down anywhere you pleased.

We all had a special job and I was assigned to the infirmary. The doctor and nurse both complimented me. The doctor said that I should have gone into professional nursing, that I gave confidence to the patients and helped them get well. I don't know about that but I've had years of practice with sick people and I like to help anybody who feels bad.

I was so happy that sometimes I couldn't sleep at night. I'd get up and click on the light and look at the furniture and the walls. It was hard to believe I had such a pleasant place to stay. I'd remember supper that night, how I'd gone back to the steam table for a second helping of asparagus with lemon and herb sauce, and I compared my plenty with those terrible times when I had slunk into supermarkets and nibbled overripe fruit and raw vegetables to ease my hunger.

Then one day here came that lawyer, not even at regular visiting hours, bouncing around congratulating me that my appeal had been upheld, or whatever the term was, and that I was as free as a bird to leave right that minute.

He told the matron she could send my belongings later and he dragged me out where TV cameras and reporters were waiting.

As soon as the cameras began whirring and the photographers began to aim, the lawyer kissed me on the cheek and pinned a flower on me. He made a speech saying that a terrible miscarriage of justice had been rectified. He had located people who testified that Mrs. Crowe had given me the box—she had told the gardener and the cleaning woman. They hadn't wanted to testify because they didn't want to get mixed up with the police, but the lawyer had persuaded them in the cause of justice and humanity to come forward and make statements.

The lawyer had also looked into the personnel record of the dead policeman and had learned that he had been judged emotionally unfit for his job, and the psychiatrist had warned the Chief of Police that something awful might happen either to the man himself or to a suspect unless he was relieved of his duties.

All the time the lawyer was talking into the microphones he had latched onto me like I was a three-year-old that might run away, and I just stood and stared. Then when he had finished his speech about me the reporters told him that like his grandfather and his uncle he was sure to end up as governor of the state.

At that the lawyer gave a big grin in front of the camera and waved goodbye and pushed me into his car.

I was terrified. The nice place I'd found to stay in wasn't mine any longer. My old nightmare was back—wondering how I could manage to eat and how much stealing I'd have to do to live from one day to the next.

The cameras and reporters had followed us.

A photographer asked me to turn down the car window beside me, and I overheard two men way in the back of the crowd talking. My ears are sharp. Papa always said I could hear thunder three states away. Above the congratulations and bubbly talk around me I heard one of those men in back say, "This is a bit too much, don't you think? Our Bat is showing himself the champion of the Senior Citizen now. He's already copped the teeny-boppers and the under-thirties, using methods that ought to have disbarred him. He should have made the gardener and cleaning woman testify at the beginning, and from the first he should have checked into the policeman's history. There ought never to have been a case at all, much less a conviction. But Bat wouldn't have got any publicity that way. He had to do it in his own devious, spectacular fashion." The other man just kept nodding and saying after every sentence, "You're damned right."

Then we drove off and I didn't dare look behind me because I was so heartbroken over what I was leaving.

The lawyer took me to his office. He said he hoped I wouldn't mind a little excitement for the next few days. He had mapped out some public appearances for me. The next morning I was to be on an early television show. There was nothing to be worried about. He would be right beside me to help me just as he had helped me throughout my trouble. All that I had to say on the TV program was that I owed my freedom to him.

I guess I looked startled or bewildered because he hurried on to say that I hadn't been able to pay him a fee but that now I was able to pay him back—not in money but in letting the public know about how he was the champion of the underdog.

I said I had been told that the court furnished lawyers free of charge to people who couldn't pay, and he said that was right, but his point was that I could repay him now by telling people all that he had done for me. Then he said the main thing was to talk over our next appearance on TV. He wanted to coach me in what I was going to say, but first he would go into his partner's office and tell him to take all the incoming calls and handle the rest of his appointments.

When the door closed after him I thought that he was right. I did owe my freedom to him. He was to blame for it. The smart aleck. The upstart. Who asked him to butt in and snatch me out of my pretty room and the work I loved and all that delicious food?

It was the first time in my life I knew what it meant to despise someone. I hated him.

Before, when I was convicted of manslaughter, there was a lot of talk about malice aforethought and premeditated crime.

There wouldn't be any argument this time.

I hadn't wanted any harm to come to that policeman. But I did mean harm to come to this lawyer.

I grabbed up a letter opener from his desk and ran my finger along the blade and felt how sharp it was. I waited behind the door and when he walked through I gathered all my strength and stabbed him. Again and again and again.

Now I'm back where I want to be—in a nice place to stay.

The More the Deadlier

Angelina was annoyed with her husband. Why was Parry being such a nuisance? Why did he have such a stubborn streak? It was his own fault that she had to murder him.

She was so placid and amiable, so much the docile companion, that even to think of murder had been unthinkable until her back was to the wall. Now she knew that there was no way out of the sweet paralysis in which she lived except to kill Parry.

Angelina readily admitted that in most ways Parry was an estimable husband and she would wholeheartedly have recommended him to a second prospective wife. But Angelina and Parry had had enough of each other and she wanted no more to do with him. Why was he so obstinate in refusing to let her go?

A divorce or legal separation, though much desired, wasn't mandatory to Angelina. She just wanted to be rid of Parry once and for all and to leave him gracefully. He was welcome to the house and she had settled much of her fortune on him when they were married, so it wasn't as if she would leave him high and dry.

He wouldn't hear of her leaving. His reaction was so violent that she decided to make no formal farewell but just to write a note and sneak off. She wasn't cruel and she didn't want to make Parry unhappy, but if she stayed with him she would be unhappy. She devised a simple escape. One morning while he was in town doing the daily errands she would put a note on his pillow and then she would walk the two miles, or however far it was, to the superhighway and flag a long-distance bus going in any direction as long as it removed her from Parry.

Why postpone the inevitable? Tomorrow would be best.

But that night after dinner when they had finished their coffee Parry said, "Angelina, when you're as close to someone as I am to you, you sense things. You've been preoccupied all day. You're planning to leave tomorrow, aren't you? Well, I won't let you."

She had been discovered in a shameful act, like an employee whose thieving hand had been discovered in the till. Such clairvoyance was unforgivably rude. Parry was taking unfair advantage of her, but his mindreading would only delay her leaving for a few days.

No two people could have been more different in background and upbringing than Angelina and Parry. "I was the only child," Angelina had told Parry during the first days of their marriage. "I wasn't only the only child, but my parents were only children too. I longed for brothers and sisters and cousins and aunts and uncles."

"Christ," Parry said. "There were so damned many of us. In the small house we lived in it seemed there were hundreds of us. Don't ever let anybody tell you the more the merrier. It's the more the deadlier. Our personalities were massacred. We were a warped lot of brats."

Angelina had to be free. She had to break out of this bondage. She couldn't wait for another natural death to set her free, and, anyway, she might die before Parry. Love and duty had kept her willingly beside her invalid mother during the time of her lingering illness, but Angelina felt neither love nor duty toward Parry. He was nice. As a matter of fact, he was rather a dear and most attentive and obliging, and for all his quietness she didn't find him dull. Indeed, there was a kind of mystery about him.

Quiet as he was, and conscientiously as he did everything, there were changes in his mood and she had learned not to let him know that she noticed shifts in his manner and behavior. It embarrassed him if she mentioned some change in the way he had prepared a recipe or noted a difference in how he combed his hair. In more intimate matters there were definite changes. His lovemaking varied in intensity and frequency; on some occasions there was an urgency and hunger about his passion, as if it were the last time the act of love would be granted to him. Which was silly, because she never refused. For heaven's sake, why should she?

He had been so acquiescent to all her suggestions that she hadn't imagined for a second that he wouldn't agree to a separation.

Angelina and Parry had promised to stay together until death parted them. More realistic persons had long since struck that vow from the marriage ceremony. But Angelina realized that she and Parry had been right to retain that part of the traditional ritual. Death, it was now obvious to her, was the only thing that could part them.

She had been drugged by the ease of their life together on their large estate in deep isolation in the country. She had been delicately corrupted by the leisure, the hours to fill as she liked, the satisfying immersion in magazines and books, and sleep that could last as long as she pleased. Self-indulgence had almost ruined her. Sloth and permissiveness had erased the demanding years when she had held two jobs and had seldom had enough sleep, had not often even sat

down to a meal but had bolted food as she was on the run from one job
to another or in the middle of a task.

"I can keep you here," Parry said. "I'm stronger than you. And who
knows we're here? We've never had visitors. The only people who ever
came were the builders and contractors and real estate agent."

That was the first time the thought of murdering Parry had entered
Angelina's mind.

The morning after that outburst, Parry was almost excessively
attentive when he served her breakfast in bed, and his voice was
seductive. "You can't possibly want to leave, Angelina. You haven't the
faintest idea of what the world is like. You haven't been hungry and
mistreated or you'd realize what a paradise we have here."

Suddenly the world seemed threatening and she doubted that even
if she were rid of Parry she would know what to do with her freedom.
She had botched her chance for freedom. Instead of sitting down and
deciding sensibly what she wanted of life after she had inherited Miss
Allison's money, Angelina had behaved erratically and precipitately
and had journeyed to what a travel folder called the Emerald Isle.
There the seven others on her deluxe tour had bolted home to the
United States instead of going to Belfast, which was under shell fire.
But Angelina could not act with their resolution. She could not budge
from Killarney, and she had grabbed at the first amenable stranger
with such intensity that she had forced him to marry her.

Since then she had done everything she could to show Parry her
appreciation for rescuing her. Well, she was sick and tired of Parry. She
wanted life. What life was she had no inkling, but she had some idea of
what it wasn't. It wasn't roses on the breakfast tray every morning. It
wasn't whiling away hours in reading. It wasn't dressing in high
fashion. It wasn't eating the most delicious food money could buy. It
wasn't making love constantly.

She had no choice but to murder Parry. She sighed. He should have
run for his life at his first sight of her in Ireland.

Angelina had been looking into the small grate fire in the Killarney
pub and had begun to weep as she sipped brandy. She felt absolutely
at the end of her tether. She didn't know how she had been able to
leave her room in the hotel and find the pub, and she was positive that
she would die there in front of the fire whose hot coals made deep red
crisscrosses on her legs. Then someone had moved from the bar to her
table and had smiled at her, and she had immediately put herself at
his mercy. She begged for help and assured him she could pay for it.
Whatever his price, he must see that she got back to the United States

because she was so confused by fear and anxiety that she could never find her way back alone.

She had been too enmeshed in her own misery to assess the situation accurately, but she soon realized that Parry, in turn, had looked to her for his salvation. She had expressed her predicament so badly that he had blurted out his own plight. He was stranded. He said he couldn't even pay for the drink in his hand. Angelina had pulled crumpled pound notes from her purse and ordered another brandy for herself and a drink for Parry, and when they had finished their drinks she invited Parry to lunch at her hotel.

They had sat at a table decorated with blatantly artificial flowers that needed dusting and looked through starched lace curtains onto a downpour of rain. Even the thought of food had nauseated Angelina for days and she couldn't remember when she had last eaten. And Parry, whose name she didn't yet know, admitted that his last meal had been a continental breakfast the day before. He told her his name was Parry and then, as if making it up, he added Brown. She told him that her name was Angelina Green, and though she was bogged down in despair it struck her as amusing that theirs was a colorful meeting if nothing else.

They were married three days after they returned to the United States. She wasn't sure whether she had mentioned Miss Allison's money to Parry before they were married, but Parry was pleased when she settled a large sum on him, and she made another sizable amount available through a joint checking account. That diminished Miss Allison's money only slightly—Angelina still had money galore for herself, and she acceded with delight to Parry's suggestion that they buy a place in the country.

Their search was leisurely and methodical until Angelina wearied of looking and was relieved when a large house in poor repair caught Parry's eye in southwest Virginia. They would have fun restoring it, he said, and its nicest feature was that it was miles from everywhere: The place was situated on property which had been sold for an expressway. Some of the land had been leveled for construction, but for some reason the highway project had been abandoned. On the western boundary there was a deep and sharp decline from which Angelina had backed away in fright, suggesting that they build a stout wall there, but Parry had said it would obstruct the magnificent view.

Parry instantly became lord of the manor. He gave orders and made decisions. He said it was his way of showing appreciation for what Angelina's money had made possible. Brick by brick and stone by stone

Angelina and Parry had helped with the restoration, and now that the house was at its most beautiful they shared the chores. At Parry's insistence he did the cooking. He didn't even want Angelina in the kitchen. Ever since he had worked as a short-order cook he had longed to be a chef, and he had extraordinary talent for it. Yet however great his gift, he sometimes lost it. Occasionally he would burn something or a dish would be too greasy or undercooked, and every now and then he appeared eager to get out of the kitchen and work in the garden or take long hikes and inspection tours around the estate.

He went into town daily to buy the groceries and do the errands and he insisted on going by himself. He also kept the grounds and cultivated roses. Gardening books were mixed with the cookbooks on the shelves he had installed in the pantry plus a few on woodworking, which was another talent he had.

This ideal life was suffocating Angelina. Damn fate for getting her into this fix. All possible choices had been open to her, and she had muffed her chance for liberty because Parry had appeared like a genie out of a brandy bottle in Killarney.

She had tried to explain to Parry. "I didn't question my life during the years my mother was an invalid. I earned what I could as a typist, and at night I went to the nursing home where my mother was and helped with the chores there to reduce the fees for her care. That was my patch. My furrow. Then my mother died and soon after that Miss Allison left me all her money and I went to Ireland and we met."

"Yes," Parry said, "and I'll always be with you. This is the first happiness I've known. I owe it all to you. It makes up for all the hell I suffered during my rotten childhood."

Damn Parry and his miserable childhood. Her own childhood had been idyllic. She had been the cherished darling of a fond father and an even fonder mother. Parry was intent on hoarding his unhappy memories and capitalizing on them. He spouted rancorously about his childhood, how he had been crammed in with all those yattering children. He didn't specify how many there were and Angelina pictured dozens, even hundreds, of competing, clawing youngsters. After harping on his misery his face would light up. "God," he would say, "the miracle of walking into that pub and ordering a drink I had no money to pay for and finding you."

He often talked about the wretchedness of being poor.

"I've been poor too, Parry. I was desperate for money for my mother's care."

Parry made no obeisance to her poverty. It was his own poverty he flaunted.

Angelina owed her misery to Miss Allison. Fabulously generous Miss Allison was to blame. Why didn't a woman with that enormous fortune leave it to a home for stray cats? What was there about Angelina that had persuaded Miss Allison that Angelina could be entrusted with a fortune? Instead of having been left the whole kit and caboodle, it would have been fairer and more plausible if Angelina had ended up down at the bottom of a long list of beneficiaries: "and to Angelina Green for her kindness and attention in my last illness I bequeath the sum of one thousand dollars" or five thousand at the most. And why did a woman with all that money choose to die in such a modest nursing home?

Angelina must be resolute about murdering Parry, and it was only decent to prepare him for death.

"Who is your next of kin, Parry?"

"You are."

"I mean blood kin."

"I've told you I have brothers and sisters—lots of close kin. So close that we suffocated each other."

"What I want to know is, whom should I get in touch with if you die?"

"What makes you think I'm going to die? I'm young and healthy."

"People who are young and healthy die every day."

"While we're on the subject, who is your next of kin—besides me?"

"I haven't any."

"So we're even."

Dinner that night was excellent, lamb with a garland of small potatoes around it, salad, a cheese tray, and fresh pineapple for dessert.

The hours until bedtime seemed long and empty to Angelina. She said to Parry, "Maybe we ought to learn to play some games." She loathed herself for her duplicity. Parry wasn't going to have much time for anything, especially games.

"I don't think either of us would enjoy games," Parry said. "Neither of us has the killer instinct. Anyway, games are just to kill time. Time goes too quickly as it is. The days here with you gallop past." He talked like someone under sentence of death.

And of course he was.

Angelina had to get down to specifics—the time, the place, the method. Shooting was unthinkable. She thanked heaven that there was no gun on the premises. What about stabbing? A direct and clean puncture of the heart might not be too bad, but there must be no gushing blood. A stab in the back might be most diplomatic, not for selfish reasons but to save Parry's feelings. He wouldn't like to know that she had murdered him. But she wasn't very adept with her hands. It would be just her luck to make a few ineffectual cuts.

She might shove Parry downstairs, but he would probably end up with only a broken back or paralysis, in which case in all honor she would have to spend the rest of her days nursing him.

What about shoving him into the freezer? It was large, but was it man-size?

No, she couldn't have Parry die all shut up in the cold and dark, shivering and with his teeth chattering.

Damn the man. How was she going to kill him?

Above all, his murder must be committed in such a way that no one could suspect her of having done it. That rather stumped her, for if Parry was found murdered it would be impossible for her to suggest to the authorities that anyone besides herself could be guilty since she and Parry spent their time solely with each other. There were no callers or guests, no servants, no delivery men.

Regarded in cold blood, murdering Parry seemed an unattainable feat. She almost gave up hope.

Why couldn't she be lucky? Why couldn't the whole thing be taken out of her hands? Why couldn't Parry be in the last throes of some deadly disease? And if natural causes didn't carry him off, there was still a chance that he might be killed in a traffic accident. Thousands died every day in them.

Why must she be forced to kill Parry? Wouldn't it be easier to fall in love with him? But that would be the cowardly way out. She wanted to find out what life was, not how to be in love with Parry.

Then after all her woolly and hopeless musing on how to dispose of Parry, he himself most accommodatingly handed Angelina his death on a platter, or at least in a picnic basket.

"Let's have a picnic," he suggested. "It will be our supper."

She was always compliant with his suggestions, though she privately had misgivings that if they picnicked they would be beset by ants, mosquitoes, gnats, bees, and an assortment of unidentified insects, and no doubt a snake or two would slither in the underbrush.

Parry packed all sorts of delicacies, including two bottles of champagne. Each carried a basket and they stopped several times to rest and look at a view.

"Where are we going?" Angelina asked, a little tired from all the hiking.

"To the most beautiful place on the estate."

Angelina was somewhat frightened when it turned out that Parry meant they were going to the steep drop left from the abandoned highway construction. Her timidity had no effect on Parry. She couldn't budge him from his decision, and with wifely submissiveness she followed him to the very brink of the sharp decline.

Right off, Parry opened a bottle of champagne and handed Angelina a glass.

"I can't get enough of all this space," he said. He walked very close to the precipice and began to drink his champagne. "It's so beautiful here with you, Angelina. I've felt crowded all my life—until I married you."

Parry served her a chicken breast, two ham biscuits, and some asparagus spears. She ate greedily, and complimented Parry on his foresight in bringing two bottles of champagne.

Angelina delved into one of the baskets for fruit and handed some to Parry. They drank more champagne and became a little giddy. Parry told Angelina to open her mouth and close her eyes, and when she obeyed she was surprised to be struck in the face by a grape.

"Sorry," Parry said, "I missed."

"Now it's my turn," she said, and she threw a grape that missed him and then she tossed a large overripe peach that smashed against Parry's forehead.

"That's not fair," he said, and when she saw him pick up a peach and aim it at her she jumped up and began to run. Parry leaped up and chased her and shouted, "Guess what I intend to do when I catch you." She suddenly stopped and held out her arms to Parry, and in that instant of waiting for him to embrace her she realized that this was what she had been trying to devise for weeks. If she could somehow get him nearer the precipice. She began to run again and forgot all her fear of the steep incline.

It was child's play to manipulate Parry past her shoulder as she swerved from his embrace. She stepped aside at the perfect instant and Parry plunged into the abyss.

Angelina looked far down the decline at Parry's body. She waited for him to move and pull himself up and climb toward her. She was about to lose her foothold and she grasped for something to cling to so that she wouldn't pitch headfirst and join Parry. A bush gave her a handhold and she gripped it and looked again at Parry.

He was absolutely inert. She realized that he was, as the unfeeling cliché had it, as dead as a doornail. He could lie there forever and no one would know.

Parry was dead and she was rid of him at last.

Angelina waited for an appropriate reaction of guilt to overwhelm her, but she had only a sense of freedom and well-being.

What was so very fortunate was that there could be no complications. Parry had told her he had no next of kin, or at least that he knew nothing of his relatives' whereabouts. There was no one to be informed of his death.

She was experiencing none of the dread that ought to ravage a murderer, because of course she had murdered Parry by enticing him to the precipice. Maybe it was just an illusion that Parry was dead. She glanced once more at his still body. Of course he was dead. There was no question about it. She had spent too much time among the dying and the dead in the nursing home not to recognize death.

"Rest in peace, Parry," she said.

She left the precipice and stooped over the remains of the picnic and began to clear away the dirty dishes and to put caps on jars. She and Parry had been loaded down, and it would take at least two trips for her to get the baskets and other picnic paraphernalia back to the house.

Her new freedom made her spirits soar and she was singing happily to herself as she picked up a basket cluttered with leftovers and started toward home. It was inhuman of her to feel no regret. No one had ever died in the nursing home without arousing her sympathy. Yet in complete honesty she had to admit that she felt nothing but relief over Parry's death. She was rid of him at last and of her own shallow life. The paths now open to her seemed infinite. She must be careful to choose the right one, though she was young enough to have time to experiment. And there had been no need for Parry to be her victim He had only to let her leave. It was his own fault that he was lying dead at the bottom of the precipice.

Angelina neared the house, and it had never seemed so attractive to her. She entered the kitchen and stood at the sink and washed some dishes. For a while she wasn't going to think about anything. A little later she would telephone the police and there couldn't possibly be any complications—no shadow of doubt could touch her. Parry's death had resulted from an accidental fall.

Time passed. Hours might have elapsed. She only wanted to sit and enjoy the quiet.

There was a sound from outside, and an icy hand might have fallen on her shoulder. Footsteps were approaching. The door to the east entrance was being opened, and Parry entered the living room. He was breathing hard and his hands were scratched. There was dried blood on his left arm and his slacks were torn and dirty. Leaves and twigs were caught in his hair. He stood in an apologetic attitude like a guest who is late and must make an excuse for a tardy appearance.

Damn the man. Damn Parry Brown and his resurrection. She had thought he was dead. Well, he obviously wasn't dead and she must make the best of it, and the poor thing needed to be attended to.

"Parry, you're hurt and you need a bath. I'll draw the water for you."

He followed her upstairs and into his bedroom. She turned on the water in his bathtub, helped him out of his shirt and slacks, and when he settled into the tub she began to soap and sponge his back. She got a comb and worked on the tangles in his dark hair. When he emerged from the tub she embraced him in a huge towel and rubbed him down, then patted powder into his light scratches and oil into the deeper ones. She took an orange stick to remove the dirt from beneath his fingernails. Then she went downstairs for a cup of milk and added rum and took it to Parry. He wanted to be babied and she held the cup while he sipped the milk, and between sips he smiled at her.

As composure came back to Parry it deserted Angelina. She almost dropped the cup. Her hands were shaking and her throat was constricted by Parry's return from the dead.

A generous splash of neat bourbon somewhat restored her, and she was able to think clearly.

Of course this failure to kill Parry altered nothing. She still must murder him. And quickly.

The next day Parry made no reference to the picnic or to his fall. He walked without limping and didn't complain of sore muscles. He acted as if everything was normal. Or was the daft man truly unaware that she had tried to kill him?

It was time for him to make his usual morning trip into town.

"Do you want anything special?" He asked his customary parting question in his customary way, and he and his Porsche were still in sight when she began to weep in frustration that Parry would soon return.

Why wasn't he at the bottom of the ravine where he ought to be?

No interval seemed to have elapsed before Parry was back, smiling and handing her a stack of new books, saying he hoped she would enjoy them and that lunch would be ready in a few minutes. Of course, the food prepared by her intended victim should have choked her.

Instead, it tasted so good that she asked for seconds.

After lunch Angelina took the new books to her room, plumped up the pillows on her bed, and lay down to read. An irritating noise disturbed her. At first she failed to identify it and then she realized that Parry was in his basement workshop. It had been a long time since he had done any woodwork. Once he had finished what was necessary to get the house in shape he seemed to have little interest in his shop, and when she asked for some minor repair he would procrastinate in doing it. The shrill screech of the electric saw annoyed her and she got up to close the door. The noise still penetrated the room, but the closed door muffled the sound so that instead of being piercing it became a monotonous humming, an odd kind of lullaby, and she dozed. At dinner she wanted to ask Parry what he was making in his workshop, but it was no doubt a surprise for her and she didn't ask.

Parry said good night at ten, and Angelina bathed, and got into bed to finish her book. Soon she was so drowsy she couldn't hold the book and she turned out the light. She was almost asleep when she heard Parry leave his room and tiptoe downstairs. In a few minutes there was the sound of a machine. Parry was back in his workshop. She fell asleep again, but much later heard Parry cautiously mounting the stairway. Angelina turned on the lamp to look at her clock. It was four.

Spying was despicable, but nothing could keep Angelina from snooping now. The moment Parry drove off on his morning errands she headed for the basement.

The steep back stairs leading to the basement were quite dark. There was a light somewhere, but Angelina was unfamiliar with this part of the house and couldn't find the switch. She groped her way to the bottom of the stairs and pushed open the door to the workshop. The basement had access to the outside and three small windows let in light from the east.

Everything was in order. There was no sign of any work in progress. The tools were in place and the machines were neatly covered. But Parry had been working on something and it had to be somewhere. She peered on shelves and opened cabinets, and then in the shadow of the ell she saw something draped in heavy canvas. She pulled the canvas back to reveal a long narrow box with a hinged lid. It was a simple piece but it showed Parry's fine craftsmanship. There were strong, carefully carved handles at the head and foot so that it would be easy to move. It must be a chest for storage.

It was a surprise for her, just as she had thought. And Parry was very dear to make it. She smoothed the canvas over the box and looked around to make sure nothing had been disturbed that would betray her intrusion, and then she went upstairs.

Angelina and Parry were finishing a bottle of very dry sherry. Angelina's tongue lingered on the last drops in her glass. She had never felt so uninhibited. Above all, she was a person of honor. She couldn't let her attempted murder of Parry just hang there; spoiling the atmosphere.

"Parry, I tried to kill you."

Parry laughed. He couldn't stop laughing.

"But it's true. It was my fault that you fell down the precipice."

"Don't be ridiculous, Angelina. I tripped and lost my footing. It was my fault. I'm ashamed of myself for being so clumsy."

He said it with conviction. He must believe it. No doubt it was for the best that he refused to believe she had tried to kill him. It would make it simpler for her next attempt—and she must get on with it. But how was she to do it?

People with real purpose had no trouble in surmounting any difficulty. There had to be a simple and easy way to dispose of Parry.

And then she realized that there *was* a simple and easy way—and one that was safe, bloodless, and painless. She had been a dolt not to think of her mother's pills as a perfect instrument of murder. Her stupidity was beyond belief.

The pills were the only things belonging to her mother that Angelina had kept. Everything else—the slippers, two housecoats as good as new, nightgowns, backrest, bedside clock—had been handed on to grateful patients in the nursing home. Angelina had kept the round squat bottles of pills as evidence of her mother's bravery and endurance. Often her mother would refuse the ease they offered, and the doctor had warned that even a slight overdose would be fatal.

The only way Angelina could give the pills to Parry was in food. But how could she put them in food when Parry did all the cooking and serving?

What a bother.

Then poor guileless Parry accepted her invitation to a picnic which she prepared while he went to town on his errands. The kitchen bewildered her. It belonged solely to Parry and she didn't know where anything was. She pulled trays and containers from the refrigerator and freezer and tried to concoct something lethal yet appetizing.

Nothing went right. First she made beef sandwiches, but the garish yellow and red pills, crushed as finely as she could manage, were too conspicuous. Parry would be sure to ask what all that red and yellow stuff was.

Bother the beef sandwiches. Angelina put them in the garbage. If only Parry liked catsup she could easily have disguised the pills in it. But Parry detested catsup. If only he liked cookies she could have sprinkled the pills on the icing. She became more and more frustrated. She put pills in the cottage cheese but they discolored it. She opened a can of vichyssoise but the crushed pills refused to sink.

She must be sensible. There had to be some way to get the pills inside Parry.

Wine! Of course! She would dissolve the pills in the wine, and she would take along beer for herself—Parry was a snob about beer.

They took a long ramble around the estate and found a lovely picnic spot on level ground. They both seemed purposely to shy away from the precipice. It had pleased Angelina to see Parry's pride of ownership as they had sauntered along—she was glad that his last hours were happy.

The long walk had made them hungry and Parry wolfed his food. But he would not drink. The wine bottle might just have been labeled POISON or LETHAL. Angelina took a long refreshing drink of beer and hoped it would incite Parry to drink. A ray of sun shot through the heavy branches of the trees and highlighted the bottle of wine. Parry ignored it.

"You'll choke to death, Parry, if you don't have something to drink." He kept munching on a chicken sandwich, and then when she had given up hope he reached for the wine and poured a large portion into a glass.

Angelina began to hiccough.

Parry was concerned. "I know a cure for the hiccoughs," he said. "Did you bring any sugar?"

"Yes, it's in the yellow bowl."

Parry removed the cover from the dish and measured out a level spoonful of sugar, which he handed to her. It struck Angelina as monstrous that Parry was trying to cure her hiccoughs while she was trying to murder him. She swallowed the sugar with effort. Moments passed, and Angelina smiled. Her hiccoughs were gone.

Parry smiled at her smugly. He refilled his empty glass and drank the wine with dispatch, then poured more.

The beer had made her drowsy and she dozed. When she awoke it was to silence. There was no sound at all, not even of Parry breathing.

Angelina crawled toward him. He was absolutely still. She dared not believe that he was dead. After all, she had miscalculated on that other occasion. And then the picnic site suddenly seemed alive with sounds— the breeze swayed bushes and limbs, it swept the leaves, it made a pickle jar resound against an olive jar, it rattled a knife against a plate.

She leaned over Parry. She bent more closely and laid her ear against his chest. There was no heartbeat. She picked up his wrist. The pulse didn't throb. Parry was dead beyond any doubt.

The wind was rising and she was getting chilly.

Parry had no need of anyone and she could leave him there in the clearing in the twilight. She stooped over him once more to make doubly sure that he was dead, and then she straightened and began to walk toward the house. Her route led her past the rose garden, and the fragrance of the blossoms had never been so sweet. Remorse was what she should have felt, yet in all honesty she felt nothing but peace. Now she would have the life alone she wanted. It was a pity that she had been forced to commit murder to achieve it.

Disposing of Parry's body would be a nuisance, but she would have to manage as best she could. Now she had to give in to the compulsion to sleep. She might have been the one who had taken the sleeping pills. Perhaps it was her great relief that Parry was dead that made her so relaxed. She nodded in the bathtub, and then she somehow managed to get out and dry herself and put on her pajamas. She was asleep by the time she touched the bed.

The next morning Parry appeared as usual with Angelina's breakfast tray.

Her sleep had been so deep that Angelina automatically reached out for the tray, and then she dropped it.

Parry smiled at her indulgently and picked up the pieces of the broken cup and returned the roses to the overturned vase. Then he retrieved the toast from the various places it had landed and excused himself to go prepare another tray.

Angelina pulled the covers over her head and screamed, damning herself for being so inept.

Having decided to kill Parry, she should have done it once and for all. She should have gone down the incline when he was lying there stunned and committed the *coup de grâce* or whatever it was they called the final merciful killing on the field of battle. Since she had failed in the first instance, she should have made doubly sure in the second.

She was disgusted with herself and with Parry. Any other man would have died decently and finally the first time. Damn Parry for bobbing up like a Jack-in-the-box.

There was nothing to do but thank him when he brought up the second tray, apologize for her awkwardness, and ask him how he was.

"I'm fine," he said, "but I didn't sleep very well. I suppose my long nap after the picnic interfered with my regular sleep."

Angelina sighed. Instead of killing him, the pills had given him a nice long nap.

"I think it would be a good morning to clear the grounds where we had our picnic yesterday," he went on. "I noticed that they're much too overgrown."

So while she had been doing her utmost to kill Parry, the lord of the manor had been casting a critical eye about his estate and making plans to tidy it. "Would you like me to help?" It was the only thing she could think to say under the circumstances. But he took her offer as only a pleasantry and left without her.

He looked exhausted when he returned. He didn't seem to have energy enough to open the door, and Angelina opened it for him. He stumbled into the room.

"You've worked too hard, Parry. I'll get lunch."

He waved her aside. "You don't know how to cook."

"I won't have to cook. We'll have sandwiches."

Parry was absolutely spent. She got the Scotch bottle and poured a strong drink for him. He leaned against the counter when she handed it to him and sagged slightly. Perhaps, she thought with wildly throbbing hope, the drugs she had given him the previous afternoon were at last taking hold. Maybe he was at last really and truly dying.

She couldn't have been more mistaken. The Scotch only revived him and by the time he had eaten a chicken sandwich, his strength and vigor had returned.

Angelina was embarrassed by her failures to murder Parry, but she would not be a quitter. His murder could be done. It must be done.

Meantime Parry prospered. His good humor increased. His good health mocked her.

One morning, as usual, Parry asked if there was anything special she wanted in town. There never was anything special she wanted in town. The only thing special she wanted was to dispose of Parry.

"Just pick up the cleaning, please," she said. "Dear."

While he was gone she wondered how she would ever manage to murder him. But when he returned he very obligingly handed her the instrument of his death.

Angelina took the plastic bag of dry cleaning from him and when she hung it in the closet she read the warning. The bag was dangerous, the large, clear print said. Children should not be allowed to play with it.

Angelina was desperate, yet inspired. There must be a third picnic. Parry would be suspicious, but she must try. And three was a magic number. A third attempt to murder Parry should be successful. It had to be successful.

There were still some of her mother's pills left, and when Parry was drugged she would apply the cleaning bag. This time his murder would be accomplished without any possibility of failure.

Angelina's optimism soared.

And Parry was obligingly gullible. Another picnic was exactly what he wanted—the other two had been such fun. He was like a lamb being led to slaughter. He *was* a lamb being led to slaughter.

Angelina packed the food in the picnic baskets and the cleaning bag lay primly folded beneath the slices of baked ham. And Parry's bottle of wine had been generously infiltrated by the pills. Angelina had been as careful as a mother fixing a formula for a baby. When she called to Parry he bounded down the stairs from his bedroom, looking especially handsome. It was a pity that she must kill him, but she reminded herself that he had only himself to blame.

They enjoyed the food and Angelina drank beer. As before, it made her drowsy. She chided herself for being so unfeeling as to doze in the middle of committing murder. She had read of the banality of evil, and she realized that she was a perfect example of it as she yawned and stretched and brushed dried leaves from her hair. The trouble was that a picnic was relaxing and murder wasn't appropriate on such a beautiful afternoon.

Parry poured some wine and sniffed it. "This smells funny," he said.

There went the murder.

"Let me see." She poured a small amount of the wine into her glass and like a professional wine taster she sipped and swished the draft around in her mouth. "It tastes all right to me," she said.

Parry frowned and swallowed his glass of wine quicky as if it were medicine. Then he poured another glass which he drank with equal speed.

"That's absolutely the worst wine I've ever drunk," he said.

Those were his last words. He managed to smile at her as he said them and then he lay flat on the ground. He was so still Angelina was positive he was dead. But then, she thought wryly, she had been sure he was dead those other times too. She must take special precaution now. She reached for the cleaning bag in the bottom of the picnic basket, knelt before Parry, and applied the folded bag to his nostrils. He did not resist. Even so, she didn't release the pressure for some moments. Then, satisfied he was dead, she folded the bag and put it back in the basket.

Back at the house, as she entered the living room, she thought with gratitude that Parry's death had had dignity. He had died out in the open in a beautiful spot after a meal he had relished. His body hadn't been mutilated in war or broken by an accident. He had not been racked by pain. Surely any sensible person would envy Parry's death. The minutes passed blissfully as she sat in the living room. She felt calm yet exhilarated.

Then she heard a sound on the terrace that was unmistakable. Parry was returning. He had outwitted her again.

This time he looked angry and indignant. She had never seen such an expression on his face. Where had his sweet temper gone?

Well, *she* had reason to be angry and indignant too. All her efforts to murder Parry had come to nothing. What sort of person was he anyway—a grown man playing games and pretending to be dead. God only knew how he had feigned it, because he had certainly looked dead to her.

Parry braced himself in the stance a batter might take and then he struck Angelina. She stumbled backward and her head hit the wire screen in a window. A marble ashtray was within her reach. She grabbed it and smashed it against Parry's jaw. "Don't you ever strike me again as long as you live," she said. "I will not have violence in this house."

The blow crumpled him. He backed toward a chair and his large body seemed to disappear. Sobs shook him. It startled her to see him give himself up to tears. She went to the kitchen and dampened a dishcloth, then returned and knelt beside him, wiping his eyes and his jaw. "You'll make yourself sick, Parry," she said. "You mustn't cry anymore."

All the thanks she got was to be shoved aside, and Parry stalked upstairs. After a while she heard the sound of running water. He must be taking a bath.

Angelina became terribly miffed. The nerve of him—pretending to lie—leading her up the garden path for the third time—striking her—shoving her!

Where was the Scotch? She poured a glassful even knowing Scotch would not ease her. There were heavy steps on the stairs. The stairway might be disintegrating beneath those menacing footsteps. An ogre from a bloody Grimm Brothers fairy tale might have been approaching. Parry swept the glass of Scotch from Angelina's hand. He looked large and strong and threatening and very healthy.

He stared down at her. She couldn't think of a thing to say and she was angry at him. Her jaw hurt. It was probably broken and she was sorry not to see any mark of the ashtray on his face.

He left her and stormed into the kitchen. She heard him tear an ice tray from the refrigerator. The cubes made a thundering clatter as Parry dislodged them. He added ice cubes to the Scotch and drank deeply, then splashed more Scotch into the glass and gulped it down. "Monster!" he shouted at her. "Bitch!"

What was wrong with the foolish man? Why was he so cross with her? He had never been impolite before. She would ignore his remarks. She would restore order and equilibrium by making a sensible suggestion.

"I think we'd better go to bed," she said.

"There'll be no going to bed tonight."

"I'm going to bed."

"I've other plans for you."

"I don't know what's got into you, Parry. Why are you out of sorts?"

He bellowed at her. "I've cooked for you! I've shopped for you! I've run errands for you! I've cleared the grounds and planted flowers and shrubbery and painted walls."

"I helped paint the walls. I helped clear the grounds. I'd have helped with the cooking and errands but you insisted you wanted to do it alone. You're being rude and impolite." Parry had nothing in the world to complain about. He was fortunate to be alive. She had done everything she could to kill him and nothing had come of it. He ought to thank his lucky stars. "I'm tired of your bad temper. I'll say good night and go to bed."

"I suggest you go upstairs and put on some jeans and loafers."

"You're crazy. I'm not going anywhere with you."

Parry grabbed her hand and jerked her toward the door. He pulled her down the front steps and across the side lawn. He flicked on a flashlight but its beam was dim and unsteady. Angelina was sure that Parry was mad. There had always been something strange about him.

Along the way she lost her satin slippers and the rocks were biting into her bare feet. Briars snatched at her caftan while Parry pulled her forward. At last they stopped and Parry shoved a spade toward her. He gave a sharp order. "Dig."

The ground was like iron and it hurt to use her foot against the shovel to force it into the earth, but she made progress.

"Harder," Parry said. "Put more muscle into it."

She tried to obey, but her palms stung and her feet throbbed. She was sick and tired of Parry's oafishness. "If you want any more digging done, you can do it yourself." She threw the shovel at his feet. Parry picked it up and thrust the flashlight into her hands. "Keep it steady," he said. Angelina watched Parry dig and the depression grew deeper. Finally she dropped the flashlight and began to run. Parry dashed after her and dragged her back, but his mood shifted from macho to beseeching. "I need you, Angelina. Please help me."

Since he had asked politely, she walked toward him—and stumbled over someone's foot: The illumination from the flashlight was dim, yet it unmistakably showed a dead body. "Take his feet, Angelina," Parry said. She did as she was told, and when they let go there was the most final sound she had ever heard.

Parry began to spade the earth into the grave, and when she realized that he had no more need of her she turned and headed home. She entered by way of the kitchen and stopped at the sink to wash her hands. The water was like fire on her blisters. She went upstairs for unguents to soothe her cuts and scratches and put on pajamas. Then she went back downstairs and poured another drink. She sipped it slowly for what seemed to be hours, yet Parry didn't return. Finally, she went to her room and climbed into bed, where she fell into deep sleep.

When she woke she was surprised to see that it was mid-morning. It was the first time since they had moved to the estate that Parry hadn't served her breakfast in bed. She wondered where he was, and then remembered the dead body. How strange and ironic that after she had made her bungling attempts to murder Parry he had committed a real murder. Of course he couldn't have served her breakfast in bed as usual. He was an honorable man and would have gone to town to give himself up for having killed someone. She had no doubt that Parry was in jail, and jails were such crowded places. Once more he would be jammed in with other human beings just as he had been during his miserable childhood.

She sat up in bed, shocked by memory. Parry had called her a monster and a bitch. She should be indignant, yet she almost smiled. The words were almost welcome after a lifetime of being called a sweet little thing and an angel. And capable and industrious and loving and devoted and unselfish beyond belief.

A car was approaching. It was no doubt the police, come to interrogate her about Parry's crime. A wife wasn't forced to give evidence against her husband, thank heaven, and Parry could count on her to keep her mouth shut. I'll stand beside you, Parry, she thought, whatever you've done. Or was the correct phrase "behind you?"

But that was hardly a suitable greeting for the confident Parry who emerged from the car with his arms encompassing bags of groceries. "Hold the door open, Angelina," he called. "I'm loaded down."

Ordinarily he asked her what her choice for lunch was or he would say he was preparing a surprise, but he showed no such courtesy now as he plopped a greasy package in front of her. "That's a hamburger for your lunch," he said. "I ate downtown."

As a matter of fact, she enjoyed the hamburger. She had practically lived on hamburgers until she had inherited Miss Allison's money. But Parry's behavior was bizarre, to say the least. After tossing the hamburger in her direction he went to his room and locked the door. After that the house had been as quiet as a tomb.

Parry must have tiptoed down the stairs. She hadn't heard a sound, yet there he was all of a sudden, directly in front of her chair in the living room. He almost scared the wits out of her.

His manner had shifted from arrogant to contrite. "Angelina, I must apologize for my behavior. I can't tell you what I've been through. You must have thought I'd lost my mind. I had in a way. It's been hell since I saw him lying on the picnic ground. At first I blamed you, but now I realize it couldn't have been your fault, no matter how it appeared. You wouldn't hurt a fly. And all the while I was hating you and trying to take the loss out on you, I was wildly happy because you belong to me now—just me." He stopped to kiss her and his lips were dry, yet passionate.

What was the demented man talking about? Angelina shook her head in bewilderment.

He took her hand gently, pulled her to her feet, and led her from the house, along the path they had taken when he had dragged her to help him dig the grave. She saw one of her satin slippers slue-footed along the gravel walk, and the second one not far away, pigeon-toed in a small gulley. Torn strips of her caftan dangled from a holly bush. After a while they came to an opening where the terrain was flat. Parry walked to a place covered with vines and freshly cut roses.

"Why are all the roses here?" Angelina said.

"They're covering the graves."

Graves. What did he mean? She had helped dig a grave, not graves. Parry's efficient hands reached for tendrils and removed the vines, uncovering three mounds.

"Don't you see, darling? Surely you understand."

What she wanted and needed was to sit quietly with some wine or spirits nearby while she listened to Parry elaborate.

Once they had sat down in the living room she chose brandy to steady her.

How could she have known that there were four of him, of Parry? She had dismissed herself as a cobbler at murder, and she had turned out to be remarkably deft and efficient in committing it. The murders she had thought she was botching had, on the contrary, been perfectly contrived. The first Parry had died on the precipice, enticed there by her invitation to sex. The second Parry had succumbed from her mother's pills, as had the third Parry—there had probably been no need of the cleaning bag *coup de grâce*.

But how had they managed it? How had they fooled her into thinking they were one? When the first Parry had died, why did they let her continue her carnage? Why had Parry cursed her only after the third murder when after the first two he had been meek and loving? But he had already explained that. He had been overwhelmed with guilt when he realized that he was the only survivor.

It was true that she had sensed there was something mysterious about Parry in spite of his wholesomeness, that she had often noticed changes in his behavior.

"My God, Parry, I can't believe I was married to four men!"

"We all loved you, Angelina. We were devoted to you. What woman has ever been so coddled and pampered?" Parry took her limp right hand and kissed it.

The evidence was there, if only she could accept it. She remembered the continuous whining of the electric tools in Parry's basement workshop. The long box she had found there and had assumed was to be a gift for her was actually a coffin. But only one had been made, and there had been more than one Parry who needed a coffin. That meant that the Parry who did woodworking had been the second one to die.

The sole surviving Parry, like an eminent professor willing to impart esoterica to an eager but not too bright student, had gladly answered every question she asked. While the other Parrys were in waiting, or on the bench, so to speak, they had lived in a small house in a rural isolated area on the other side of town. When Angelina had talked about leaving, a second Parry was usually somewhere nearby on the estate, as they had no intention of letting her get away. They were determined to be vigilant until she came to her senses. The stand-ins had been immediately alerted to the deaths of the others.

At that point. Parry said, "Angelina, I don't ever want to hear another word about you leaving. Do you understand?"

She ignored the question and proposed one that made her blush from immodesty. "How on earth could I satisfy four men?"

"Don't you see, Angelina? We'd never had anything before. Our parents exploited us. We were quadruplets and from the time we were born our pictures were used for endorsements. They wanted us to support them and all the other kids. We rebelled and left home when we were eighteen, but we had little education and less skill. Life was hell, multiplied by four. We swore that if anything good ever happened to one of us it would happen to us all, and a miracle happened when Parry found you."

There was another kiss of her limp right hand.

"Angelina, listen, darling, I have something to confess. I am the only one who couldn't cook. The others were truly good chefs. When it was my turn with you, whoever was leaving would put all sorts of food in the refrigerator and freezer for me to use. So we had to keep you out of the kitchen. We knew that if you ever came in when I was cooking you'd know I didn't have the vaguest idea how to cook. Breakfast wasn't so bad, though sometimes I'd ruin half a dozen eggs before I could bring one up to you. Cooking is an unbelievable chore for me. I don't intend to go into the kitchen again as long as I live. It's all yours from now on."

Parry yawned. The yawn was catching, and Angelina yawned too. She went into the kitchen and prepared a cold supper and they yawned and dozed over their plates. Shortly afterward, when Parry came to her room, Angelina's response to his lovemaking surprised her. But her mind was engaged in more serious matters. Her situation was intolerable, and what she had been subjected to was base and demeaning. She was more determined than ever to leave, and she realized that it could only be accomplished by Parry's death. In for a penny, in for a pound. Since, without knowing it, she had committed three murders, she must commit a fourth. The fourth was the most necessary of all. And the sooner the better.

Late the next morning when Parry greeted Angelina jauntily on his return from doing the errands in town, she asked him what he would like for lunch. Food was food, he shrugged, and anything she wanted to fix was fine.

In all the neat packages and containers of food in the freezer and refrigerator prepared and left by the provident Parrys there were bound to be a dozen dishes whose colors matched her mother's pills. She ran upstairs and brought down the bottles with their remaining contents. When she returned to the kitchen she called out to Parry in the living room, "Get yourself a drink, Parry, while I prepare lunch. It won't take long."

The Disappearance of Mrs. Standwick

"Why on earth didn't you tell me I was going to stop over in Richmond?" Ellen Williams asked her travel agent as she picked up her tickets and itinerary for her five-day tour of Colonial Williamsburg.

The agent looked at her in astonishment. For years now Mrs. Williams had been sheeplike in accepting without complaint or comment the trips he had arranged for her. She wasn't like other tourists who badgered him with questions about climate, what to wear, what to buy, how much to tip, telephoning him any hour of the day or night about matters he had already covered fully. "I met a very nice woman from Richmond when I was in Ireland in June," Ellen Williams continued. "If I'd known I was staying over tomorrow night I'd have planned to see her. It's too late now."

Though exactly how Ellen Williams might have arranged to see Mrs. Standwick, who had seemed to disappear into thin air, was something else again. Mrs. Standwick had not said goodbye, nor had she given Ellen Williams her address. The only reason that Ellen Williams knew she lived in Richmond was a tag on her suitcase printed succinctly STANDWICK, RICHMOND, VIRGINIA.

"I'm sorry," the agent said. "But the inn in Williamsburg didn't have a room for tomorrow night and I couldn't change your transportation, so I got a reservation for you in Richmond. Anyway, I thought you'd like to stop over in Richmond. Lots of people think it has the most beautiful capitol in the country and there are other interesting sights. Besides, it'll make a nice break for you before you go on to Williamsburg. Surely you can telephone your friend when you get to Richmond and explain why you weren't able to give her any warning."

That was an apt suggestion, surely, and Ellen Williams thanked the agent for it. Yes, she would telephone Mrs. Standwick on her arrival.

Ellen Williams said good afternoon to the agent and went home to pack and do all the last-minute things that had to be done before she began her trip the next morning.

She was a reluctant traveler. If she had her way she would never go any farther from her apartment than she could walk. She wanted nothing more in life than to enjoy middle age in her three rooms, devoting her time to her plants, going to the hospital two days a week to do volunteer work, visiting her neighbors, ministering to her cat Thaddeus, of no particular lineage but with very aristocratic airs and tastes. Then when night came and she finished her supper and washed the dishes, she liked to settle down and scare herself to death by reading novels of mystery and suspense.

That simple routine was to Ellen Williams the ideal life.

But her two sons had taken it into their heads that she wanted to travel, that she had an insatiable passion for going places, and every time they saw a travel poster that suggested a new place to visit they made plans for her usually two long trips each year and additional shorter ones, like the upcoming tour of Williamsburg.

They were the kindest, most generous sons alive. They simply did not realize how they disrupted their mother's life by sending her to the four corners of the earth on independent tours or packaged tours or group tours. Mrs. Anderson down the hall was sweet enough to water Ellen Williams' flowers but she really had no knack for it and half of them died by the time Ellen returned.

Thaddeus the cat was made furious by having to stay at the vet's and it took weeks of cajoling him with special dishes such as lobster and kidneys before he would so much as deign to sit in the same room with her again.

Everything about traveling was much too upsetting, but she couldn't get out of it. Once she had tried to lie herself out of a trip by making a vague complaint about her health, and her sons had promptly sent her off to a famous clinic where all the tedious and exhaustive tests showed that she was in perfect health, and after all that she ended up, as booked, attending every performance of the Salzburg Festival when she didn't even like music.

Well, her sons were wonderful and when they were small they had obeyed her and now she had to obey them. She was proud of their success—Frank was a lawyer and Joseph a banker—and they had both married good-hearted, sensible girls of whom Ellen Williams was very fond. If only her sons would think of something for her to do besides travel! That was their only flaw.

Her flight to Richmond was short and uneventful and the travel agent had known what he was talking about when he recommended the Capitol. She couldn't remember having seen a simpler, more pleasing building anywhere. After walking around the Capitol grounds she had returned to her hotel in the late afternoon.

The hotel was an old and elegant one and her room was perfectly nice, except that nothing about it suited her. The light was too dim and, besides, the lamp wasn't situated properly for reading. The chair didn't fit her back, the flowers in the wallpaper were purple, the framed engraving of St. John's Church was crooked, and the mirror made her look fat when she weighed only 130 pounds—well, maybe 132.

She was disgruntled and at odds with herself when she thought how nice it would be to see Mrs. Standwick. She riffled through the telephone directory. Only one Standwick was listed, thank goodness. It would have been awkward to go down a long list of Standwicks asking for the one who had been in Ireland in June.

She dialed the number. There was no answer. She got up and straightened the engraving of St. John's Church, but it slid right back to its awry position. She tried to make the armchair more comfortable by putting a bed pillow in it, but that didn't work either. She pulled a paperback from her carryall and began to read, only to find herself yawning. She had never in her life yawned over a murder novel. It was time to take herself in hand. So she wrote postcards to her sons and daughters-in-law telling them of her safe arrival, then went to the coffee shop and ordered an omelet and green salad.

When she got back to her room she telephoned the Standwick number again, but there was still no answer. Maybe Mrs. Standwick, poor thing, like Ellen Williams had been sent by relatives on another tour. Ellen Williams looked at herself in the mirror and appeared to have gained ten pounds, in spite of her light supper. She frowned at her appearance and at everything. If only she could be home with Thaddeus and her plants and her bright lamps and her comfortable chairs and a selection of brand-new mystery novels from the public library.

She was one of the luckiest women in the world, yet now she felt like one of the most miserable. She never got into such a mood when she was at home where she belonged. In desperation she left the hotel and window-shopped on Grace and Broad Streets and then she returned to her room and once more dialed the Standwick number. Somehow she hadn't expected an answer, so she was startled when she heard a woman's voice.

"Hello."

"May I speak with Mrs. Standwick, please?"

"This is Mrs. Standwick."

"I hope you're the Mrs. Standwick I know. This is Ellen Williams."

"Who?"

For heaven's sake, Ellen thought, I've never had any trouble with anyone understanding my name before. Ellen is as easy as Mary, and Williams is as simple as Jones or Smith.

"Ellen Williams. I'm at the Adams Hotel briefly and I want to talk with the Mrs. Standwick who was my fellow traveler—"

But Mrs. Standwick did not let her finish. "Yes, yes," she said and then there was a long silence and she said, "I'm afraid you have the wrong number." And abruptly the connection was broken.

Anger made Ellen's hand tremble as she put the telephone back on the hook. She had never been subjected to such unaccountable behavior, the very idea, pretending that Ellen Williams had got a wrong number! Of course that was the Mrs. Standwick she knew. It was Mrs. Standwick's voice and that last sentence gave her away: "I'm afraid you have the wrong number." That was a speech habit of Mrs. Standwick—she often prefaced her statements with "I'm afraid." Ellen Williams remembered so well that she would say, "I'm afraid I'll have to ask you for the butter," or "I'm afraid I'll have to ask you to let me pass." I'm afraid this, I'm afraid that.

Nothing distressed Ellen Williams as much as rudeness. Human beings had to live in the same world, whatever they might think of each other, and they could at least be polite even if they had to lie a little. If Mrs. Standwick didn't want to see her she could at least have made a plausible excuse and managed to exchange a few civil words.

Still Ellen must admit that in their short time together she had become very fond of Mrs. Standwick. True, she was a mousy and colorless woman. Come to think of it, Ellen Williams had no idea how old Mrs. Standwick might be. She was the washed-out type that would look about the same whether she was thirty or fifty. Her clothes had no style to them; the material was nice enough, but nothing she wore flattered her and there wasn't enough variety. She had worn one suit and she had only two dresses for dinner. Not that anybody needed many clothes for a five-day tour from Dublin to Cork to Killarney and then back to Dublin.

Ellen thought of Mrs. Standwick's plain, wistful face. No, whatever the reason for Mrs. Standwick's strangeness on the telephone, she wasn't unkind. There was something shy about her—even sad—and she had seemed to depend on Ellen. They hadn't talked much, except to oh and ah over the Irish scenery, but they always sat together on the bus and at mealtime. Ellen Williams had felt protective toward her, and then on that last morning in Dublin when everyone was saying goodbye, Ellen had tried to find her but she couldn't. Of course it was a time of confusion, with everybody heading in different directions, eager to make travel connections, yet everyone had managed a farewell except Mrs. Standwick.

Ellen Williams had felt sure that Mrs. Standwick had left a message for her with someone and that in the hurly-burly of leave-taking it had been forgotten. Ellen had worried about her—well, not really worried, but thought about her on the way home—and then she'd found six of her prettiest African violets dead and Thaddeus sulking even more than usual and the volunteer chairman at the hospital miffed because the substitute volunteer hadn't been conscientious about taking over, so she hadn't got around to writing any letters. And when she had finally settled down, she saw that Mrs. Standwick hadn't written in her address book, though it had been handed round to everyone and all the other tourists' names were there. Moreover, Mrs. Standwick hadn't passed around an address book of her own—at least, not to Ellen Williams.

The faint light in the hotel room seemed to grow dimmer. Shadows lurked in the corners. The night wind stole in and rattled the blinds. Ellen shivered and glanced at the menacing cover on the mystery paperback. Never before had she applied any of her mystery reading to events in real life. Oh, once she had thought how exciting it would be if Mrs. Randolph, who lived on the second floor and was the most ordinary person in the world, turned out to be a double agent, or how exciting it might be if Mr. Watkins, who made a fool of himself in doting over his wife, was secretly poisoning her.

But somehow her feeling about Mrs. Standwick was altogether different. It wasn't vicarious fear. It was real. She sensed that Mrs. Standwick was scared—badly scared. The telephone conversation, if you could call it a conversation, had been odd, to say the least. First she had said yes, she was Mrs. Standwick, and then in almost the next breath she said that Ellen had the wrong number, and had hung up.

Yes, there was something fishy about it, and if Ellen Williams had been at home she would have gone straight to the police. But she couldn't very well go to the police in Richmond and say she'd telephoned someone and had been told she had a wrong number. That would be ridiculous. Perhaps there was only some slight misunderstanding, but it would be awkward to make another telephone call so soon to try to clear it up. Whatever the circumstances, she somehow couldn't help feeling that Mrs. Standwick would be glad to see her—after all, they had got along so well. In all her years of touring Ellen Williams had never been so drawn to a fellow traveler as she had been to Mrs.

Standwick.

There was only one thing to do—to go see for herself. It might be foolish to set out in the dark in a strange city to find someone under such mysterious conditions, but Ellen was lonely and the night was long, and, above all, she felt uneasy about Mrs. Standwick.

Downstairs in the hotel entrance, the doorman pointed in the direction of the street that Ellen inquired about. "It's just a short walk," he said. "About five or six blocks. Go straight down Franklin—your street crosses Franklin."

Ellen Williams set out briskly and traffic soon thinned. She noticed without concern that she was the only pedestrian. She supposed that Richmond had its share of muggings and that she ought not to risk being out alone in the dark, but the air was bracing and the townhouses she passed interested her they were substantial and well kept, and their interiors—which she glimpsed between the slats of Venetian blinds or half drawn draperies—were colorful and attractive.

Earlier than she expected she reached Mrs. Standwick's street. The house she was seeking was on a corner. It had the same dignity and substance of the other residences she had been admiring and its number was spotlighted in graceful, slender brass figures.

At her touch the iron gate swung open and Ellen Williams quickly covered the short walk and mounted the steep steps of the Georgian house. For an instant she caught her breath, then she pushed the bell and it sounded like an alarm. She started at the commotion she had created in the cold silence.

After a while the front door was opened. Ellen Williams had hoped that Mrs. Standwick would greet her and invite her inside for a visit, exclaiming in delight over their reunion. Instead, the woman standing there intimidated Ellen. She seemed disdainful in her perfection. She wore an elaborately complicated hairdo and an elegantly simple evening dress. Her throat and left hand were on fire with diamonds.

"Good evening," Ellen said. "I'd like to see Mrs. Standwick, please."

The woman said nothing—she and her diamonds glowered at Ellen Williams.

"Mrs. Standwick does live here, doesn't she?" Ellen Williams' manner was timid and she took a half step in retreat.

A man's voice filled the house, shouting, "Who is it?"

The woman turned and walked down the hall toward the gracefully curved stairway and called up the stairwell in answer to the man. "It's someone who has come to see about a contribution."

That remark astonished Ellen. Her retreat ended. She crossed the threshold and approached the woman. "You've misunderstood me," she said. "I certainly don't want any contribution. I just wanted to say hello to Mrs. Standwick. She and I were on a trip together and I—"

There were heavy footsteps and before Ellen knew what was happening or could finish what she was saying she was shoved inside a room and the door was closed after her.

"I'll be back in a moment," the woman said through the door.

Ellen glanced around the room. It was large and elegant, its furniture was in the French style, and the brilliant chandelier flashed as blindingly as the woman's diamonds. Ellen Williams sat down on a delicate tapestried settee and squinted against the bright lights.

Time seemed to slacken, and then she decided that it was not so much that time was passing slowly as that a lot of time had passed. Studying her watch, she tried to calculate how long she'd been in the house. She had left the hotel at 7:00. Even though she had sauntered to look at the houses, it couldn't have taken her more than fifteen minutes to reach the Standwick residence.

It was now 7:50. So she had been left alone to cool her heels for more than half an hour. If this was the Richmond brand of Southern hospitality she wanted none of it. She would leave this splendid room immediately and she was tempted to slam the front door behind her.

She grabbed at the slender gold handle of the door; it did not move. She tried to turn it, first to the right and then to the left. It must be stuck. She pulled and pushed.

The door was locked from the outside.

Ellen looked around frantically for another exit. There was no other door. She walked over to the window and pulled the brocaded draperies apart. Darkness lapped outside the window and as her eyes grew accustomed to that darkness she saw that light from a street lamp faintly illuminated the yard. The ground was too far beneath her to risk jumping.

She went back to the door and beat on it. "Let me out," she yelled. "Let me out at once!"

From somewhere behind her a hand reached out and clutched her. Ellen Williams screamed and turned to find the woman there. A panel had opened beside the fireplace. There had been another door, after all, its outline concealed by the carving of the wainscoting.

Ellen Williams' voice rose in indignation. "What is the meaning of all this? I only wanted to see Mrs. Standwick. She and I were good friends on a tour of Ireland."

The woman ignored what Ellen had said.

"Come this way," she ordered. She grasped Ellen Williams by the arm and led her through two unlighted rooms down a narrow passage, and before Ellen Williams was aware of her predicament she was pushed into a small dark room and the door was locked after her.

Everything had happened too quickly. All she could think was that she had been treated like a child who had misbehaved badly and had been shut up in a closet for punishment. For it was a closet to which she had been banished, as she discovered when she reached out to explore her prison and touched various garments hanging from a double row of rods.

She tiptoed and lashed out and came in contact with a shelf crowded with luggage. There must be a light somewhere, but its switch must be outside the locked door—not that a light would do her much good, but she hated the dark.

She groped again. She tapped the wall in every direction, still trying to find a switch, and she cried out in surprise and triumph when she found it and the closet was drowned in light.

Her eyes were dazzled by all the high fashions regimented as to coats, suits, evening dresses, and day clothes. Then Ellen glanced up at the shelf filled with suitcases. One of the cases might as well have shouted Mrs. Standwick's name. She would have recognized it anywhere—she had helped Mrs. Standwick stow it on the rack in the bus every morning and take it down in the late afternoon during their trip. It was shabby and worn, like all luggage that has undergone the rigors of a bus tour. It was proof that Mrs. Standwick lived here, was somewhere in this house, and that the awful woman who had pushed her into the closet was trying to keep them apart.

The light pained Ellen Williams' eyes. She was tired from her long day and indignant over what had happened, but there was nothing she could do about her plight for the moment. She must try to make herself as comfortable as she could. She must save her strength so that at the next encounter with that woman she could shove instead of being shoved.

Ellen pulled a mink coat from a hanger and spread it on the floor; then she took a sable coat and folded it up for a pillow. She turned off the light and lay down.

Something wakened her. She sat up and wondered where she was. A feeling of panic overtook her as it often did when she was away from home and woke up and tried to decide exactly where she was. The fur beneath her startled her. She extended her arms and the hanging clothes swung out as if to attack her—and then she remembered that she was a prisoner in a closet in Richmond, Virginia.

She scrambled up, turned on the light, and put the fur coats back on their hangers. Her nap had refreshed her and she was ready for action. She intended to scream her head off and to batter at the locked door of the closet until someone came. She tugged at the door and it opened immediately. No doubt that woman was lurking somewhere in the dark, waiting to push Ellen Williams behind another locked door. But Ellen was onto her tricks and ready to give instead of to take—and she intended to find Mrs. Standwick, who had to be somewhere in this strange house.

With resolution, Ellen stalked out of the closet and invaded one luxurious room after the other, calling Mrs. Standwick's name. There was no answer. The house was empty. The elegant woman had left. The man who had shouted from the upstairs had gone. Mrs. Standwick was nowhere in the house.

Ellen Williams left the opulent house with its tomblike silence and walked without fear along the deserted streets. Nothing that might happen to her outside could be as terrifying as what she had already experienced. She was indignant and outraged, and as soon as she could sit down and collect her wits she must decide what to do.

It astonished her to see from the clock in the hotel lobby that it was only 9:00. When she asked for her key, the clerk looked at her with concern. "Are you all right, Mrs. Williams?" he asked. "A woman who didn't give her name telephoned about five minutes ago. She said you had been to her house and seemed upset and she wanted to know if you had got back all right."

Anger like a spasm shook Ellen Williams. Her voice squeaked. "Well, if she calls again, please tell her that I've never felt better in my whole life in spite of the extraordinary welcome she gave me."

When Ellen Williams awoke later than she had intended the next morning, she felt rested and full of purpose. Her duty was clear. Instead of visiting the Valentine Museum, as her typed itinerary prescribed, she intended to see the police. It was the only sensible thing to do. Mrs. Standwick had disappeared and very peculiar things had happened to Ellen when she had made inquiries about her.

The police must be informed and she mustn't waste another second. She'd better go to them even before she ate breakfast.

She had just put on her hat and was peering out the window to decide whether to take her umbrella when a knock sounded on her door. Someone called her name. She caught her breath when she opened the door and saw who her visitor was.

Mrs. Standwick stood there, dressed in her neat, nondescript suit. The battered suitcase in her hand reminded Ellen of those mornings in Ireland when Mrs. Standwick had come by her room holding her suitcase exactly like that, ready to set out for their next destination. The anxiety which had troubled Ellen ever since she had attempted to see Mrs. Standwick suddenly left her, and though she was not usually a demonstrative person she embraced Mrs. Standwick warmly. "I'm so happy to see you," she said. "I've been terribly worried. I was on my way to the police. Oh, I can't tell you how relieved I am to see that you're all right! I didn't know what that terrible woman had done to you."

Mrs. Standwick was so moved by Ellen Williams' welcome that she began to cry. Tears ran down her cheeks. "I'll try to explain," she said. "Excuse me for a minute." From her handbag she withdrew a plain white handkerchief and dabbed at her reddened eyes. Then she picked up her suitcase and went into the bathroom.

Thank heaven she's safe, Ellen thought, and that was all that mattered—though Mrs. Standwick ought to be persuaded to leave that bizarre household where unsuspecting callers were mauled and thrust into closets …

Time passed but Mrs. Standwick did not emerge from the bathroom.

She's disappeared again, Ellen Williams thought wildly. "Are you all right?" she called out.

The bathroom door opened. But Mrs. Standwick did not come out. It was that other woman, heavily made up and dressed in a Chanel suit. Hung across her arm was the same mink coat on which Ellen had dozed in the closet.

"Your Mrs. Standwick doesn't exist any longer," the woman said. "I wanted to tell you last night but I couldn't. I was terrified when you telephoned—my husband was in the library with me and I didn't dare let him know I was talking to someone I'd traveled with in Ireland. He didn't know I'd been there. He thought I'd visited my sister who lives in Italy.

"I mustn't bother you with my problems, but my husband won't give me a divorce and he's pathologically jealous. I'm in love with someone and I had a brief, wonderful meeting with him in Dublin before I took the tour. I dressed for it as I'd like to dress all the time—in plain, comfortable clothes—but my husband insists that I wear high fashion.

"I was so sad over saying goodbye to John and you were so kind to me. There was no way to thank you for your sweetness and I didn't even try. I didn't dare give you my address because my husband reads all my mail and I knew that if you wrote he'd find out that I'd been in Ireland. Last night I locked you up to keep you out of his way until we left for a party. He heard you in the sitting room and that's why I moved you to the closet.

"I sneaked back from the party and unlocked the closet door, but my husband missed me and followed me and I rushed back out at once to keep him from coming inside. So I couldn't apologize to you. The party wasn't over until after two and I didn't want to disturb you then. But the very moment my husband left for his office this morning I came to see you. You must forgive me for everything, Mrs. Williams. You must."

Ellen smiled at the beautiful, troubled woman. Of course she forgave her. But this person was a stranger. The woman Ellen Williams had liked so much had disappeared forever.

Back For a Funeral

John Whyte kissed his sister Alice goodbye. It was a delicate peck just at her left eyebrow. They weren't demonstrative in their family and yet they were deeply bound to each other. When John was young his devotion to his parents and his profound sense of obligation to them had been overpowering.

In those long-ago years of his childhood and adolescence, children's lives at least in the particular class to which he belonged—had been centered on their parents. Obedience had been expected and duty had been exacted. He hadn't ever once gone against his parents' wishes. Why had he been so acquiescent when they had demanded that he give up Lucy? Why hadn't he protested their extravagant statement that Lucy would be the death of him?

He was fond of Alice and proud of her beauty and fine qualities as a human being. They were the only children. She was younger by enough years to have kept them from being close when they were growing up, but since middle age had claimed them the difference in age hadn't mattered. What kept them apart now was distance. His law practice in Washington was so demanding that he came back to Kingborough only on special occasions—Christmas and Thanksgiving, graduations and weddings in the family and among close friends, and funerals. The death of Lloyd Roberson, Alice's husband, had brought him home this time.

Alice was bearing her loss with dignity and composure. John admired that, just as he had admired the way Alice and Lloyd had taken over the Whyte family mansion and maintained its elegance begun by their grandparents and sustained by their parents. How Alice and Lloyd had contrived to find expert plasterers and woodworkers and upholsterers mystified him. John and his wife Jenny were invariably annoyed by the shoddiness of the repairs to their house in Georgetown.

He walked toward the front door while Alice mounted the stairs to rejoin their Aunt Maud. The dining room had only a few minutes before been cleared of the buffet set out for the guests after the funeral, and he and Alice had managed to have a few quiet moments together when he had offered his help in settling Lloyd's estate. She thanked him but said that Lloyd had been as foresighted as their father and had arranged everything long before his death.

Alice and John both turned to face each other for a last goodbye. Alice was on the landing and her resemblance to their mother startled him. Their features weren't very much alike but their gestures and voice inflections were almost identical. It might have been his mother blowing him a kiss.

He had refused Alice's offer of a ride to the airport to catch the Washington plane. He had said he would go to the James Madison Hotel just around the corner where limousine service to the airport was available, and he intended to go there eventually, but first he wanted to see Lucy's house. Of course it wasn't her house now and hadn't been in the long years since her death. No matter, he felt he must see it.

On his many previous returns to Kingborough he had thought of going by Lucy's house but he had always been accompanied by one or other of his wives and it had seemed inappropriate and even slyly rude to take them out of the way to a place where he had known so much joy with another woman. Though he had visited Lucy for only a few months while he was a student at the university, the happiness he had known with her had sustained him all his life. Lucy had been the lodestar, the *sine qua non* of his life.

Of course he had been fond of his wives—indeed, he had loved them very much. There had been three. Anne, his first wife, had died, and Lynne, his second, had found someone she loved more and there had been a discreet divorce. She still lived in Washington and they moved in the same circles and often saw each other at parties and receptions. They still liked each other. Jenny, his present wife, was a darling. They were devoted to each other and respected each other's differences. Just now she was abroad—though he had her itinerary both at home and at the office he wasn't sure of her exact location. She was addicted to travel and he abhorred the confusion of airports, the discomfort of long flights and trying to live out of a suitcase. Besides, his demanding law practice wasn't amenable to long absences and being out of touch in Afghanistan or all those other remote places that attracted Jenny. So Jenny traveled alone.

What compelled him toward Lucy's house? And it was a compulsion—there was no other word to describe it. He found himself walking vigorously and with as much pleasure as he had felt when he was 19. He remembered that he sometimes walked slowly, even deliberately loitered, to add to the final delight of seeing Lucy.

His parents' objection to Lucy had stunned him. He hadn't expected it, and even now after all those years he found it difficult to understand. But the world was different then. Who in the present, when all liberties and licenses met with acceptance if not approval, would believe that parents would object to a prospective daughter-in-law because she had been divorced and was ten years older than their son?

His mother's attitude had been outrageous. She would greet him at the front door, "Son, you haven't been to see that woman, have you?" His mother didn't even name Lucy. Lucy was "she." And when he answered yes, his mother said, "She will be the death of you." And his father was equally melodramatic. "She will be the death of you," he had repeated. And Uncle John, for whom John was named and whose heir he was, had also said that Lucy would be the death of him. John didn't mention the bitterness of his parents' feeling to Lucy, but he did tell her of their strenuous objection, and Lucy quite understood. She had accepted it without question. She was almost as addicted to the straitlaced mores of the pre-World War II South as his parents were.

John had met Lucy in the university library where she had a job. Most of the time she worked at the front desk, and she had showed him how to make out call slips and how to use the catalogue and where the reserve shelves were. Some days later she had smiled at him when they were sitting separately in the university cafeteria over a late lunch. Once he had offered to help take a stack of books to her apartment and she had invited him in and had made iced tea for them. Every now and then she invited him to her apartment and prepared supper.

They became deeply fond of each other. He couldn't explain their feeling for each other then and he couldn't explain it now, but he had never known such an affinity for another person in his life, and the joy of it had stayed with him until that very moment. No affection for his parents or his sister or his wives had ever compared in the slightest degree with his profound feeling for Lucy.

The house couldn't be much farther. It depressed him to see that the neighborhood had deteriorated. When Lucy had lived there it had been an area of small neat houses and apartments. He passed askew signs announcing BAD DOG—FURNISHED ROOMS—FOR SALE—MAKE US AN OFFER, and the cracked uneven sidewalks were littered with cans and broken glass.

A boy on a bicycle nearly ran him down as John arrived at Lucy's house, and he glanced up at the second floor. A lamp with a torn angled shade lighted the window of what had been her living room. He wanted to dash upstairs as he had so often done and knock on the door. Instead he stood very still and looked up and remembered all the happiness he had known there.

For a long time he didn't move and then he walked over to the street light and glanced at his watch. He would miss the plane he had intended to take.

Well, there were other planes. He didn't want to leave Lucy's house just yet.

It was strange. He couldn't remember any of their conversations and yet they had talked endlessly. He couldn't even remember the color of Lucy's eyes or of her hair or how tall she was. He could only remember what she had meant to him, the absolute joy of being with her, and he thought again of the outrageous statements made by his parents and uncle.

His parents knew nothing of Lucy's gentleness and generosity. Because of Lucy he had been happy. She had given him joy.

But they had said, "She will be the death of you." It was like something ordained, irrevocable, not to be escaped. They might have been characters in a Greek drama pronouncing a curse. "No," he said.

He had never said no to his parents, but now they seemed to be behind him and he had begun to protest violently, and then in one hideous moment of illumination and pain he realized that what his parents had said had been prophetic. His love for Lucy had brought him here to his death.

"For Pete's sake, Joe, hurry! We've got to get out of here. He really put up a fight, didn't he? Look at that watch. Have you ever seen anything like it? And all this money in the billfold. Come, on let's drag him in the alley."

Murder at the Poe Shrine

The last visitor of the day had just left the Edgar Allan Poe Shrine in Richmond, Virginia.

Miss Wilson, the Shrine's lecturer, guide, and curator, went to the small table where the brochures and postcards were displayed; she rearranged them into neat stacks: *A Walk Around the Edgar Allan Poe Shrine, Historic Guide to Richmond and James River*, the colored reproductions of the Old Stone House and garden; the black and white prints of the daguerreotype made of Poe when he had gone to Providence in November 1848 on a frantic lover's visit to Mrs. Helen Whitman, one of the numerous Helens in his life.

Miss Wilson sat down at the desk where all the guests registered. She was exhausted; there had been an unusual number of visitors that Sunday afternoon; the pace had been hectic and tiring; she had barely been able to get one person or group on its way through the Old Stone House, the garden, and the Memorial Building, before the bell at the front door had rung and she had to rush back to admit others, collect their entrance fees, and start them on their rounds. The number of guests had been uncommonly large because an instructor at one of the local colleges had assigned a visit to the Poe Shrine as one of the requirements for a course in American literature, and many students in the turtle-like completion of their summer school work had waited until the last day before their reports were due to visit the Memorial.

Miss Wilson was tired, but pleasantly so; she had a sense of accomplishment. At the end of every day she felt good that a number of people had for the first time in their lives seen mementoes connected with Poe; had looked at manuscripts written in his beautiful, meticulous handwriting; had touched furniture that had been in the Allan household where he had had his precarious tenancy; had examined the trunk that had accompanied him on so many of his sad wanderings; had glanced at the desk he had used as editor of the *Southern Literary Messenger*; had seen the cane he had carried with such an air of elegance; and in the display case had viewed the precious edition of his first published work, *Tamerlane and Other Poems* (By A Bostonian).

There were several small tasks she had to do before she could go home—chiefly the closing of windows and locking of doors.

The Shrine consists of the Old Stone House, the garden, and the Memorial Building. She left the Old Stone House and walked into the garden. In the springtime the flowers Poe loved were planted there, among them the two she thought were especially appropriate, forget-me-nots and heart's ease. Poe … who would never be forgotten so long as the love of literature persisted, and whose own heart had never known ease.

Her brisk steps then took her to the Memorial Building. She did not go upstairs in that building except at the end of each day's work; the stairs were steep and it was too long a walk from there to the Old Stone House when the bell rang announcing new callers.

As she ascended the staircase she looked up at Carling's series of illustrations in India ink for *The Raven*; they embodied for her the spirit of the poem, so long worked upon and finally completed at the Brennan home on Bloomingdale Road in New York City.

When she got to the head of the stairs she stopped to catch her breath. At this time every day she often reviewed what had happened. Today had been perfect, she thought; though it was still summer the late August days were borrowing their flavor more and more from autumn; it was a day streaked with shadow and sunshine and quick winds, a day that might have come from Poe's lonesome October or even the bleak December that had always haunted him.

Miss Wilson looked across the room at the head of the stairs. Her glance stopped at Ellen Glasgow's photograph, signed in her distinctive writing. She considered handwriting and wondered if it really were an index of character; she thought of the handwritten specimens of Poe on exhibit at the Shrine, all that careful, painstaking formation of letters. But there were other examples, written in times of distress and despair, when Poe's writing had wavered and wandered, like some hastily scrawled signpost to madness. Certainly she was more than ordinarily interested in handwriting; often when she had time she went over the signatures of the visitors who had registered in the guest book; handwriting was so intimately connected with a person, it must, she felt, have deep significance. She had even sent off a specimen of her own to a graphologist for comment; the answer had been on the whole pleasant but rather noncommittal; what had delighted her was the mention of her powers of analysis. Poe would have approved of that, she thought; he had emphasized that particular quality in his four detective stories.

But her thoughts were making her dawdle. This dilly-dallying had to be stopped. She must look briefly into the room where the rest of *The Raven* illustrations hung, the raven itself was mounted and set on a dark table, and where the bust of Pallas sat, if not quite above the chamber door—that line had given them some trouble—at least on a stand near the door. On the threshold Miss Wilson stopped.

"Why, Mr. Poe," she said.

Her feet would not settle on the floor; they stood uncertainly on tiptoe while fingers of fear pricked at her neck.

In the late afternoons when she had the Shrine to herself like this she had often felt in communion with Poe. But then, she told herself, people were often in communion with the dead: the reader of Shakespeare, the viewer of paintings by Klee or Cézanne—whoever looks with a receptive heart at the works of artists no longer living is in communion with the dead.

"Mr. Poe," she said again, her fear changing to curiosity.

Because Edgar A. Poe himself sat at the table.

His hair was done in the style shown in the familiar daguerreotype; everything about him was like that picture—his mustache, his cravat, his neat clothes. His arms were stretched out, his head was bent forward, and he stared with a most horrible expression.

Miss Wilson walked toward him, then backstepped to turn on the light switch.

A more distinct view merely confirmed what was before her.

Edgar A. Poe was in fact sitting at the table; he had a heavy cord around his neck and the cord was tied to the back of the chair in such a way as to keep him from toppling. Just out of his reach on the table stood the raven.

She wanted to shriek, to run, to dissolve into hysteria. Her gaze would not leave Poe and her mind had stopped functioning.

"Margaret Ellen Wilson," she commanded, "control yourself!"

With tremendous effort she deserted Edgar Allan Poe and returned to the Old Stone House.

No one could have entered that afternoon without paying the entrance fee and signing the register. Whatever her tormented brain was inclined to think, Edgar A. Poe could not be in the upstairs room of the Memorial Building. Whoever was there had deliberately masqueraded as Poe but his right name or an assumed name must be in the guest book.

Darkness had claimed the Old Stone House. Miss Wilson turned on the lamp near the register. She fluttered through the book until she came to the page beginning with the visitors on that Sunday afternoon in August. Her eyes sought and then would not go beyond two entries:

Eddie Poe, Main Street, Richmond, Virginia
Gus Dupin, Faubourg St. Germain, Paris

She felt the healthy emotion of justified indignation. Not even Edgar A. Poe; not even C. Auguste Dupin. Eddie and Gus. Gay, flippant hoaxers had written that—arrant leg-pullers committing a schoolboy's prank. But murder was no hoax. Death by violence was no prank.

This might mean ruin for the Shrine, she thought frantically; at best it would mean notoriety; but as a citizen she had no choice. Her finger ran down the telephone book until she reached *Police Department*. She went to the telephone and dialed the number listed. When there was an answer her message was on the verge of hysteria …

While she waited for the police she copied out the names of the persons who had visited the Shrine that afternoon; surely the investigators would need them; as far as she could see it would be all they would have to go on. The last name was barely set down in her fine, even calligraphy when the police arrived.

Their leader was an amiable, matter-of-fact young man. His name was Williams, his rank, lieutenant. Miss Wilson told him all that she could; then she led the way to the Memorial Building and returned alone to the Old Stone House.

Soon Poe's imposter left the Shrine in a horizontal position, assisted by two men.

"Lieutenant Williams," Miss Wilson said, when the door had closed on the body of the impersonator, "I have a favor to ask of you. It's not just for me—it's for Richmond—for everyone who admires Poe. This story would be sensational—a man dressed as Poe murdered at the Poe Shrine. It has all kinds of possibilities for exploitation. Can't you just make a report that an unidentified man has been found dead under suspicious circumstances on East Main Street? If you have to give an exact address you can say 1916 East Main Street—I don't think most people would identify that number as the Poe Shrine. That really won't be suppressing news but it would protect one of the country's great literary shrines. If there is any unfavorable publicity it might mean an end to the Shrine. People would come don't you see?— not from love of Poe but to look at a room in which someone was murdered."

Lieutenant Williams understood. "I think you're right. I'll do what I can. Meantime, thanks for the list of the people who visited the Shrine today. A lot of them seem to be from out of town. They may have just been passing through Richmond. I mustn't waste any time trying to reach them."

"When you've finished with them you must come to see me," Miss Wilson said. "I've nothing to say now that could possibly help, but I may think of something later."

Their earnest, worried expressions were almost identical as they said goodbye and promised to meet again within a few hours.

As Miss Wilson left the Shrine and locked its doors on the remnants of murder she did not examine her emotions. She must get away, that was essential; then she could think. She remembered taking a bus, asking for a transfer, and later she had some slight recollection of waiting to transfer across from the Telephone Building. The bus had traveled to West Grace and Laurel Streets before she decided to get off and visit one of the girls' dormitories of Wellington College; it was not far from her apartment on West Franklin Street and she just might learn something from one of the students who had been to the Shrine that afternoon.

The hostess admitted her and Miss Wilson asked if any of the girls who had visited the Shrine were in. She was given the name and room number of a student and directed upstairs.

A qualm overtook her then. This might very well be usurpation of the Police Department's domain. But she must think about the murder and try to analyze it; and to do this she needed facts.

Mary Johnson, the student, was barefooted and wore only a slip.

"Golly," she said, "I'm sorry not to be decent. I thought it was one of the kids. Please excuse me." She grabbed for a robe.

"You may not remember," Miss Wilson said, "but I'm the guide or lecturer—whatever you want to call it, at the Edgar Allan Poe Shrine. I was wondering if anything out of the ordinary happened while you were there this afternoon."

"Gosh, I don't know. I don't *think* so. Except of course I was awfully disappointed about the room where the raven is. Some of the students had said they liked it best of all. It's what I get for waiting till the last minute, I suppose."

Miss Wilson tried not to let her eyes glisten in anticipation; she tried not to wet her lips.

"What do you mean you were disappointed?"

"Well, the door was shut and there was a sign saying 'Temporarily Closed.' I hated to miss it because some of the kids said it was about the spookiest thing they'd ever seen—all those drawings of *The Raven* and the raven itself there on the table."

"You didn't by any chance see anyone who looked like Poe?"

"Golly, no!"

Miss Wilson thanked Mary Johnson and left the dormitory.

She made a determined, thought-free walk to her apartment; she insisted on keeping her mind inactive until she could cook a light supper for herself.

Catarina, named after Poe's cat (Miss Wilson's only surrender to Poe associations in her own household), waited for her at the door. There was only the most formal greeting between them; Catarina disliked being fondled.

Miss Wilson found it hard to refrain from thinking about the murder. It took the strictest discipline to make her mind behave while she prepared an omelet and a salad of lettuce, endive, watercress, and asparagus. She did not usually drink coffee at night—it kept her awake; but tonight she would need to be kept awake. She got out the percolator that she used only when she had guests, filled it, and set it on the stove. Then she ate. Ordinarily she did not leave dirty dishes in the sink; but this was no ordinary occasion. The coffee burbled cheerfully as it rose in the pot; she watched it gain blackness; then she poured a cup. When she had set it on a table beside her favorite chair she drew the drapes and sat down.

The time had come to think.

Miss Wilson's hand reached for a lamp, but she suppressed her impulse to flood the room with light.

The hour had come to think of Poe and Dupin and of the help they could offer her. Darkness was the atmosphere each of them encouraged; hadn't Dupin himself insisted in *The Purloined Letter*: "If it is any point requiring reflection, we shall examine it to better purpose in the dark?" Then let her, as a willing disciple, follow the master's rule.

She let her mind trot and scamper like a dog that hates the leash. Perhaps she was a silly woman and too full of pride, but as much as anything in life she had wanted Poe to be proud of her. That was an idiotic way to put it—wanting someone dead for more than a hundred years to be proud of you. But he had suffered so deeply at so many hands—possibly, most of all, at his own hands—that she felt very close to him. Poor Poe! All his life he had been protected by women, from the gracious Frances Valentine Allan to the time of his last dreadful agony when Mrs. Moran, the wife of the doctor at the Washington Hospital in Baltimore where he died, had ministered to him. Margaret Ellen Wilson wanted to protect him now.

It was just possible, she thought, that she felt closer to Poe than anyone now alive. Oh, she wasn't in love with him in the way Fanny Kemble had been in love with Byron or Amy Lowell with Keats. But she was the chatelaine of Poe's shrine in Richmond; she was his protectress, and nobody had any business coming on the premises and committing murder, especially committing murder on the person of someone dressed like Poe. The names in the register incensed her— Gus Dupin and Eddie Poe! Levity, no respect … It was outrageous.

Miss Wilson pulled her feelings up. Anger was not an indulgence she could allow herself now. She must stop such foolish meanderings and get on with her thoughts.

Handwriting. She came back to that. Again she recalled that the graphologist had written that she had powers of analysis. Poe's critique and extolment of analysis were in *The Murders in the Rue Morgue* and *The Purloined Letter*. Analysis was the one quality he had seemed to revere above all others. At times in his life he had even overestimated his ability to analyze, perhaps because he knew he was a person of violent emotions and liked to cherish, even if somewhat falsely, an ability unrelated to passion.

Poe had in fact attempted to solve a real-life crime, fictionalized in *The Mystery of Marie Rogêt*, before the police. Good lord, Miss Wilson asked herself, is that what I am proposing to do, with Poe's help? It was, indeed! Then start at the beginning, she urged herself. Two men. They had signed themselves Dupin and Poe, and one had ended up dead. Two friends on a lark, but only one had left the Shrine alive.

What did that remind her of?

Two friends, conversing pleasantly—one tricked into doing something but not aware that he was being tricked.

The Cask of Amontillado, of course. Fortunato and Montresor. Two friends. But one was not a friend. And he had duped the other through vanity, through his palate, his knowledge of wines, into meeting a horrible death.

Fortunato and Montresor. Eddie Poe and Gus Dupin.

If two men came as friends to the Poe Shrine for a lark, a hoax, it must have been carefully planned.

But no man carefully plans his own murder.

Leave the two friends for a minute, she instructed herself. Leave *The Cask of Amontillado*. Just consider the fact of the man's death—the man dead in the room, the raven a few inches from his outstretched hands.

What did that suggest?

But her mind, the dog she had unleashed, would not pick up the scent. It would not sniff. It withdrew. It refused to pursue the quarry.

Very well, then, she thought, don't insist that the mind do what it balks at. Go back to the two friends, the two who signed their names as Poe and Dupin; two friends on a prank; they must have winked at each other as they signed the register, as she waited to conduct them through the Shrine.

But she found herself thinking of Poe's parents instead. They were desperately poor. His mother, after his father's death or desertion … heavy with child, returning to the stage as soon as she could get up after the birth of her daughter Rosalie … Miss Wilson felt a deep sadness as she recalled Elizabeth Poe's plight. She supposed she should have grown accustomed to the tragedy of everything and everyone related to Poe, but there was never a moment when she could not be saddened by it. Poe, who gave so much to the world and had so little, who was defeated and starving—one of the few authentic starving poets in literary history….

Miss Wilson commanded her brain to stop its melancholy reflections. Get back to the murder, she admonished it sternly.

All she really knew was that two people had entered the Shine that afternoon and had signed the register as Poe and Dupin.

Wait! Whoever had done the murder must surely have registered in the guest book on a previous occasion. He must have familiarized himself with the setting; he would have to know about the room where *The Raven* illustrations were hung.

Then his name must be in the register twice!

After five telephone calls Miss Wilson located Lieutenant Williams. She told him she was sure she could be of help if he brought the Shrine guest book to her immediately.

When Lieutenant Williams's knock sounded on her door Miss Wilson was sitting in pitch darkness. She blinked against the lights as she turned them on to admit him. For an instant Lieutenant Williams seemed illuminated.

He handed her the register.

"Here's the book," he said.

Book. Williams.

He handed her a book and his name was Williams.

She trembled as if a revelation were about to occur. But no revelation came. She invited him in and poured some coffee. He took it eagerly and drank it in three gulps.

He had nothing to report. "No luck. I found a few of the people who visited the Shrine this afternoon still in Richmond. A lot of them were tourists, I guess, who have already left town. None of those I saw could tell me anything we don't know, and we haven't even been able to identify the victim. There's nothing about his clothes to tell us who he is. He had on a wig, by the way. Actually, he's rather bald. The mustache was false, too. He even wore makeup. Seemed funny for a man to be wearing makeup."

A wig. A mustache. Makeup.

Joy and exultancy possessed Miss Wilson. Poe and Dupin were guiding her accurately. But she must take herself in hand. She must proceed logically.

"Now, Lieutenant Williams, before I begin I want you to know that I respect the police. I don't share Dupin's opinion—well, I'm not sure he felt that way about the police in general, perhaps only the one with whom he was involved at the time. I mean I don't think you're capable— in Dupin's words—oh, well, I suppose it's gentler in French: *de nier ce qui est, et d'expliquer ce qui n'est pas*—to deny what is and to explain what is not."

"Go right ahead," Lieutenant Williams said. "I'm not following you, but I sure am interested."

"All I'm saying is that you must be doing a good job or you wouldn't be a lieutenant. You're competent and trustworthy. But you see, I feel that I must help solve this crime because—well, because it happened where it did and because the place points rather logically to who did it. Not that I know his name yet or where he is or how you can find him, but I think I'll know soon. Of course, all the hard work will be left to you. But I want you to know what I've been thinking.

"First, though, I want to look at the register. The murderer has been to the Shrine before and fairly recently, I think."

Miss Wilson grappled with the large register, actually an old-style ledger.

"It's the handwriting of the man who registered today as Dupin that I've got to find."

She thumbed through the leaves, stopped, went back to that day's entries, shook her head, started again, consulted more entries; then she stopped again, gazed hard, sighed, and said, "There it is—I'm sure of it. The man you want is named Horace Manchester."

Lieutenant Williams set his cup down. He was impressed; in fact, he was astounded, and trying very hard not to be overwhelmed. He said, "Was this Horace Manchester thoughtful enough to write down his address and telephone number?"

"He's given his address as New York City."

"New York is a big place."

"We can narrow it down for you."

"Can we?"

"May I go back for a moment?"

"Anything you say, Miss Wilson."

"I was thinking of the two men as Montresor and Fortunato—the two characters in *The Cask of Amontillado*. I'd like to go ahead and call them that, though we know that our Montresor is Manchester. Curious, isn't it?—the same initial.

"My mind wouldn't go any further when I started to think of Elizabeth Poe. She was an actress. Then when you came and handed me the ledger I felt there was a revelation in the making. But all I did was to ask you in and then I poured the coffee. I know now what my subconscious was reaching for. A book. Handed to me by a man named Williams. And that reminded me of Emlyn Williams and a book. He did readings from Dickens dressed as Dickens. Impersonation. Actor. Don't you see? Somebody dressed like Poe reading *The Raven* in the Poe Shrine. These two men must be actors. Ordinary persons might not know where to buy wigs and mustaches, might not know about makeup. Their minds wouldn't run in theatrical channels.

"Actors. There have been dozens of stock companies in and around Richmond; the summer season is about over and actors are getting back to New York for fall casting. Actors might have come to the Shrine from Washington, Norfolk, Williamsburg, Abingdon, or anywhere around Richmond. But actors must have rehearsals. They're not at all impromptu persons. One of the friends, or both of them, would have had to be at the Shrine before—in fact, Horace Manchester was here in June. Otherwise he wouldn't have known the floor plan. He wouldn't have realized that the room upstairs could be shut off from the rest of the Shrine while the staging was being prepared. It's even possible that Manchester had no plan for staging a murder at Poe's Shrine when he first visited the Shrine.

"So this crime probably involves two actors who played Richmond or somewhere in the vicinity this summer. I'd guess that for our two men the season ended last night. These two actors were leaving the vicinity and heading for New York. One felt deep hatred for the other—I don't know why, but we can assume, if murder was committed, there must have been an intense loathing.

"Maybe the victim, whom I'll continue to call Fortunato because we still don't know his name, had planned to do some readings dressed as Poe—in the way that Emlyn Williams did readings from Dickens. Manchester appeals to his friend's vanity. What a publicity stunt to come to the Shrine and read *The Raven* in the very room where the bust of Pallas is, and all *The Raven* illustrations are hung. How shocked and thrilled the visitors at the Shrine would be. The papers would carry feature stories about it. Engagements and bookings would pour in. All right, Fortunato says. They come to the Shrine and Fortunato brings his makeup. A brief time is needed to dress, but Manchester has thought of everything—he has brought a printed sign saying 'Temporarily Closed,' which he tacks to the outside of the door, so they won't be disturbed. Then when Fortunato has completed his Poe makeup and thinks the door should be opened and he should begin to do his reading of *The Raven*, his friend proves to be not his friend but his murderer. A cord. Strangulation. Manchester escapes. He is now en route to New York—unless he took a plane, in which case he's already there. He is smug and triumphant. But he has forgotten something: his right name is in the register! And actors can be located through Actors' Equity. Actors' Equity, did you know, helped place a monument on the unmarked grave of Poe's mother in St. John's Churchyard?

"Now then, Lieutenant Williams, that's the best Poe and Dupin and I can do. Try to locate Horace Manchester through Actors' Equity, and perhaps you can even get some help here from the newspaper critics who followed the summer theatrical season."

On Wednesday afternoon Miss Wilson escorted a small group through the Shrine. It seemed uncannily appropriate that they had suggested detective fiction as a topic for discussion.

She told them in some detail of Poe's contribution: the eccentric, infallible detective; the narrator who is something of a dunderhead and has to have the genius's deductions explained; the ineffectual police.

"So you see," she concluded, "not since Poe's invention of the modern detective story has there been any important addition."

One of the young men called out, "Oh, but you're wrong. What about blondes and sex? They're additions, aren't they?"

Miss Wilson smiled at him. "No," she said, "they aren't additions. They're aberrations."

The sympathetic laughter buoyed her. She had been apprehensive and depressed since Sunday night. She withdrew from the guests and they went their separate ways around the Shrine.

The ringing of the telephone summoned her.

"Is this the Edgar Allan Poe Detective Agency?" someone asked. "I'd like to speak to Operative Wilson, please."

She recognized the voice of Lieutenant Williams.

"Hello," she said. "How are you?"

"Dead on my feet. But as soon as I get a little rest I want you to enroll me in the Beginners' Class in Deduction. I've been on the chase you suggested and it didn't turn out to be a wild goose. In fact, Miss Wilson, even if it is the Twentieth Century, I think it's just as well that you live in Richmond. If you were in Salem they'd use the old gallows tree on you—they sure would!"

His voice dropped. "We located Horace Manchester—or Montresor, as you and Poe would say. Thanks for what you did. We might never have got him if not for you."

It wasn't I, Miss Wilson thought humbly as she hung up the receiver. It was Edgar A. Poe.

Recipe for a Happy Marriage

Today is just not my day.

And it's not even noon.

Maybe it will take a turn for the better.

Anyway, it's foolish to be upset.

That girl from the *Bulletin* who came to interview me a little while ago was nice enough. I just wasn't expecting her. And I surely wasn't expecting Eliza McIntyre to trip into my bedroom early this morning and set her roses down on my bedside table with such an air about her as if I'd broken my foot for the one and only purpose of having her arrive at seven-thirty to bring me a bouquet. She's been coming often enough since I broke my foot, but never before eleven or twelve in the morning.

That young woman from the *Bulletin* sat right down, and before she even smoothed her skirt or crossed her legs she looked straight at me and asked if I had a recipe for a happy marriage. I think she should at least have started off by saying it was a nice day or asking how I felt, especially as it was perfectly obvious that I had a broken foot.

I told her that I certainly didn't have any recipe for a happy marriage, but I'd like to know why I was being asked, and she said it was almost St. Valentine's Day and she had been assigned to write a feature article on love, and since I must know more about love than anybody else in town she and her editor thought that my opinions should have a prominent place in the article.

Her explanation put me more out of sorts than her question. But whatever else I may or may not be, I'm a good-natured woman. I suppose it was my broken foot that made me feel irritable.

At that very moment Eliza's giggle came way up the back stairwell from the kitchen, and it was followed by my husband's laughter, and I heard dishes rattle and pans clank, and all that added fire to my irritability.

The one thing I can't abide, never have been able to stand, is to have somebody in my kitchen. Stay out of my kitchen and my pantry, that's my motto. People always seem to think they're putting things back in the right place, but they never do. How well I remember Aunt Mary

Ellen saying she just wanted to make us a cup of tea and to cut some slices of lemon to go with it. I could have made that tea as well as she did, but she wouldn't let me. I couldn't tell a bit of difference between her tea and mine, yet she put my favorite paring knife some place or other and it didn't turn up until eight months later, underneath a stack of cheese graters. That was a good twenty years ago and poor Aunt Mary Ellen has been in her grave for ten, and yet I still think about that paring knife and get uneasy when someone is in my kitchen.

Well, that young woman leaned forward and had an equally dumbfounding question. She asked me just which husband I had now.

I don't look at things—at husbands—like that. So I didn't answer her. I was too aghast. And then again from the kitchen came the sound of Eliza's giggle and Lewis's whoop.

I've known Eliza Moore, now Eliza McIntyre, all my life. In school she was two grades ahead of me from the very beginning, but the way she tells it now she was three grades behind me; but those school records are somewhere, however yellowed and crumbled they may be, and there's no need for Eliza to try to pretend she's younger than I am when she's two years older. Not that it matters. I just don't want her in my kitchen.

That young woman was mistaking my silence. She leaned close as if I were either deaf or a very young child who hadn't paid attention. How many times have you been married? she asked in a very loud voice.

When she put it like that, how could I answer her? Husbands aren't like teacups. I can't count them off and gloat over them the way Cousin Lutie used to stand in front of her china cabinets, saying she had so many of this pattern and so many of that.

For goodness sake, I had them one at a time, a husband at a time, and perfectly legally. They all just died on me. I couldn't stay the hand of fate. I was always a sod widow—there weren't any grass widows in our family. As Mama said, it runs in our family to be with our husbands till death us do part. The way that girl put her question, it sounded as if I had a whole bunch of husbands at one time like a line of chorus men in a musical show.

I didn't know how to answer her. I lay back on my pillows with not a word to say, as if the cat had run off with my tongue.

It's sheer accident that I ever married to begin with. I didn't want to. Not that I had anything against marriage or had anything else special to do. But Mama talked me into it. Baby, she said, other women look down on women who don't marry. Besides, you don't have any particular talent and Aunt Sallie Mae, for all her talk, may not leave you a penny. I don't think she ever forgave me for not naming you after her, and all her hinting about leaving you her money may just be her spiteful way of getting back at me.

Besides, Mama said, the way she's held on to her money, even if she did leave it to you, there would be so many strings attached you'd have to have a corps of Philadelphia lawyers to read the fine print before you could withdraw as much as a twenty-five-cent piece. If I were you, Baby, Mama said, I'd go and get married. If you don't marry you won't get invited anyplace except as a last resort, when they need somebody at the last minute to keep from having thirteen at table. And it's nice to have somebody to open the door for you and carry your packages. A husband can be handy.

So I married Ray.

Well, Ray and I hadn't been married six months when along came Mama with a handkerchief in her hand and dabbing at her eyes. Baby, she said, the wife is always the last one to know. I've just got to tell you what everyone is talking about. I know how good you are and how lacking in suspicion, but the whole town is buzzing. It's Ray and Marjorie Brown.

Ray was nice and I was fond of him. He called me Lucy honey, exactly as if it were one word. Sometimes for short he called me Lucyhon. He didn't have much stamina or backbone—how could he when he was the only child and spoiled rotten by his mother and grandma and three maiden aunts?

Baby, Mama said, and her tears had dried and she was now using her handkerchief to fan herself with, don't you be gullible. I can't stand for you to be mistreated or betrayed. Should I go to the rector and tell him to talk to Ray and point out where his duty lies? Or should I ask your Uncle Jonathan to talk to Ray man-to-man?

I said, Mama, it's nobody's fault but my own. For heaven's sake let Ray do what he wants to do. He doesn't need anyone to tell him when he can come and go and what persons he can see. It's his house and he's paying the bills. Besides, his taking up with Marjorie Brown is no discredit to me—she's a lot prettier than I am. I think it's romantic and spunky of Ray. Why, Marjorie Brown is a married woman. Her husband might shoot Ray.

I don't know exactly what it was that cooled Ray down. He was back penitent and sheep-eyed, begging forgiveness. I'm proud of you, Ray, I said. Why, until you married me you were so timid you wouldn't have said boo to a goose and here you've been having an illicit affair. I think it's grand. Marjorie Brown's husband might have horsewhipped you.

Ray grinned and said, I really have picked me a wife.

And he never looked at another woman again as long as he lived. Which unfortunately wasn't very long.

I got to thinking about him feeling guilty and apologizing to me, when I was the one to blame—I hadn't done enough for him, and I wanted to do something real nice for him, so I thought of that cake recipe. Except we called it a receipt. It had been in the family for years—centuries, you might say, solemnly handed down from mother to daughter, time out of mind.

And so when that girl asked me whether I had a recipe for a happy marriage I didn't give the receipt a thought. Besides, I'm sure she didn't mean an actual recipe, but some kind of formula like let the husband know he's boss, or some such foolishness.

Anyway, there I was feeling penitent about not giving Ray the attention he should have had so that he was bored enough by me to go out and risk his life at the hands of Marjorie Brown's jealous husband.

So I thought, well, it's the hardest receipt I've ever studied and has more ingredients than I've ever heard of, but it's the least I can do for Ray. So I went here and there to the grocery stores, to drug stores, to apothecaries, to people who said, Good Lord, no, we don't carry that but if you've got to have it try so-and-so, who turned out to be somebody way out in the country that looked at me as if I asked for the element that would turn base metal into gold and finally came back with a little packet and a foolish question as to what on earth I needed that for.

Then I came on back home and began grinding and pounding and mixing and baking and sitting in the kitchen waiting for the mixture to rise. When it was done it was the prettiest thing I had ever baked.

I served it for dessert that night.

Ray began to eat the cake and to savor it and to say extravagant things to me, and when he finished the first slice he said, Lucyhon, may I have another piece, a big one, please.

Why, Ray, it's all yours to eat as you like, I said.

After a while he pushed the plate away and looked at me with a wonderful expression of gratitude on his face and he said, oh, Lucy honey, I could die happy. And as far as I know he did.

When I tapped on his door the next morning to give him his first cup of coffee and open the shutters and turn on his bath water he was dead, and there was the sweetest smile on his face.

But that young woman was still looking at me while I had been reminiscing, and she was fluttering her notes and wetting her lips with her tongue like a speaker with lots of things to say. And she sort of bawled out at me as if I were an entire audience whose attention had strayed: Do you think that the way to a man's heart is through his stomach?

Excuse me, young lady, I wanted to say, but I never heard of Cleopatra saying to Mark Antony or any of the others she favored, here, won't you taste some of my potato salad, and I may be wrong because my reading of history is skimpy, but it sounds a little unlikely that Madame de Pompadour ever whispered into the ear of Louis XV, I've baked the nicest casserole for you.

My not answering put the girl off, and I felt that I ought to apologize, yet I couldn't bring myself around to it.

She glanced at her notes to the next question, and was almost beet-red from embarrassment when she asked: Did the financial situation of your husbands ever have anything to do with your marrying them?

I didn't even open my mouth. I was as silent as the tomb. Her questions kept getting more and more irrelevant. And I was getting more stupefied as her eyes kept running up and down her list of questions.

She tried another one: What do you think is the best way to get a husband?

Now that's a question I have never asked myself and about which I have nothing to offer anybody in a St. Valentine's Day article or elsewhere. I have never gone out to get a husband. I haven't ever, as that old-fashioned expression has it, set my cap for anybody.

Take Lewis who is this minute in the kitchen giggling with Eliza McIntyre. I certainly did not set out to get him. It was some months after Alton—no, Edward—had died, and people were trying to cheer me up, not that I needed any cheering up. I mean, after all the losses I've sustained, I've become philosophical. But my Cousin Wanda's grandson had an exhibition of paintings. The poor deluded boy isn't talented, not a bit. All the same I bought two of his paintings that are downstairs in the hall closet, shut off from all eyes.

Anyway, at the opening of the exhibition there was Lewis looking all forlorn. He had come because the boy was a distant cousin of his dead wife. Lewis leaped up from a bench when he got a glimpse of me and said, Why, Lucy, I haven't seen you in donkey's years, and we stood there talking while everybody was going ooh and aah over the boy's paintings, and Lewis said he was hungry and I asked him to come on home with me and have a bite to eat.

I fixed a quick supper and Lewis ate like a starving man, and then we sat in the back parlor and talked about this and that, and about midnight he said, Lucy, I don't want to leave. This is the nicest feeling I've ever had, being here with you. I don't mean to be disrespectful to the dead, but there wasn't any love lost between Ramona and me. I'd like to stay on here forever.

Well, after that—after a man's revealed his innermost thoughts to you—you can't just show him the door. Besides, I couldn't put him out because it was beginning to snow, and in a little while the snow turned to sleet. He might have fallen and broken his neck going down the front steps and I'd have had that on my conscience the rest of my life.

Lewis, I said, it seems foolish at this stage of the game for me to worry about my reputation, but thank heaven Cousin Alice came down from Washington for the exhibition and is staying with me, and she can chaperone us until we can make things perfectly legal and aboveboard.

That's how it happened.

You don't plan things like that, I wanted to tell the girl. They happen in spite of you. So it's silly of you to ask me what the best way is to get a husband.

My silence hadn't bothered her a bit. She sort of closed one eye like somebody about to take aim with a rifle and asked: Exactly how many times have you been married?

Well, she had backed up. She was repeating herself. That was practically the same question she had asked me earlier. It had been put a little differently this time, that was all.

I certainly had no intention of telling her the truth, which was that I wasn't exactly sure myself. Sometimes my husbands become a little blurred and blended. Sometimes I have to sit down with pencil and paper and figure it out.

Anyhow, that's certainly no way to look at husbands—the exact number or the exact sequence.

My husbands were an exceptional bunch of men, if I do say so. And fine-looking, too. Even Art, who had a harelip. And they were all good providers. Rich and didn't mind spending their money—not like some rich people. Not that I needed money. Because Aunt Sallie Mae, for all Mama's suspicions, left me hers, and there was nothing spiteful about her stipulations. I could have the money when, as, and how I wanted it.

Anyway, I never have cared about money or what it could buy for me.

There's nothing much I can spend it on for myself. Jewelry doesn't

suit me. My fingers are short and stubby and my hands are square—
no need to call attention to them by wearing rings. Besides, rings
bother me. I like to cook and rings get in the way. Necklaces choke me
and earrings pinch. As for fur coats, mink or chinchilla or just plain
squirrel—well, I don't like the idea of anything that has lived ending
up draped around me.

So money personally means little to me. But it's nice to pass along.
Nothing gives me greater pleasure, and there's not a husband of mine
who hasn't ended up without having a clinic or a college library or a
hospital wing or a research laboratory or something of the sort founded
in his honor and named after him. Sometimes I've had to rob Peter to
pay Paul. I mean, some of them have left more than others and once in
a while I've had to take some of what one left me to pay on the
endowment for another. But it all evened itself out.

Except for Buster. There was certainly a nice surplus where Buster
was concerned. He lived the shortest time and left me the most money
of any of my husbands. For every month I lived with him I inherited a
million dollars. Five.

My silent reminiscing like that wasn't helping the girl with her St.
Valentine's Day article. If I had been in anybody's house and the hostess
was as taciturn as I was, I'd have excused myself and reached for the
knob of the front door.

But, if anything, that young lady became even more impertinent.

Have you had a favorite among your husbands? she asked and her
tongue flicked out like a snake's.

I was silent even when my husbands asked that question. Sometimes
they would show a little jealousy for their predecessor and make
unkind remarks. But naturally I did everything in my power to reassure
whoever made a disparaging remark about another.

All my husbands have been fine men, I would say in such a case, but
I do believe you're the finest of the lot. I said it whether really thought
so or not.

But I had nothing at all to say to that girl on the subject.

Yet if I ever got to the point of being forced to rank my husbands, I
guess Luther would be very nearly at the bottom of the list. He was
the only teetotaler in the bunch. I hadn't noticed how he felt about
drink until after we were married—that's when a thing you've
overlooked during courtship can confront you like a slap in the face.
Luther would squirm when wine was served to guests during a meal,
and his eyes looked up prayerfully toward heaven when anybody took
a second glass. At least he restrained himself to the extent of not

saying any word of reproach to a guest, but Mama said she always expected him to hand around some of those tracts that warn against the pitfalls that lie in wait for drunkards.

Poor man. He was run over by a beer truck.

The irony of it, Mama said. There's a lesson in it for us all. And it was broad daylight, she said, shaking her head, not even dark, so that we can't comfort ourselves that Luther didn't know what hit him.

Not long after Luther's unfortunate accident Matthew appeared—on tiptoe, you might say. He was awfully short and always stretched himself to look taller. He was terribly apologetic about his height. I'd ask you to marry me, Lucy, he said, but all your husbands have been over six feet tall. Height didn't enter into it, I told him, and it wasn't very long before Matthew and I were married.

He seemed to walk on tiptoe and I scrunched down, and still there was an awful gap between us, and he would go on about Napoleon almost conquering the world in spite of being short. I started wearing low-heeled shoes and walking hunched over, and Mama said, For God's sake, Baby, you can push tact too far. You never were beautiful but you had an air about you and no reigning queen ever had a more elegant walk, and here you are slumping. Your Aunt Francine was married to a midget, as you well know, but there wasn't any of this bending down and hunching over. She let him be his height and he let her be hers. So stop this foolishness.

But I couldn't. I still tried literally to meet Matthew more than halfway. And I had this feeling—well, why shouldn't I have it, seeing as how they had all died on me—that Matthew wasn't long for this world, and it was my duty to make him feel as important and as tall as I possibly could during the little time that was left to him.

Matthew died happy. I have every reason to believe it. But then, as Mama said, they all died happy.

Never again, Mama, I said. Never again. I feel like Typhoid Mary or somebody who brings doom on men's heads.

Never is a long time, Mama said.

And she was right. I married Hugh.

I think it was Hugh.

Two things I was proud of and am proud of. I never spoke a harsh word to any one of my husbands and I never did call one of them by another's name, and that took a lot of doing because after a while they just all sort of melted together in my mind.

After every loss, Homer was the greatest solace and comfort to me. Until he retired last year Homer was the Medical Examiner, and he was a childhood friend, though I never saw him except in his line of duty, you might say. It's the law here, and perhaps elsewhere, that if anyone dies unattended or from causes that aren't obvious, the Medical Examiner must be informed.

The first few times I had to call Homer I was chagrined. I felt apologetic, a little like calling the doctor up in the middle of the night when, however much the pain may be troubling you, you're afraid it's a false alarm and the doctor will hold it against you for disturbing his sleep.

But Homer always was jovial when I called him. I guess that's not the right word. Homer was reassuring, not jovial. Anytime, Lucy, anytime at all, he would say when I began to apologize for having to call him.

I think it was right after Sam died. Or was it Carl? It could have been George. Anyway, Homer was there reassuring me as always, and then this look of sorrow or regret clouded his features. It's a damned pity, Lucy, he said, you can't work me in somewhere or other. You weren't the prettiest little girl in the third grade, or the smartest, but damned if from the beginning there hasn't been something about you. I remember, he said, that when we were in the fourth grade I got so worked up over you that I didn't pass a single subject but arithmetic and had to take the whole term over. Of course, you were promoted, so for the rest of my life you've been just out of my reach.

Why, Homer, I said, that's the sweetest thing anybody has ever said to me.

I had it in the back of my mind once the funeral was over and everything was on an even keel again that I'd ask Homer over for supper one night. But it seemed so calculating, as if I was taking him up on that sweet remark he had made about wishing I had worked him in somewhere among my husbands. So I decided against it.

Instead, I married Beau Green.

There they go laughing again—Eliza and Lewis down in the kitchen. My kitchen.

It's funny that Eliza has turned up in my kitchen, acting very much at home, when she's the one and only person in this town I never have felt very friendly toward—at least, not since word got to me that she had said I snatched Beau Green right from under her nose.

That wasn't a nice thing for her to say. Besides, there wasn't a word of truth in it. I'd like to see the man that can be snatched from under anybody's nose unless he wanted to be.

Eliza was surely welcome to Beau Green if she had wanted him and if he had wanted her.

Why, I'd planned to take a trip around the world, already had my tickets and reservations, and had to put it off for good because Beau wouldn't budge any farther away from home than to go to Green River—named for his family—to fish. I really wanted to take that cruise—had my heart especially set on seeing the Taj Mahal by moonlight; but Beau kept on saying if I didn't marry him he would do something desperate, which I took to mean he'd kill himself or take to drink. So I canceled all those reservations and turned in all those tickets and married him.

Well, Eliza would certainly have been welcome to Beau.

I've already emphasized that I don't like to rank my husbands, but in many ways Beau was the least satisfactory one I ever had. It was his nature to be a killjoy—he had no sense of the joy of living and once he set his mind on something he went ahead with it, no matter if it pleased anybody else or not.

He knew good and well I didn't care for jewelry. But my preference didn't matter to Beau Green, not one bit. Here he came with this package and I opened it. I tried to muster all my politeness when I saw that it was a diamond. Darling, I said, you're sweet to give me a present, but this is a little bit big, isn't it?

It's thirty-seven carats, he said.

I felt like I ought to take it around on a sofa pillow instead of wearing it, but I did wear it twice and felt as conspicuous and as much of a show-off as if I'd been waving a peacock fan around and about.

It was and is my habit when I get upset with someone to go to my room and write my grievances down and get myself back in a good humor, just as I'm doing now because of that girl's questions; but sometimes it seemed like there wasn't enough paper in the world on which to write down my complaints against Beau.

Then I would blame myself. Beau was just being Beau. Like all God's creatures he was behaving the way he was made, and I felt so guilty that I decided I ought to do something for him to show I really loved and respected him, as deep in my heart I did.

So I decided to make him a cake by that elaborate recipe that had been in our family nobody is sure for how long. I took all one day to do the shopping for it. The next day I got up at five and stayed in the kitchen until late afternoon.

Well, Beau was a bit peckish when it came to eating the cake. Yet he had the sweetest tooth of any of my husbands.

Listen, darling, I said when he was mulish about eating it, I made this special for you—it's taken the best part of two days. I smiled at him and asked wouldn't he please at least taste it to please me. Really, I was put out when I thought of all the work that had gone into it. For one terrible second I wished it were a custard pie and I could throw it right in his face, like in one of those old Keystone comedies; and then I remembered that we were sworn to cherish each other, so I just put one arm around his shoulder and with my free hand I pushed the cake a little closer and said, Belle wants Beau to eat at least one small bite. Belle was a foolish pet name he sometimes called me because he thought it was clever for him to be Beau and for me to be Belle.

He looked sheepish and picked up his fork and I knew he was trying to please me, the way I had tried to please him by wearing that thirty-seven-carat diamond twice.

Goodness, Belle, he said, when he swallowed his first mouthful, this is delicious.

Now, darling, you be careful, I said. That cake is rich.

Best thing I ever ate, he said, and groped around on the plate for the crumbs, and I said, Darling, wouldn't you like a little coffee to wash it down?

He didn't answer, just sat there smiling. Then after a little he said he was feeling numb. I can't feel a thing in my feet, he said. I ran for the rubbing alcohol and pulled off his shoes and socks and started rubbing his feet, and there was a sort of spasm and his toes curled under, but nothing affected that smile on his face.

Homer, I said a little later—because of course I had to telephone him about Beau's death—what on earth is it? Could it be something he's eaten? And Homer said, What do you mean, something he's eaten? Of course not. You set the best table in the county. You're famous for your cooking. It couldn't be anything he's eaten. Don't be foolish, Lucy. He began to pat me on the shoulder and he said, I read a book about guilt and loss and it said the bereaved often hold themselves responsible for the deaths of their beloved ones. But I thought you had better sense than that, Lucy.

Homer was a little bit harsh with me that time.

Julius Babb settled Beau's estate. Beau left you a tidy sum all right, he said, and I wanted to say right back at him but didn't: Not as tidy as most of the others left me.

Right then that young woman from the *Bulletin* repeated her last question.

Have you had a favorite among your husbands? Her tone was that of a prosecuting attorney and had nothing to do with a reporter interested in writing about love for St. Valentine's Day.

I had had enough of her and her questions. I dragged myself up to a sitting position in the bed. Listen here, young lady, I said. It looks as if I've gotten off on the wrong foot with you—and then we both laughed at the pun I had made.

The laughter put us both in a good humor and then I tried to explain that I had an unexpected caller downstairs who needed some attention, and that I really was willing to cooperate on the St. Valentine's Day article; but all those questions at first hearing had sort of stunned me. It was like taking an examination and finding all the questions a surprise. I told her if she would leave her list with me I'd mull over it, and she could come back tomorrow and I'd be prepared with my answers and be a little more presentable than I was now, wearing a rumpled wrapper and with my hair uncombed.

Well, she was as sweet as apple pie and handed over the list of questions and said she hoped that ten o'clock tomorrow morning would be fine; and I said, yes, it would.

There goes Eliza's laugh again. It's more of a caw than a laugh. I shouldn't think that. But it's been such a strange day, with that young reporter being here and Eliza showing up so early.

Come to think of it, Eliza has done very well for herself, as far as marrying goes. That reporter should ask Eliza some of those questions.

Mama was a charitable woman all her life and she lived to be eighty-nine, but Eliza always rubbed Mama's skin the wrong way. To tell the truth, Eliza rubbed the skin of all the women in this town the wrong way. It's not right, Baby, Mama said, when other women have skimped and saved and cut corners all their lives and then when they're in their last sickness here comes Eliza getting her foot in the door just because she's a trained nurse. Then the next thing you hear, Eliza has married the widower and gets in one fell swoop what it took the dead wife a lifetime to accumulate.

That wasn't the most generous way in the world for Mama to put it, but I've heard it put much harsher by others. Mrs. Perkerson across the street, for one. Eliza is like a vulture, Mrs. Perkerson said. First she watches the wives die, then she marries, and then she watches the husbands die. Pretty soon it's widow's weeds for Eliza and a nice-sized bank account, not to mention some of the most valuable real estate in town.

Why, Mrs. Perkerson said the last time I saw her, I know that Lois Eubanks McIntyre is turning in her grave thinking of Eliza inheriting that big estate, with gardens copied after the Villa d'Este. And they tell you nursing is hard work.

I hadn't seen Eliza in some time. We were friendly enough, but not real friends, never had been, and I was especially hurt after hearing what she said about me taking Beau Green away from her. But we would stop and chat when we bumped into each other downtown, and then back off smiling and saying we must get together. But nothing ever came of it.

And then three weeks ago Eliza telephoned and I thought for sure somebody was dead. But, no, she was as sweet as magnolia blossoms and cooing as if we saw each other every day, and she invited me to come by that afternoon for a cup of tea or a glass of sherry. I asked her if there was anything special, and she said she didn't think there had to be any special reason for old friends to meet, but, yes, there was something special. She wanted me to see her gardens—of course, they weren't her gardens, except by default, they were Lois Eubanks McIntyre's gardens—which she had opened for the Church Guild Benefit Tour and I hadn't come. So she wanted me to see them that afternoon.

It was all so sudden that she caught me off guard. I didn't want to go and there wasn't any reason for me to go, but for the life of me I couldn't think of an excuse not to go. And so I went.

The gardens really were beautiful. And I'm crazy about flowers.

Eliza gave me a personally guided tour. There were lots of paths and steep steps and unexpected turnings, and I was so delighted by the flowers that I foolishly didn't pay attention to my footing. I wasn't used to walking on so much gravel or going up and down uneven stone steps and Eliza didn't give me any warning.

Then all of a sudden, it was the strangest feeling, not as if I'd fallen but as if I'd been pushed, and there Eliza was leaning over me saying she could never forgive herself for not telling me about the broken step, and I was to lie right there and not move until the doctor could come, and what a pity it was that what she had wanted to be a treat for me had turned into a tragedy. Which was making a whole lot more out of it than need be because it was only a broken foot—not that it hasn't been inconvenient.

But Eliza has been fluttering around for three weeks saying that I should sue her as she carried liability insurance, and anyway it was lucky she was a nurse and could see that I got devoted attention. I don't need a nurse, but she has insisted on coming every day, and on some days several times; she seems to be popping in and out of the house like a cuckoo clock.

I had better get on with that reporter's questions.

Do you have a recipe for a happy marriage?

I've already told her I don't, and of course there's no such thing as a recipe for a happy marriage; but I could tell her this practice I have of working through my grievances and dissatisfactions by writing down what bothers me and then tearing up what I've written. For all I know it might work for somebody else, too.

I didn't hear Eliza coming up the stairs. It startled me when I looked up and saw her at my bedside. What if she discovered I was writing about her? What if she grabbed the notebook out of my hands and started to read it? There isn't a thing I could do to stop her.

But she just smiled and asked if I was ready for lunch and she hoped I'd worked up a good appetite. How on earth she thinks I could have worked up an appetite by lying in bed I don't know, but that's Eliza for you, and all she had fixed was canned soup and it wasn't hot.

All I wanted was just to blot everything out—that girl's questions, Eliza's presence in my home, my broken foot.

I would have thought that I couldn't have gone to sleep in a thousand years. But I was so drowsy that I couldn't even close the notebook, much less hide it under the covers.

I don't know what woke me up. It was pitch dark, but dark comes so soon these winter days you can't tell whether it's early dark or midnight.

I felt refreshed after my long nap and equal to anything. I was ready to answer any question on that girl's list.

The notebook was still open beside me and I thought that if Eliza had been in here and had seen what I had written about her it served her right.

Then from the kitchen rose a wonderful smell and there was a lot of noise downstairs. Suddenly the back stairway and hall were flooded with light, and then Eliza and Lewis were at my door and they were grinning and saying they had a surprise for me. Then Lewis turned and picked up something from a table in the hall and brought it proudly toward me. I couldn't tell what it was. It was red and heart-shaped and had something white on top. At first I thought it might be a hat, and then I groped for my distance glasses, but even with them on I still couldn't tell what Lewis was carrying.

Lewis held out the tray. It's a St. Valentine's Day cake, he said, and Eliza said, we iced it and decorated it for you; then Lewis tilted it gently and I saw L U C Y in wobbly letters spread all across the top.

I don't usually eat sweets. So their labor of love was lost on me. Then I thought how kind it was that they had gone to all that trouble, and I forgave them for messing up my kitchen and meddling with my recipes—or maybe they had just used a mix. Anyway, I felt I had to show my appreciation, and it certainly wouldn't kill me to eat some of their cake.

They watched me with such pride and delight as I ate the cake that I took a second piece. When I had finished they said it would be best for me to rest, and I asked them to take the cake and eat what they wanted, then wrap it in foil. And now the whole house is quiet.

I never felt better in my life. I'm smiling a great big contented smile. It must look exactly like that last sweet smile on all my husbands' faces—except Luther, who was run over by a beer truck. I feel wonderful and so relaxed. But I can hardly hold this pencil. Goodness, it's

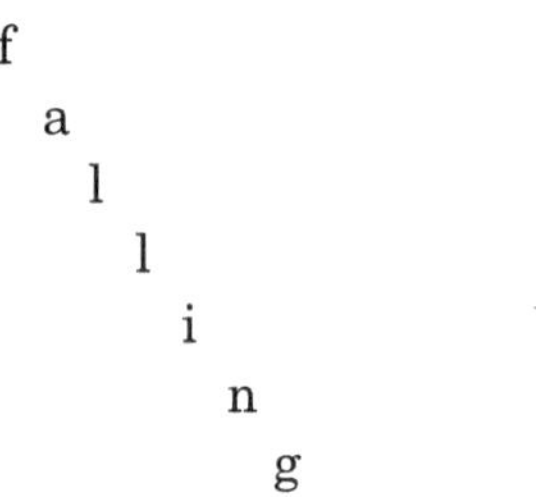

A Murder is Arranged

Mary must murder her husband.

There was nothing else to do. She hadn't the slightest doubt about it.

She had forgiven John everything except for his actions these last few weeks.

No, that wasn't putting it accurately. She hadn't forgiven him anything. Until recently, there had been nothing to forgive, no matter what people might have thought.

John was the ideal mate for her. What would her life have been without him? When she thought of the husbands of her friends— those dull, earnest, aspiring types—she shuddered. How blessed she had been to have John instead of one of them.

John was exactly right for her.

Her mother, her sisters, aunts, cousins and friends had said that she was too good for John; though, mind you, they admitted that he was fascinating, a real charmer, the best company in the world. What they deplored was that John wrapped her around his little finger. That was what they all harped upon. She did what he wanted, she danced to his tune.

They twitted her that no matter what she thought, John didn't put the sun in the sky. They were wrong—John had put the sun in her sky; he *was* the sun in her sky.

If only they could have realized what had happened. She was no longer dancing to John's tune. She wasn't being twisted around his little finger.

She was about to murder him.

The only hindrance was that she had no idea how to murder John. Exactly how did a self-respecting woman go about killing her husband?

Why hadn't she learned how to shoot from her father and brothers? Marksmen all, they could so easily have taught her how to reach John's heart with one bullet—but there would be an awful noise and no doubt a great deal of blood. Besides, if she shot John, her relatives and friends would no doubt say that John had got his just deserts at last. Nor did she have any intention of being tried for John's murder—that would defeat her purpose. John's death must be made to look either natural or accidental.

It had been foolish for people to insist that she was too good for John and she did not intend that anyone should crow or gloat over John's death. Because, for all his infidelities, he was everything she wanted. When they were together at dinners and parties his eyes didn't wander. Of course he greeted other women, exchanged pleasantries with them, complimented them on their clothes and appearance, but his arm embraced Mary all the while.

In contrast, how inexcusable was the behavior of the other husbands. At dances at the club, at cocktail parties in private homes, those other men began to make passes with the first whiff of Scotch, while John was beside Mary feeding her cream cheese-and-chives dip and asking if she wanted more ice in her drink. His lapses might have been many, but they were all done with finesse while she was out of sight. He was careful to see that she lost no face. There was no flaunting of any of his encounters. Whenever he had been away with someone else he had acted like a dutiful son, sending flowers to Mama, writing cards and letters, assuring her that his love for her was deep and eternal. For a brief time he was, figuratively, only a jaunty dog gamboling down the street for a short trot and would return soon; and when he did return his arms were loaded with lavish presents.

Well, if people called that being twisted around John's little finger she preferred it to the sordid, sneaky liaisons indulged in by other men in their social group.

All this mulling was getting her no closer to dispatching John. She must murder him in a quiet, unobtrusive way. She much preferred that there be no blood.

What about suffocating him?

No, that wouldn't do. The poor man would gasp and would turn purple and John was much too handsome to spend his last moments in such an agitated manner. Besides, she doubted that she had sufficient strength to strangle or suffocate him.

How sad that it had come to this—that her love for him, her devotion, infatuation, commitment, whatever it was, anyway her total absorption in him had been ruined.

His character, attitude and persona had altered entirely. He had become messy and slovenly. The impeccable, faultlessly groomed John had disappeared altogether, and he had begun to act like a satyr. When he accompanied her on shopping trips he would stop in the middle of a sidewalk to ogle a young girl. At the checkout counter he would make a pass at the clerk. John had always drunk well. He could drink for hours and not show it. Now his speech was often slurred. He even walked unsteadily.

His manners had become boorish. He didn't compliment Mary any longer on her cooking, but would scrape the food to one side of the plate as if it were beneath his contempt.

He had begun to speak harshly to her. *Dear, darling, beloved*, all those endearments with which he had addressed her, had been deleted from his conversation as if they were obscene. Formerly he had hung upon every word she uttered. Now he often pretended he I hadn't heard what she said. Twice he had told her to shut up—this from John who had never raised his voice in speaking to her! Now he had become a bully and a ruffian.

She was chagrined and mortified.

But how on earth was she to murder him?

There were no long flights of stairs down which she could send him spinning.

There was no swimming pool in which she might conveniently drown him.

More than anything, his new grossness disgusted her. How had he contrived that leer? When had she ever refused him? When hadn't she welcomed him with open arms? How dare he use those earthy, demeaning approaches when he wanted to make love? When had she ever been coy? Love was an open, defenseless plain upon which lovers met without reservation or pretense and he was behaving now as if their passion were vulgar and degrading. He made her feel cheap.

For the first time ever he had forgotten her birthday, and on their wedding anniversary, instead of taking her to the customary champagne dinner and showering her with dozens of roses and carnations and an exquisite chiffon nightgown, he had yawned and said he was much too tired to go out—a ham sandwich and a bottle of beer in the kitchen were all that he wanted. Then he had said in an offhand but cutting manner that there had been enough celebrations of an event so long in the past and he was sure she was as weary of them as he was.

Finally, what set a limit to his few remaining days on earth was his cruel reference to their having no children. "It's damned bleak, isn't it, not to have any children? Nothing but the two of us."

He really was a brute. Just the two of them was what he had insisted upon! He had said he did not want children who would only come between them and their happiness. They were complete in themselves. They needed nothing and no one else.

John must die immediately for rejecting that premise on which so much of their joy had been based. She must get this caricature that her husband had become into the ground immediately.

Yet she owed him something for the happiness that they had shared and so, to honor that debt, she would murder him decently and quietly by giving him an overdose of sleeping pills.

Why had it taken her so long to think of the one perfect method? It seemed stupid of her not to have arrived at it long before, but perhaps she had needed to be goaded by that final insult of not having borne him any children.

John knew he hadn't deserved Mary, but he had made her happy. He believed in love and rapture, and he had loved her completely. He was a romantic. Men were the romantics of this world and women were the practical ones.

There had been many women in his life, but Mary had come first and she knew it. He went out of his way to show her. Not that he had exploited the others. He had reason to think that he had made them happy, too. Mary, though, was his life. His flirtations had never brought shame to Mary or made her feel neglected. They had been minor skirmishes, and only added piquancy to the passion he felt for Mary. He wished he could have given her the world, but he had no knack for business, and he was grateful to his grandfather who had set up a trust fund for him shortly before he and Mary were married, and had then promptly and conveniently died. Also, Mary had her own tidy annuities gleaned from several rich and thrifty great-aunts and some cousins twice removed. He was grateful to them all. He loved women, no matter how old or young they were so long as they were pleasant.

He had a gift for love and dalliance.

But he had no courage and he could not endure pain, and he could not abide sympathy. Illness robbed a man of everything. He could not confront agony and anguish. Perhaps that was why he had punished himself when he was younger by doing volunteer hospital work in the wards filled with the hopelessly ill. He had seen so many die hideous deaths of what he now had—but he refused to accept that painful, lingering death for himself. Perhaps he had thought that he could trick life into giving him an easy death if he helped others in pain. Well, life couldn't be manipulated; fate wouldn't oblige.

Mary, however, could be manipulated.

All those relatives and friends had joked over the years that John could twist Mary around his finger. It was true. He could have, but he hadn't. Yet now that he needed to manipulate her, he knew that he could.

John might have taken his own life, but that would have been cowardly. It would have been an affront to Mary, who had made him completely happy—the life she had given him was more than happy, it had been blissful. To the world his suicide would have negated their perfect years together, and it would have placed upon Mary a terrible, unendurable burden of guilt. Mary must be made to give him death. An easy one. A quick one.

He knew her so well and was precisely aware of how she responded to him and what there was about him that attracted her. It would be a matter of only a few weeks until he could make her take his life.

The days had gone as he had predicted and Mary's disgust had flourished. He knew the exact moment when she had accumulated enough sleeping pills, and the next morning he pushed himself across the bed and nudged her—she had taken to sleeping as far away from him as the width of the large bed allowed. His voice was sharp and demanding, "I want a large glass of orange juice and I want it immediately."

Mary sprang out of bed and grabbed her robe and hurried to the kitchen. She was gone only a little while and John saw her hand quiver as she set a small tray holding the orange juice on the bedside table. He rudely jerked the glass from the tray and gulped the juice.

Only then could he trust himself to smile at her. "Thank you, darling," he said, but she had already left the room and did not hear him.

The Gentle Miss Bluebeard

Miss Mary Anne Beard was not of a reflective or probing disposition, and so it did not occur to her to dwell upon how she had developed into a murderer. A talent for murders of a discreet and delicate nature came upon her unexpectedly in early old age, a gift full-blown and quite successful. Her prowess indicated that she might have been born to do murder.

If she had been compelled to form an opinion about her connection with murder, she very likely would have said she had fallen into it for lack of anything better to do. But she would not have been offhand about it. "Pride" seems a bizarre word to use as descriptive of the attitude she took toward her proficiency, and it lacks accuracy; yet she did regard her gift, her knack, her faculty—whatever it might be termed with feeling approaching pride and wonder.

Her aptitude for murder first showed itself six months after her sixty-fifth birthday. It was then that she murdered for the first time. Her wits were about her; her purpose was clear, and she did not waver. That night after she had committed murder she slept well, remorse was not even a remote bedfellow. Two days later, wearing her best dress and newest hat, she went to her victim's funeral, not to gloat over her success, but out of respect to the dead man, of whom she was fond; she nodded toward his wife, muttered some apt words of unfelt sympathy, and listened with reverence to the service for the dead. Though the deceased was only an acquaintance, she was gratified that she had gone to the funeral because few people were there, her victim was old and had been bedridden for years, his friends had dropped away, and a shrew of a wife was his only relative.

Miss Beard murdered because there was not much else to do in her retirement: the paucity of her social security check did not allow for other indulgences. That sounds callous. It is not meant to be; for Miss Beard followed her new calling with high resolve and dedication.

There was not much else that would have attracted her. Actually, she had no taste for travel, even if she had had the money for it.

Most of her previous leisure during her business career had been devoted to reading. There had never been enough time to do all the reading she wanted to do. Now that there was time her sight had begun to fail; reading closed her lids like a soporific, or else the print danced before her eyes in some intricate ballet which she was unable to follow. So reading was out.

For a short while to try to find something of interest Miss Beard sought out the old-age clubs. The members at these clubs were all pleasant enough, but Miss Beard resented being lumped with them for the sole reason that they were all elderly. She did not feel an automatic member of the aging, just because she had gotten up every day that presented itself and had lived through it the best way she could, and so by this natural and inevitable course had accumulated an impressive number of years. No, she could not identify herself with all these people. And so old-age club activities were out, along with travel and reading.

So, in a sense, because there was nothing better to do in the time of her retirement, Miss Beard took to murder.

She was modest about this gift; she must have nurtured it through the years to have become suddenly so adept at it, yet she had not once suspected this deadly and deathly trait in herself. And then the long tunnel of memory bored deep into her subconscious and she remembered that year in the third grade when the children had taken up the taunt, aping a boy—a mean, spiteful youngster—as he called after her, *Mary Anne Beard, Mary Anne Bluebeard, Bluebeard Mary Anne*, and after that many of the children out of the teacher's hearing had called her Mary Anne Bluebeard. But this name-calling had ended when her father died and her mother moved to a more modest neighborhood and Mary Anne had gone to another school, so that she and her former classmates had been lost to each other in the city's vastness. The name Bluebeard had hurt as it had been meant to hurt, yet she had forgotten it until the time of her first murder. Her talent for murder had been dormant all those years and it might very well have been that the little boy—what was his name?—something simple—she had no head for names—had been gifted with unusual intuition and had divined her true nature. Anyway, her ease and adeptness at murder sometimes amazed her.

What amazed her even more was the number of people eager for death. She had believed that, however hazardous and fraught with discontent and discomfort existence might be, people still grasped at life. It was not so. Her victims were all obsessed with the death wish. The slightest gesture in death's direction and they embraced it like a lover. She learned with astonishment that a person needs only the tiniest encouragement—only a word, a gesture, or the slightest push or shove when he or she is inclined toward death.

Her first victim's name was Smith, John Smith, and his life was as noncommittal as his name. Miss Beard had been as unaware of him as she was of the other tenants in the modest apartment house where she lived. It was a neighborly deed on her part, an offer to help in an emergency, that introduced them to each other; on their first meeting, there was no hint that their brief acquaintance would end in murder.

That afternoon Miss Beard heard the doorbells ring, the ringing progressed up one side of a corridor and down the other side. The walls of the apartments were thin, the bells sharp; it was a sound she had become accustomed to since her retirement—solicitors, salesman of one kind of another, making their rounds, neglecting no one, going from apartment to apartment, seldom getting an answer because it was a domicile of working people. The sound of steps approached and diminished, with the spitting buzz of the bells blaring in between. Her turn came. She answered the door. A woman flushed by irritation stood there. "I've got to leave the house," she said, "and the man who promised to come stay with my husband just phoned he can't come. I must go. It's urgent. Can you come?"

There was nothing tentative about the request; it was a command. "Of course," Miss Beard said, as if the question were politely put, "I'll be glad to come."

And so she was admitted to the presence of her first victim: to Mr. John Smith. He lay there on the bed, a captive of heart disease.

Mrs. Smith barked an introduction to them and then busied herself in a bluster of leave-taking. The apartment was a glory of silence when she left, and then Miss Beard turned to Mr. Smith. From his bleak dominion he summoned up a smile for her. She answered him with a smile but could think of nothing to say, nor could Mr. Smith, who was like a timid child suffering a bad case of the cat had got his tongue, and so they smiled again at each other, and this exchange sealed their goodwill.

Miss Beard sat there as she was to sit on succeeding occasions when Mrs. Smith went to play bridge (card playing was the emergency that took her away, not anything more urgent than that) and she habitually called upon Miss Beard to sit with Mr. Smith, as Miss Beard came willingly and would accept no pay, whereas the man had to be cajoled into coming and charged a dollar an hour.

Though the total of their meetings were mounting at the rate of two a week, Miss Beard and Mr. Smith still found nothing to say to each other. Miss Beard was alert to any wish of his eyes glancing toward the water and she was up quickly to hand the glass to him, or a flicker of pain across his brow and she proffered a pill, and sometimes just to show her interest and concern, she would raise or lower the shade, tuck the blanket in, or remove it—and his smile would tender his gratitude. No words were spoken. He had come to mistrust words and spoken communication, and well he might, Miss Beard thought. For even during her brief stays in Mrs. Smith's presence, she had noticed the continuous barrage of Mrs. Smith's words directed against Mr. Smith. Once or twice when he had attempted an answer, Mrs. Smith had distorted what he said, a simple statement that she was not to worry he was in Miss Beard's good hands would be caught as if it were a barb and shot back at him with an arrow's speed to wound and hurt and make him cringe beneath the covers.

Then after the miracle of her departure, Miss Beard and Mr. Smith did not defile the blessed silence. Yet they had begun to plot and what they plotted was Mr. Smith's death. Those two gentle people began to collaborate on a deed of violence. No word was spoken; it was tacit planning.

There was the afternoon when Miss Beard had stolen for the first time in her life. Her theft was a rose for Mr. Smith. She had come back from the grocery store and there the rose was, leaning over a fence, tempting her; a thorn pricked her finger when she reached toward the vine, but that did not deter her in breaking off the blossom. It was the loveliest rose she had ever seen, and Mr. Smith's look of pleasure told her he thought so too when she handed it to him shyly. Though Mrs. Smith had been engrossed in dressing, her witch's heart had intuited something; she came to the door and saw Mr. Smith in the act of accepting the rose. "My, my," she said. "Nobody knows what goes on around here while I'm away." Her voice was a mockery, a taunt; nothing could possibly take place in her absence and she knew it.

And Miss Beard, aware that she was in the presence of an inquisitor, a sadist and tormenter, said to herself: Mr. Smith must get out of this at once. I must murder him right away, and Mr. Smith looked longingly at her, as if to answer, yes, you must, I can't endure this any longer.

Events proved immediately favorable; there was no need to dillydally.

That afternoon Mr. Smith had one of his attacks, and Miss Beard reached for the dosage Mrs. Smith had measured out, just in case. Miss Beard extended the glass, and in the midst of pain Mr. Smith looked at her and his lids blinked negatively, and she had taken the glass and poured the medicine down the lavatory. It would have done her no good to have had any remorse later and to have tried to replenish the glass, because she did not know from what bottle the medicine had been poured and the chest's shelves were regimented with bottles. She did not know Mr. Smith's doctor's name and so could not telephone him. Twice she tried to telephone the city hospital, but got only a busy signal. If there had been an answer she would have asked for emergency service, but she might have given an incorrect address, only to call later with a mild reproof over the fact that the ambulance had not appeared. Anyway, it would have been too late.

Her second murder was something like trying out a new recipe, wondering if it would work. Yes, it was like reading a recipe and deciding to follow it sometimes if the ingredients were available. It came about in this way.

The house next door was very close and the people living in the upstairs apartment opposite Miss Beard's used loud voices in their anger. A lovely girl whose lovely face was twisted into a hag's mask, shouted: "But Mama, has it ever occurred to you that you have these attacks only when I'm going out with Joe?"

The older woman answered: "It's no pleasure for me to suffer alone here in this grubby apartment day in and day out and then have you come home at night and scream at me and rush out, just when I've been hoping we could have a nice evening together."

"But, Mama, it's only once a week. Joe knows I have to stay with you every night but one."

"Last week it was Friday and tonight's only Tuesday. Is that once a week?"

And then Miss Beard watched the girl go to the telephone. The voice she used was the cold, bitter one of women who give up men or have been given up by them. For a long time, the girl listened to the reply she had provoked and at last said: "That's how it is, Joe. There's nothing I can do about it." So for the second time, murder was to prove an easy task for Miss Beard.

The next morning she watched the girl leave the apartment. Miss Beard joined her at the bus stop, and opened the conversation with a reference to the weather gambit, then sat down with the girl on the bus. The ride was not long, but it took no time at all for the heartbroken girl to spill out her despair to a sympathetic listener.

So it came about that instead of husband-sitting as in Mr. Smith's case, Miss Beard began to mother-sit while the girl went on dates with Joe. The woman, whose name was Brown, enjoyed Miss Beard's company and her many attentions—Miss Beard dearly loved to pamper people: a massage, a manicure, a shampoo, a cologne foot bath, an alcohol rub, pleasant conversation that lulled Mrs. Brown into sleep. Her last speech before she dozed off was invariably: "If Anne should leave me to marry Joe, I'll kill myself."

That was when Miss Beard decided to do it for her.

And yet Miss Beard was not sure just how this murder might be consummated, though she knew the deed must be done immediately, for Anne had whispered: "Joe asked me to marry him. I said yes. I don't know how to tell Mama. Help me to think of a way." And Miss Beard promised she would put on her thinking cap and try to figure out a way to break the news.

As it turned out, there was not a great deal to it. That next night Mrs. Brown complained of being chilly and asked Miss Beard to hand her a bed jacket. "It's just come from the cleaners," she said. "You'll find it in a plastic bag."

Miss Beard handed bag and all to Mrs. Brown. She watched Mrs. Brown take the jacket out and put it on and fling the plastic bag to the foot of her bed. Miss Beard talked on and on to her in her most soothing voice, and then after a while the woman's resounding snoring began. There was nothing, Mrs. Brown had bragged, that could wake her once she had fallen asleep. It was then Miss Beard recalled what she had read in the newspapers, so many unfortunate cases recently of persons, usually babies or young children, being suffocated by plastic bags. It was really hard to believe they were so lethal. Miss Beard had not seen one before; her cleaners used old-fashioned paper bags. She wondered if plastic bags were as deadly as all that. Would it work? Ought she to try it? She might as well see if all those news stories had any truth in them. Surely it was worth a try. She picked the bag up from the foot of the bed and laid it across the edge of Mrs. Brown's pillow. Just then Mrs. Brown turned over in her sleep and burrowed deeply into the plastic bag.

Miss Beard tiptoed out.

She was not invited to the wedding; it was a small, very private affair, coming so soon after a death in the family, only the closest friends and relatives were asked and Miss Beard was not among that group; she did send a present: two dessert spoons in Anne's pattern—Greenbrier.

Miss Beard encountered her third victim in the grocery store. The weather that day was perfect, the wind just right, the sun just warm enough; it did not seem possible to Miss Beard that there could be misery anywhere. But her awareness of sinister reality came back when she reached for a number two can of beets and turned to see a rapacious hand stretched toward the section marked Disinfectants. The hand belonged to a woman whose face was wracked and devastated by unhappiness; in the distraught eyes was a bald and bold lust for death.

Miss Beard, thinking only of the woman's suffering, and not of her own gift for murder, said: "My dear, you must sit down. Let's go to the drugstore next door. A sip of tea will help you."

Over the tea, the woman poured out such a pathetic account of betrayal that Miss Beard saw at once something must be done to try to comfort her. The tea grew tepid, and the tea bags, limp against the saucers, only added to the air of dismay and ruin. Something had to be done at once, the woman must not be allowed to commit suicide in the awful way she had planned, with poison causing slow, infernal pain and distortion and disfigurement.

The woman pleaded in a pathetic tone: "Do you mind walking home with me? I don't think I could cross a street without help."

"Of course, my dear, I'll be delighted."

And with Miss Beard's two shopping bags full of groceries and the woman's sack with its solitary fatal content, they walked to the dingy rooming house where the woman lived.

Inside, down labyrinthine halls filled with musty odors of days old cooking, the woman guided Miss Beard to a furnished room. The bed with its imprint of the woman's body, the pillow moist with her tears, the sink filled with coffee cups ringed with stains and grounds, the cheapness and shabbiness of everything, the solitary armchair with its stuffings bursting through, like some picador's injured horse whose belly had been ripped by a bull's horns, and the ceiling cracked and discolored, were too much for Miss Beard. All these evidences and echoes of misery were beyond her endurance.

The woman's teeth began to chatter, making hallow staccato sounds of grief.

"You must get in bed," Miss Beard urged. "You must warm yourself."

Miss Beard turned on the gas heater, and the heat made the exhausted woman relax. Miss Beard tucked her into the rumpled covers, and almost at once the woman fell asleep. Then Miss Beard saw the suicide note the woman had written earlier; it was stuck into the cracked mirror of the dresser. The woman's heavy breathing reassured Miss Beard; the room grew warmer and Miss Beard turned down the gas, and then she turned it off. The woman slept on and on and Miss Beard felt that she must leave. But the woman must not be allowed to wake in that dreary room with the newly bought disinfectant so conveniently at hand. There was a much easier way to carry off the whole thing.

Miss Beard turned the gas on. But she did not light it. She tucked towels at the window. The door fit snugly enough. The room was small; there was no reason why the gas should not take effect in a short time, and there was the suicide note to explain everything. Miss Beard had kept on her gloves—she had always worn gloves when she went out and when she worked around the house, strange that all her life she had prepared herself for a murderer's necessary precaution. Miss Beard picked up her shopping bags and left the woman's room.

She had forgotten how perfect the day was, until she walked out into the sunlight again.

As for her next murder, Miss Beard eased her fourth victim across death's threshold with a slight push, down a fire escape. And her fifth murder—no, her sixth—also involved a tiny push, this time down an embankment. Her seventh was an administering of an overdose of sleeping pills. And so they mounted: her eighth, ninth, tenth, eleventh and twelfth murders. She was most especially careful about her thirteenth—no matter how much anyone protests, everyone is superstitious about the number thirteen.

And so it went, murder only slightly premeditated—one after the other, with no malice, and no such maudlin emotion as regret; murder in these instances seemed required and Miss Beard did not flinch; she felt no sorrow for what she had done and the persons she murdered benefited from her action.

There were no complications at all, though every now and again after her fourteenth endeavor she would have a strange, somewhat unsettling sensation that she was being watched, yet no one could possibly be watching her. What could any of those deaths mean to anyone living—all her victims had been emotional outcasts, no one had taken any notice of them except to wish them out of the way. Still the feeling of being watched persisted, and in an eerie fashion she half-expected the little boy whose name she had not been able to recall to dart out at her in some dim hall and shout, *Bluebeard Mary Anne, old Mary Anne Bluebeard,* and then to chant, *I told you so, I told you so, I've always known you were a murderer.*

One afternoon, after her fifteenth murder, the impression of being watched was so overwhelming she decided she needed a rest, her trouble must be that she had grown fidgety from overwork. Besides, all the chores were getting behind in her apartment. She should soft-pedal the murders for a while; she had been overdoing them, zeal was triumphing over zest and that would never do. One or two crimes a month were all that she should reasonably expect of herself, whereas that last week she had disposed of three poor wretches.

A change of pace did prove helpful. She enjoyed her vacation from murder. Tidying, dusting, cleaning out drawers, puttering around, shifting furniture were most satisfying. And then time began to pall; she must get her hand back in; that poor love-torn lady on Sixth Street urgently needed attention and the poor dear alcoholic gentleman on Seventh had suffered too long. Well, then, another day or two of pampering herself with all that leisure and she must get back at it.

Unaccountably, and for the first time, she began to doubt her gift. She even began to think that she might be caught. This had not occurred to her before, and because she had never told a lie in all her life, she knew that if she were ever questioned about any of the people she had helped along death's route, she would answer truthfully. So to be prepared for any emergency, however remote, that was the morning she took her light blue silk dress to the cleaners to have ready, just in case she should ever be brought to trial.

It was the last day of her holiday from her delicate craft that the bell rang. She went merrily to answer it; what she needed to put her in the mood for getting back to work was diversion.

A man was standing just outside her door when she opened it. She greeted him and he gave his name, but she was so poor when it came to names she did not notice what he said. A thought slightly strange and unsettling, but on the whole stimulating, rushed through her mind: I know this man quite well. And at the same moment, she realized that she had never seen him before. He was quite nice, a person in either late youth or very early middle age with a re- laxed, assured air. He complimented her on her geraniums and primroses and asked if he might talk with her. At her invitation he settled himself on the sofa, then he said:

"Miss Beard, I want to talk with you about crime. Are you interested in it?"

It was another survey, she thought. People were eternally making surveys on every subject and object; only the week before, she had answered a long list of questions about soaps, washing powders, and detergents.

"I don't quite know what you mean," she said and smiled. "If you're asking whether I like to read about crime, I can't say that I do. I've never been a detective novel fan, not even when my eyes were good. I don't read about crimes in the paper either, except maybe the headlines."

He gave a small, polite nod to acknowledge her answer. "I meant to be more specific than that," he said. "I meant to ask you if you were aware of the sharp increase in crime in this immediate neighborhood—a radius of five blocks. It's phenomenal—the increase in accidental deaths and so-called suicides. Have you noticed?"

She did not answer. She could not lie, falsehood outraged her principles. She would give the man an answer soon, but not just then; and he rushed in to fill the conversational lag, as if he were the host and she the guest to be put at ease.

"Well, I'm interested in crime," he said. "My whole family is. It started with my father. Before his death my father was a criminal psychologist. He had what some authorities called a 'genius for probing the criminal mind'—particularly murderers. He went off the deep end just once. My father knew dozens of murderers, but he said the only mass murderer he ever saw in his life he recognized when he was a child—she was a little girl in his class at school. Do you know he made very discreet investigations of that little girl throughout her adult life, and all the poor lady ever did was build up a fine record as a stenographer? Until the day my father died ten years ago, I kept twitting him about her. I told him Lombroso or anything resembling his theories was for the birds, that no one could possibly discover a murderer just by looking at her. He still insisted that respectable lady was a mass murderer. He went to his grave believing it. And he wouldn't tell me her name; he said it would make headlines someday. Aside from that one instance, my father was right on every criminal he ever dealt with but he really was off the beam about that little girl. It was the only time anyone ever caught him out. Now, you see Miss Beard—"

And just for a moment she did not pay any attention. Now she knew the little boy's name. Now she knew why the man in front of her looked so familiar. For months she had tried to remember a name and in that instant she knew it as well as she knew her own. The little boy's name was Bobby. Bobby Williams. And this man, his son, had said that he was Lieutenant Williams. Yes, that was the name he had given when he entered her apartment. She began to listen again.

"Miss Beard, in the Police Department we can't intuit anything. My father wouldn't be of much help in making inferences for us. We have to have proof. So when there's a marked rise in the rate of suicides and accidental deaths, we have to know why, and when those deaths occur within a small area and when most of them happen in the daytime in a neighborhood where nine-tenths of the people are away from home all day working, we still may have a tedious job, but it's something we can handle. So we start looking for someone who doesn't work, and one day one of our men notices a pleasant elderly lady who always wears white gloves and who is conveniently near after a suicide is reported, and then when we're almost positive it's she, why her suspicions are aroused and she doesn't go out any more on her little errands and for two weeks there aren't any suicides or accidental deaths. So that makes us sure she's the one. Do you see how it is?"

She did not mean to justify herself; she had no need to justify what she had done, but he was waiting for her to say something. "But don't you see," she said. "Those people were miserable. They had to die. They would have killed themselves if I hadn't done it for them."

He glared at her; it was the only time he showed any temper. "Miss Beard, people in this world have the right to their unhappiness." He was so angry he repeated himself: "Miss Beard, people in this world have the right to their unhappiness just as they have the right to their happiness. You can't go around killing people just because they're unhappy."

They talked on for a while, and once during the rest of their conversation she thought of her blue dress and was glad that it was cleaned and ready; it was a good thing that she had been foresighted enough to think of it. And then she thought of the love-torn lady on Sixth Street and of the alcoholic gentleman on Seventh whom she had not disposed of. Poor darlings, they would just have to manage the best they could.

Then Lieutenant Williams offered her his arm, and Miss Beard, the gentle Miss Bluebeard, who had done everything quietly her whole life long, went quietly with him.

Another Turn of the Screw

The Atmosphere in the staff lounge of the Concord Social Service Agency seemed heavy with conspiracy and intrigue. Actually the whispers and furtive glances which the seated women made toward the hall door were signs of dismay and of fissures in morale.

Mrs. Watkins spooned more sugar into her coffee and began to give to the other caseworkers her usual 10:15 A.M. report on what she had overheard. She was not a congenital eavesdropper, and had not previously paid the slightest attention to what had been said in the office next to her own. Recently, however to be specific, for the two months that Miss Prentice had been working for the agency—Mrs. Watkins had turned informer.

The agency's quarters were a remodeled townhouse and Mrs. Watkins' office was formerly a small dressing room whose connecting door fitted loosely into the master bedroom, which had been converted into the Director's office. Random words from very loud conversations would sometimes seep through to Mrs. Watkins' desk, but if she placed her ear against the door, as she, to her shame, now did habitually when the Director and Assistant Director had their daily conference, she could hear every single remark with absolute clarity.

"I feel like a spy," Mrs. Watkins said. "I *am* a spy. But the things she says to her about her get worse and worse—more fantastic and inexcusable."

By now, in Mrs. Watkins' recitals, the three principals had all become "she" or, in the objective case, "her." Mrs. Rugby, the Director, was "she." Mrs. Matthews, the Assistant Director, was "she." So was Miss Prentice, the new worker. All the agitated listeners knew precisely to whom Mrs. Watkins referred in her inexplicit statement: the first "she" was Mrs. Rugby, the first "her" was Mrs. Matthews, the last "her" was Miss Prentice. It was as if Mrs. Watkins had said: "But the things Mrs. Rugby says to Mrs. Matthews about Miss Prentice."

"It's all so terribly unfair," Miss Sloan said. Next to Miss Prentice, who was the object of Mrs. Rugby's unprecedented persecution, Miss Sloan was the newest staff member. "I got through my first months here all right. I mean, there was no constant discussion of my weak points, no daily tearing my professional self limb from limb. I couldn't have survived if Mrs. Rugby had been half as critical of me as she is of Miss Prentice! A new person is naturally insecure, and it's bound to take time to fit into a new routine."

Mrs. Green as usual bristled with indignation. "We're lucky to have Miss Prentice. It's not as if she couldn't get another job just like that." The snap of her fingers emphasized Mrs. Green's resentment. "Of all people, social workers can pick and choose."

It was then Mrs. Andrews' turn to comment. She sat next to Mrs. Green on the sofa and she set her coffee down so violently that it splashed onto the table. Mrs. Andrews' master's thesis had been titled *Manifestations of Covert Hostility*; she had written it hurriedly and much too succinctly and she had among her voluminous and unused notes all sorts of tidbits that she kept regretting she hadn't included; she liked to present one or two at such critical times as these morning coffee breaks. "None of this has anything to do with Miss Prentice really. It's all a matter of Mrs. Rugby's deep-seated resentment of Mrs. Matthews. Mrs. Rugby is furious over retiring in the fall no matter how much she's carried on these last two years about looking forward to freedom and having time to herself, and she's trying to find any possible excuse to make Mrs. Matthews, who is to succeed her, appear incompetent and muddling in having employed Miss Prentice. It's simply repressed hostility."

With vigorous shakes of their heads and deep frowns they all acknowledged the obvious truth of Mrs. Andrews' remarks. Mrs. Moore, the next one to speak, did not offer her opinion in Mrs. Andrews' psychiatric terms. "Mrs. Rugby is plain mean and childish to talk as she does about Miss Prentice. I'd rather be a salesclerk standing on my feet eight hours a day and with sales tax to figure than be in Miss Prentice's shoes."

And though they were in one of the largest cities in the Middle Atlantic States, Mrs. Singer dug into the Deep South for a figure of speech when she commented. "I'd rather chop cotton from sunup to sundown than to be subjected to what Miss Prentice is facing."

While the reactions were verbalized in various ways, their tenor was identical: unanimous resentment. The facts were these. Mrs. Rugby was scheduled to retire within a few months after twenty-five years as Director of the Concord Social Service Agency, and Mrs. Matthews, her assistant for ten years, had already been named as her successor. Mrs. Rugby had attended a conference in New York for a week and had come back to find that in the meantime Mrs. Matthews had employed

Miss Prentice. The vacancy had been long unfilled, the shortage of caseworkers was acute, and Mrs. Matthews had acted with the dispatch she had considered urgent, since Miss Prentice had many attractive offers.

Returning and learning of Miss Prentice's appointment, Mrs. Rugby had said there hadn't been all that much rush about filling the position and that the entire matter could have been postponed until she got back. Her efforts since then had been centered on trying to force Mrs. Matthews to admit that Miss Prentice was incompetent.

Mrs. Calvin, next in line in that morning's ring-around-the-rosy, was noted for being romantic and dramatic and yet as shrewd as they come. "What's needed," she said, "in fact, the only thing that would solve this whole mess and prove that Miss Prentice has the resourcefulness and ability that Mrs. Rugby denies, would be for Miss Prentice to do something spectacular—like rescuing a child from a burning building or overtaking bank robbers and snatching their loot or solving a murder that has stumped the police."

"But it would have to be in a casework setting," said Mrs. Andrews, professional to the end.

They all agreed with Mrs. Calvin. Her solution was the perfect one. It was inspired. But it could never happen. Not in real life. Fate was obstinate, not to be manipulated either by wishes or by necessity.

Their spoken regrets over the perversity of fate were suddenly silenced by the sound of footsteps. They all looked up toward the door to see Miss Prentice, the target of Mrs. Rugby's criticism, enter the lounge. They couldn't treat her as one of themselves, able to fend for herself. Their sympathy for her and their outrage at Mrs. Rugby's behavior made them oversolicitous; they offered Miss Prentice peanut butter crackers, homemade cookies, fruit, coffee, cigarettes; the room reeked with false jauntiness and false bonhomie.

Miss Prentice refused their offers and inserted a dime in the soft drink machine. She upended a bottle and they all watched as she gulped. She set the empty bottle in the rack where it rattled, and then she hurried out just in time to bump into Mrs. Rugby on the threshold. "I beg your pardon, Mrs. Rugby," she said. "I'm so sorry." They all saw that the incident had clearly been Mrs. Rugby's fault.

Mrs. Rugby dominated the lounge. No one could think of a word to say. The silence opened great potholes of embarrassment into which they all fell. Then like nursery school children they greeted her in unison.

Mrs. Rugby went to the coffee urn to fill her cup and then she swept out with it.

"This is ridiculous," Mrs. Green said. "This situation has reduced us all to ninnies—acting like idiots when our newest staff member comes in and bleating like sheep when the Director appears."

"It's intolerable," Mrs. Calvin said. "But there's nothing we can do. We're helpless."

"Yes," Miss Sloan said. "The solution will have to come from either Mrs. Rugby or Mrs. Matthews or Miss Prentice. It's strictly in their hands."

Miss Phillips had not spoken until then. She cleared her throat and said, "I have a horrible foreboding that it will all end in blood and violence."

She might have been an oracle intoning a prophecy. Cymbals might have clashed after she had spoken. No one said a word. Almost ritualistically the women rose and then one by one they tossed their empty paper cups into the wastebasket and walked hesitantly, as if to a dirge, back to their offices.

When Mrs. Watkins gave her next and—though none of them at the time realized it—last report she was alternately blanched and flushed in her anger over what she had to relate.

"Exactly at nine she called her in and summarized her failings." What Mrs. Watkins meant, of course, was that Mrs. Rugby had called Mrs. Matthews in and summarized Miss Prentice's failings. "She said that Miss Prentice had no self-control—that in an emergency she would go all to pieces. She said Miss Prentice was unable to establish rapport with a client, that no one would want to unburden problems on her. She said Miss Prentice has no insight, she isn't observant, she has neither intuition nor common sense."

"What Mrs. Rugby wants," Mrs. Andrews said, "is for Mrs. Matthews to say *mea culpa*, to prostrate herself and ask forgiveness for dressing up in Mrs. Rugby's clothes, figuratively speaking, while Mrs. Rugby was away and daring to hire a new worker. Then on the basis of Mrs. Matthews' incompetence Mrs. Rugby will go to the Board and postpone her retirement."

And Mrs. Rugby would get away with it; they all knew that, for Mrs. Rugby had the Board in the palm of her hand. Years ago she had helped the Chairman's son through a sticky period of juvenile delinquency, and she had steered the Personnel Chairman's daughter through a time referred to delicately as "running around." The Board would do whatever their darling Ruggie suggested. They would stretch any of the rules for her. No matter that she was long beyond retirement age, if she decided to stay on as Director until she was ninety-nine a way would be found to let her.

"What did Mrs. Matthews say?" Miss Sloan asked.

"Well, you know she usually doesn't answer Mrs. Rugby's accusations. Her attitude is more of a mother trying to soothe an angry child. But this morning she said very emphatically and very coldly, 'I don't agree with you at all, Mrs. Rugby.' And Mrs. Rugby said, 'Very well, Mrs. Matthews'—you know all these years they've called each other Matty and Ruggie—'I'll have to prove my point to you. I'll make home visits with you and Miss Prentice this afternoon and I'll show you Miss Prentice's lamentable shortcomings.'"

The statement immobilized the women. Coffee cups stopped on their way to mouths. Matches midway to cigarettes burned so long they scorched fingers. Eyebrows were such sharply inverted v's that they almost disappeared into hairlines.

Miss Sloan was the first to recover enough to speak. "My Lord, you don't mean that the three of them will go out together this afternoon!"

"Nobody could do casework with a Director and an Assistant Director at her elbow," Mrs. Green said.

"Something should be done to stop it," Mrs. Singer said. "I've never heard of anything so preposterous!"

The remainder of the morning was a shambles: clients in need of emotional sustenance faced caseworkers in even more pressing need. Lunches went uneaten, noontime errands were neglected. Miss Prentice's approaching ordeal was all that anyone could be concerned about. Someone learned that the first visit would be paid to a nursing home subsidized by the agency. This meant another turn of the screw. Miss Prentice must meet her trial with the nursing staff and attendants and other patients within earshot of her interviews with her clients.

At 2:50 the silent, apprehensive staff, their office doors open, their ears frenziedly alert, heard Mrs. Matthews say to Mrs. Rugby, "Are you ready?"

The caseworkers listened to the footsteps of the three departing women, then they crowded around the office windows that overlooked the parking lot.

The three women being watched paid no attention to each other as they walked toward the staff car. Once they had reached it Mrs. Rugby waved grandly to Mrs. Matthews and Miss Prentice to sit in front. As if one were the chauffeur and the other a footman, they crawled in as directed while Mrs. Rugby sat arrogantly alone in back.

Mrs. Matthews drove slowly and painstakingly as if she headed a procession of mourners, and when the car rolled beyond the view of the watchers upstairs they shook their heads in dismay; more than one shuddered remembering Miss Phillips' remark that it would all end in blood and violence.

And Miss Phillips' foreboding was fulfilled.

For the issue did indeed end in blood and violence on that mild afternoon in spring, but none of the caseworkers was ever to know the full truth—not even from the newspaper, television, and radio reports of the crimes and the three dead bodies and the efficient, indeed brilliant and remarkably swift action of the police.

The lips of Mrs. Rugby and Mrs. Matthews and Miss Prentice were sealed forever on the subject.

The appearance of the three women surprised Mrs. Allingham, the superintendent of the nursing home. "Isn't this an unannounced inspection?" she asked anxiously.

Mrs. Matthews and Miss Prentice waited for Mrs. Rugby to explain. When the silence dragged on uncomfortably, Mrs. Matthews said, "No. Not at all. We've come out to visit clients with Miss Prentice just to observe to see how she's getting along."

Mrs. Allingham looked displeased and unconvinced. "I don't remember that you've ever done anything like this before. Well, Miss Prentice knows where the patients are. She can show you around. I'm afraid there would be too much of a crowd if I came along with you. The afternoon rest hour isn't over and some of the people may be asleep, but go right along."

To comply with Mrs. Allingham's instructions Miss Prentice stepped forward, but Mrs. Rugby, unwilling to follow anyone, pushed past her. Miss Prentice said mildly, "Straight ahead, Mrs. Rugby, and to the left. Our clients are in that wing."

As if they were trailing royalty along the corridor, Mrs. Matthews and Miss Prentice kept a respectful three paces behind Mrs. Rugby and maintained that distance when Mrs. Rugby knocked on a door and entered without waiting to be invited in.

Suddenly her hands fluttered, then grasped melodramatically at her throat and forehead; she reeled backward and slammed the door shut. When she saw Mrs. Matthews and Miss Prentice looking at her questioningly, she strained to collect herself and faltered toward the next door. Her control returned; her hand was steady as she tapped on the door and thrust it open.

Again Mrs. Matthews and Miss Prentice, keeping their prescribed distance, saw Mrs. Rugby repeat her strange behavior. She gasped, her hands trembled, she staggered backward and jerked the second door shut.

With consternation Mrs. Matthews watched Mrs. Rugby. She felt compelled to try to account to Miss Prentice for their Director's abnormal deportment. "Mrs. Rugby must be having an attack of some kind. Or perhaps seeing clients is too much for her—it's been years since she's done anything but administrative work."

Once again Mrs. Rugby collected herself. She walked to a third room and made another entrance without waiting to be invited in.

Once more something inside repelled her; she withdrew as if routed, and having slammed the third door she clung to the knob as if whatever was inside might escape to destroy her; then she let out a shriek of hysteria.

Her wail aroused the entire nursing home.

Doors burst open. Patients in wheelchairs began trundling up and down the corridors. There was the clumping sound of crutches. Heads peered down stairwells. Nurses and attendants came running. From all directions voices yelled, "What's the matter? What's wrong?"

Mrs. Rugby shrieked one final shriek that silenced the nursing home for an instant. Then she began to gasp and mumble, and Miss Prentice patted Mrs. Rugby's face softly and gently chafed her hands. Then she turned Mrs. Rugby's care over to Mrs. Matthews and walked into each of the three rooms from which Mrs. Rugby had retreated in so fantastic a manner. Miss Prentice remained longer in each room than Mrs. Rugby had; her response in no way resembled that of Mrs. Rugby. What she saw neither repelled nor upset her. Instead it left her concerned and pensive.

She looked across all the puzzled and inquiring faces to the superintendent and said, "Mrs. Allingham, please telephone the police. There have been three murders. Miss Grandison, Mr. Kent, and Mr. Mabry are all dead."

The boldest of the onlookers rushed toward the closed doors, to be stopped by Miss Prentice's quiet air of command. "I'm afraid no one can go in. I suggest that you all go back to your rooms and your posts and leave this matter to the police."

For an instant patients and staff rebelled and surged closer to the doors, and then they obeyed Miss Prentice's quiet authority. They saw that her suggestion was the only sensible course to take. The clogged traffic of the wheelchairs was soon eased as expert hands guided the chairs down the halls; the patients on crutches swung themselves back to their rooms and wards; the nurses and attendants returned to their duties.

Even Mrs. Rugby had somewhat recovered. Mrs. Matthews, sitting beside her on the bench, was heartened enough by Mrs. Rugby's improvement to whisper to her, "But, Mrs. Rugby, you said Miss Prentice had no self-control, that she'd be no good whatever in an emergency."

Mrs. Rugby shook her head and slumped deeper onto the bench. The tip of her tongue darted in and out of her quivering mouth. Whatever she might have been about to reply was interrupted by the arrival of the police.

They moved in like invaders, took immediate command, and strode with authority in and out of the bedrooms containing the three dead persons. The officer in charge, after introducing himself as Lieutenant Forsyth, addressed the three women from the Social Service Agency. "Who found the bodies?"

Mrs. Matthews nodded toward Mrs. Rugby. Mrs. Rugby pushed her face into the back of the bench and whimpered.

Miss Prentice said, "I also went into the rooms and saw exactly what Mrs. Rugby saw. As you see, she's very upset by it, but if it would help I'll be glad to tell you what I know."

"I'm sure we saw what you saw," the Lieutenant said. "Perhaps we saw and understood a little more, since, after all, crime's our business. What we're after now is the murderer—or murderers."

"Why do you say murderer or murderers?" Miss Prentice asked.

"Because a multiple crime like this is usually committed by one person using one method. But in this case, as you must have noticed, one person was smothered to death, one person was strangled with a cord, and one person was stabbed. So it appears there may be more than one murderer."

"Poor harmless old souls," one of the policemen said as he walked over to the Lieutenant. "They had lived so long. It's a pity they couldn't have been allowed to live out peacefully whatever little bit of time was coming to them."

"They got the deaths they wanted," Miss Prentice hurried to comfort him. "Miss Grandison was killed by a jealous suitor. That's a wonderful death for an old woman, don't you think? And Mr. Kent told me when I was out here two weeks ago that he wished he could die suddenly, that he hated to see death creep up on him inch by inch. As for Mr. Mabry—"

But the glances of the police interrupted Miss Prentice. The Lieutenant shook his head, and the other men looked up from their various duties, shrugged, and might as well have said out loud that

Miss Prentice had lost her mind.

Miss Prentice, however, only stopped long enough to catch her breath. Their skepticism did not bother her. "You see," she said. "I was their caseworker. I knew them all very well indeed. They told me about themselves, entrusted their secrets to me."

"Our job, young lady, is not to find out their secrets but to find their murderer."

"Well," said Miss Prentice, "perhaps I can help. You said a moment ago that in a multiple killing the same method is habitually used. Aren't smothering and strangulation very much the same?"

"Yes."

"Then that takes care of two of the deaths. And Mr. Mabry was stabbed."

"Yes."

"Couldn't it be that the murderer was murdered by one of the persons he murdered?" Miss Prentice asked her question with such conviction that the Lieutenant was either too stunned or too polite to contradict her.

"It was a lover's quarrel," Miss Prentice continued.

Disbelief bowed the Lieutenant's head.

"Just a minute, ma'am," he said. "That lady was seventy if she was a day."

"She was seventy-five last month," Miss Prentice corrected him. "I had a piece of her birthday cake."

The Lieutenant plowed on. "And the men were even older." Again Miss Prentice proffered the exact figures. "Mr. Kent was seventy-seven in December and Mr. Mabry was eighty in February."

The Lieutenant seemed reassured by the information; Miss Prentice was enmeshing herself in her faulty reasoning. "Yet you say it was a lover's quarrel," he said. "That's a little hard to swallow."

Miss Prentice's smile was wistful; her tone was indulgent but firm. She said, "You see, sir, it's a mistake of the young to think that love dies in the old." Miss Prentice was in her mid-twenties, Lieutenant Forsyth a good fifteen years her senior; but her words seemed to reverse their ages. "Even though they were old, Mr. Kent and Mr. Mabry were still as ardent as schoolboys, and Miss Grandison was as much a flirt as if she were a teenager. She pitted the two men against each other, and in a jealous rage Mr. Mabry killed both Miss Grandison and Mr. Kent. During the rest hour today, while Miss Grandison was having a nap, Mr. Mabry went into her room and smothered her with a pillow; then he entered Mr. Kent's room to kill him—"

Lieutenant Forsyth held up his hand to silence Miss Prentice. He had had enough. He would finish Miss Prentice's story for her. He said, "And then Mr. Mabry, full of remorse over his double murder, returned to his own room where he proceeded to stab himself in the back—a physical impossibility with that long blade—"

"No," Miss Prentice said. "That wasn't it at all. The murderer was murdered by one of his victims. Mr. Kent was asleep when Mr. Mabry came in, but when Mr. Mabry put a cord around his throat Mr. Kent was roused enough to grab the knife he always kept on his bedside table, and he stabbed Mr. Mabry—I'm sure you'll find that there are no fingerprints on the knife's handle except Mr. Kent's. Mr. Mabry didn't realize that he had been mortally wounded—you'll find other cases where people mortally stabbed have still been able to carry on for a while. Well, with the knife in his back Mr. Mabry tightened the cord around Mr. Kent's throat until he had strangled him, and then Mr. Mabry went back to his own room, where he collapsed and died."

The corridor seemed to resound with the truth.

Lieutenant Forsyth knew when he was lucky enough to have a solution handed to him on a silver platter. He looked with wonder at Miss Prentice.

To a man the Homicide Squad gawked in admiration at her. "Of course you're right," Lieutenant Forsyth said. "That's got to be how it happened—it's the only way."

Mrs. Rugby began to moan. "I want to get out of here. I have to get out of here. Please, may I leave at once? Matty, you've got to take me home immediately. Officer, please, please let Mrs. Matthews take me home."

"Of course you may go," the Lieutenant said. "But I'd like to talk further with this young lady. I mean, I'd like for her to talk further with me—not that there's much else for her to say."

The men and Miss Prentice watched while Mrs. Matthews took Mrs. Rugby's arm and helped her rise from the bench and guide her toward the entrance. They all listened as Mrs. Matthews let two months of repressed resentment pour out. "But, Mrs. Rugby, you said that Miss Prentice wasn't observant. You said no client would unburden himself to her. You said she had no common sense. You insisted that she would go to pieces at the slightest crisis." Mrs. Matthews' voice was a lash of accusation, mercifully silenced when the front door slammed.

Mrs. Rugby ventured back to the agency one last time. It was the next day and a Saturday, so no one was around to watch. She took down her framed diploma showing that she had earned the degree of Master of Science in Social Work, and she took down her certificate showing that she was a member of the American Association of Social Workers; she took her three potted plants—a geranium, a cactus, and a maidenhair fern; she took her desk clock and her letter opener and pen and pencil set whose holder was inscribed with extravagant praise, a gift from the Board on her 20th anniversary as Director.

In her eagerness to leave the premises Mrs. Rugby did not say goodbye to anyone. She relinquished the glory of a farewell banquet and of testimonial luncheons and end-of-career interviews in the newspapers and on television. She dashed off a letter to the staff explaining that she felt it best to leave without fanfare. She moved to California, which was as far away as she could get in the continental United States.

Mrs. Matthews made an admirable Director, as all the caseworkers had known she would, and things settled down happily and smoothly in the Concord Social Service Agency. But the staff did not for very long include Miss Prentice. Shortly after the three murders at the nursing home she handed in her notice to become the first woman officer ever employed by the Homicide Squad of the Concord Police Department.

Tour de Couleur

Part Four

There were only a few minutes between planes for the interview with Dr. Robert Meadows, the eminent anthropologist, and John Anderson had in his hand a number of questions he intended to ask the famous scientist.

As an editor and reporter, Anderson was analytical as well as inquisitive about people and public affairs. He was also self-analytical, and he glanced down his list of questions and noticed there were none relating to color; and yet he knew he would ask about color. His question would be vague—he never seemed to be able to make it specific; but he had been acutely—sometimes it seemed to him passionately—interested in color ever since a certain event had occurred five years before. Whenever a person he talked with professionally appeared likely to have information about color, Anderson finally veered to that subject; but when he got there he found himself faltering and uncertain. He had talked about color with people in all trades and careers; some of them were friends, some were acquaintances, most of them were illustrious strangers whom he, as associate editor of the city's leading newspaper, had interviewed.

A great modern painter had once told him something of the esthetics of color; a psychologist who might someday rank just below Freud had explained how yellow was the color of madness, and green that of perversion; a historian had discussed the sumptuary laws of medieval times when certain colors, particularly purple, were restricted to use by royalty; semanticists had rambled on about color expressing emotion and how the same word could be used in contradictory senses for instance, a blue mood in contrast with a blue sky, and how red was at once the color of violence and of power.

Persons in publishing and editing had cited examples of powerful written treatments of color: Proust's use of pink; Keats's melodic employment of color, particularly in *The Eve of St. Agnes*. There was a special force to Meier-Graefe's description of Van Gogh's death— when all the colors of Van Gogh's palette came to pay him obeisance on his deathbed. Through the character of Dorothea Brooke in *Middlemarch*,

George Eliot had described the compelling emotional quality of color: *It is strange how deeply colors seem to penetrate one, like scent. I suppose that is the reason why gems are used as spiritual emblems in the Revelation of St. John.* And one author had insisted that the most effective use of color in all literature was in Edgar Allan Poe's passage describing the variously hued apartments in *The Masque of the Red Death*.

These tidbits of knowledge were interesting but they made Anderson chafe. Provocative too, they made him yearn even more for the answer he needed but never got because somehow he did not know the exact question he should ask. All this unrelated trivia simply widened the distance between the question he could not phrase and the unknown answer he longed for ...

Dr. Meadows impressed Anderson at once with his vast fund of information, with the quiet way in which he revealed his knowledge, and with his obvious gratitude for the interest that Anderson showed in anthropology.

It was something that the anthropologist said about burial customs that set Anderson's mind to recalling details of the death of the young woman, although thoughts of her death were always easily summoned. She had been in her grave for five years now. Her husband had remarried. His second wife had been a friend of the first wife; the second wife was an interior decorator whose international reputation almost matched that of her husband as a financier.

But Anderson realized he must not let his mind gambol, though it was reassuring to see that even with his thoughts elsewhere he had still been able to take down in his own brand of shorthand what the social scientist was saying.

"Will you explain simply," Anderson said, "so that I can make it clear to our readers, the difference between cultural and physical anthropology?"

The anthropologist talked precisely and Anderson's hand raced across his notebook, but his mind was a dog that would not let go of a bone; his mind wanted to dismiss anthropology and dwell only on color ... and the girl's death.

Part Two

Anderson had been on the city desk then and had taken the call when it came in. A young woman had just died suddenly. No autopsy had yet been done—her body was still where her husband had found it in the living room. The story would have been buried deep in the back pages except for the fact that the husband was rich and rising phenomenally as a banker and belonged to a prominent old family. There was pathos and reader interest too in the fact that the young wife had just returned to her newly redecorated home—she had been away to visit her ill mother on the West Coast; her return had been expected, but the exact time of her arrival had not been known, and even as she died her husband and the decorator had been at work in another part of the house, busy with last-minute details to make a triumphant welcome for the young wife. She had died alone; she had entered the house and evidently the joy of her homecoming had been too overpowering, and she had died almost instantly.

Anderson had gone to the house of death and had watched the police and the men from the city hospital do their precise duties in the impressive Georgian mansion. As he observed them he had not been able to describe what he felt; it was uncanny and pervasive, a feeling that willful violence might be abroad; as he looked into the astonished face of the husband and the strikingly handsome face of the woman who stood beside him, Anderson sensed mystery and evil; but there was nothing he could do, no accusation he could make.

Back at the paper he had sat waiting, impatient, irritable until the autopsy was completed and the medical report had become available; his voice was angry when he told the medical examiner he didn't believe the girl had died simply from a heart attack; he had said something wild and incoherent about the walls and the rugs, and the medical examiner had suggested that Anderson must have nipped a bit too freely from some bottle in his desk drawer while he waited for the medical report.

Once Anderson's copy was filed he left the office to go to his apartment, but he had stood outside the newspaper building and had looked up at the stars as if in blazing cuneiform they might spell out the answer he wanted; he stood there in the wind and the cold while the night stumbled hesitantly and unwillingly into morning; and he thought of the girl so new to death, her body being prepared even then for the ceremony burial. Clouds gathered and thickened, rain fell; his slow steps pushed through the hard, challenging rain and he longed for it to wash away his suspicion and uncertainty.

Part Three

The chapel was a small, gracious place; its cheerful atmosphere minimized death, treating it as if it were only a minor hazard in life's progress. John Anderson had gone there early the next morning; he had not known why—certainly he did not plan to stay for the funeral service. A mortuary assistant wearing a reassuring smile and mourning clothes had welcomed him as if to a reception and had led him to the place where the dead girl lay.

Anderson looked down upon her and was stunned by what he saw.

She was beautiful in death, lovely enough to evoke the fair ladies of legend: Elaine and Iseult, Deirdre and the bride in *The Song of Songs*. The soft gray of the coffin, the delicate pink of its lining fondled her; the faint orchid of the chiffon robe lay on her like a caress and made a lyric of color, obliterating the threnodic black of death's dominion; her tiny, fragile hands encircled the blue and pink fragrance of a bouquet of forget-me-nots and sweetheart roses; every tone, every shade, every color near her or touching her elaborated with the skill of a generous but unflattering portraitist—the soft pastel blonde beauty of the dead girl.

And then Anderson was not alone; two other watchers were there—he had not noticed when they had joined him. They paid no attention to him, but they were mourners, he knew that; and then he recognized them as the two persons in the house the night before—the girl's husband and the decorator. In a strange, wild, fantastic way they seemed to complete the composition in the chapel: the gentle colors of everything about the dead girl were made into a whole picture by those two in their colorless, shocked silence of grief—the handsome man in his oxford-gray suit, the young woman in her black coat and black hat with her masklike face that indicated sorrow so much more than features distorted by weeping.

As Anderson left the chapel he was possessed by a macabre feeling that somehow color had been used beyond the borders of art and in a way that approached diabolism.

Part One

Mary stood looking at the stately, impressive Georgian house; her bags were clustered around her on the lawn—she had refused the taxi driver's offer to take them to the entrance; and she thought, in the soaring peace of fulfillment, that her true marriage was just beginning the months before were simply a happy prologue. As she speculated on the future, the bags at her feet might have been her children gathered around her, or even her grandchildren—it was a house that had lasted many generations and would last generations more, a place of permanence and pleasure and contentment.

She noticed that the front of the house was dark but from somewhere in the back there seemed to be a light; perhaps Arnold was there having a snack or doing some last-minute chore to make the house ready for her; he had not known when to expect her—the course of her mother's illness had been unpredictable—physical seesaw, now better, then worse; but at last her mother had recovered and the doctor had said Mary might leave. The joy at this moment, she thought, may be greater than when I see my husband—emotion and elation will take over then. The capricious wind descended once more—its strength made even her heavy suitcases sway; the name plates attached to their handles chattered against the locks, and still she did not go in— she hesitated outside like someone too struck with awe and thankfulness to enter. She had so much, she had everything: a distinguished, successful husband, attentive and generous; a fine old house now in its new splendor after being decorated by the famous Katrin, her own Kate, her closest friend at college, her roommate, celebrated now in all the fashionable centers as one of the world's outstanding decorators. Kate's fabulous success had not surprised Mary. Kate—Katrin, whatever she chose to call herself—had always known what she wanted; her ambition was even greater than her remarkable talent, and she did not let anything stand in her way.

That first day at college, when they had been assigned to the same room, Kate had said even before she acknowledged the introduction by the house mother: "Take off that red sweater at once and get a pale pink one. Don't you know red eats you up, destroys you? Haven't you any idea what strong colors do to you?"

They had roomed together for four years, and though Kate supervised the buying of everything Mary wore, Mary never came to have any intimate knowledge of Kate; there was no exchange after dates of what he said and I said, what he did and I did, because Kate didn't have dates; she didn't want any—she said she couldn't waste the time, she had to get on with her work; if ever she saw the man she wanted she would know what to do, and until then she would concentrate on her career. Later there were the years when Kate was out of the country, first in Europe, then in South America, recently in the West Indies, always doing brilliant work on important hotels and houses; while she was away she had missed Mary's wedding, hadn't even met Arnold. Then by the greatest of good luck Kate, long since known professionally as Katrin, had come back just when the house was ready to be redecorated; Mary had begged her on the telephone to do it, and Kate had come from New York and had spent long hours talking with Mary and Arnold, together and separately, before she had accepted the job.

Now the house was ready and waiting to receive her, to enclose her in its new graciousness, and the cold night was pushing Mary forward, its bite and bitterness insisting that she enter. Her key dangled from a small golden heart encrusted with pearls—Arnold's engagement present; it slipped easily into the lock and she called out gaily as the door opened; but there was no answer. It didn't matter—her eagerness was like a joyful fountain inside her; after all it might be more fun to see the house alone.

Her hand found the light switch.

It was as if the lights had given a signal for a detonation and a savage attack. Silent forces burst around her; her eyes were assaulted, her breath snatched from her. The deep rancid green of the wallpaper in the entrance hall swirled around her. She swayed and stumbled, plowing through it as through billows of water rushing upon her in gigantic waves; she tried to cry out but the green was suffocating her, muffling her outcry as it pressed against her lungs; wildly she grabbed at the banisters as the bright green of the carpeted stairs, like a sea monster of overwhelming strength, snapped and gnawed at her ankles.

In despair she pulled herself upstairs, but again she walked in turmoil and her feet were now in the frightening mire of a blood-red carpet; then the brilliant yellow of the guest room assailed her, choking off whatever air there was, and she ran in terror to another room. She looked with horror at its walls painted like a garish circus tent and recognized it as the room she had intended for a nursery, and on the wainscoting the brightly painted animals of a caged menagerie might have come to life and suddenly escaped their bars—they seemed to jump at her and overwhelm her.

Mary clawed against the walls until she felt bits of plaster beneath her fingernails; nausea descended upon her—and panic. She closed her eyes against the onslaught and moaned the names of Arnold and Kate—but there was no answer, except from somewhere deep in the house there seemed to come the murmur of voices and of laughter. Wildly, her hysteria soaring, she looked for escape. There must be some place where she could hide, some closet where the colors could not reach her; but she could find no door to open, and she faltered along the hallways until she came to the upstairs sitting room. There her fear became even more hysterical—the walls painted in chocolate and chartreuse stripes might have been whips to flay her.

A prayer was on her lips but she had no strength to say it. She knew then that her life was in jeopardy and through the merciless barrage of color she struggled back downstairs, using as her guide in the swirling labyrinth of color the laughter she heard faintly from somewhere. The sounds might have been the voices of the Lorelei or of the sirens beckoning her to disaster. Yet surely in that place from which the voices came, the library, she would find help—Kate and Arnold were there; she knew it, but destruction raced toward her like a demented lover and jerked her into its ghastly embrace. All the hideous colors suddenly combined and joined forces, converged upon her, and then the mauve of the living room made the ultimate attack. It rained down from the walls and inundated her; she collapsed onto the thick pile of the maroon carpet in a finality of terror …

Part Five

The flight had just been announced and the passengers with their packages, magazines, and luggage bolted toward the waiting plane. Dr. Meadows picked up his briefcase, held out his hand, and thanked Anderson for his kindness in coming to talk with him.

At that moment Anderson knew that the question had at last formed itself—his brain gave birth to the query that had so long been in gestation if only his lips could say it; but now there was no time for tentativeness—the plane waited, the anthropologist must board it and leave.

Miraculously, the question was spontaneous. Anderson said, "In all your experiences with various cultures and races have you ever come upon an instance in which color has been used lethally?"

Dr. Meadows considered the question, then he asked one of his own to be sure that he had understood. "Do you mean color used in the deadly sense that Dorothy L. Sayers used the bells in *The Nine Tailors*—as the actual instrument of death?"

"Exactly. Can color be used to commit murder?"

"I've never heard of it."

The answer was unqualified. And it was no.

Anderson watched the anthropologist enter the plane. Then he stood while the plane lifted itself from the field and lost itself in the night's low swarming clouds.

After all those years he had been able to ask that fantastic question—and the answer had been negative. But as he walked back through the crowds arriving and departing he realized that he had found the answer he wanted, that he had given it to himself. It might seem like fantasy or aberration but it was true. He knew of one instance in which color had been the instrument of death—the murder weapon.

THE END

Nedra Tyre Bibliography
(1912-1990)

Crime Novels

Mouse in Eternity (Knopf, 1952; reprinted as *Death is a Lover*, Mercury
  Mystery, 1953)
Death of an Intruder (Knopf, 1953)
Journey to Nowhere (Knopf, 1954)
Hall of Death (Simon and Schuster, 1960; reprinted as *Reformatory Girls*,
  Ace, 1962)
Everyone Suspect (Macmillan, 1964)
Twice So Fair (Random House, 1971)

Collections

Red Wine First (Simon & Schuster, 1947)

Short Stories (alphabetical)

Accidental Widow (*Alfred Hitchcock's Mystery Magazine*, Apr 1976)
An Act of Deliverance (*Ellery Queen's Mystery Magazine*, Aug 1971)
Another Turn of the Screw (*Ellery Queen's Mystery Magazine*, Dec 1969)
The Attitude of Murder (*Alfred Hitchcock's Mystery Magazine*, Oct 1969)
Back for a Funeral (*Ellery Queen's Mystery Magazine*, Oct 1978)
Beyond the Wall (*Alfred Hitchcock's Mystery Magazine*, June 1968)
Carnival Day (*Ellery Queen's Mystery Magazine*, July 1958)
A Case of Instant Detection (*Ellery Queen's Mystery Magazine*, May 1967)
Color Me Dead (*Ellery Queen's Mystery Magazine*, mid-July 1983)
Cousin Anne (*Mystery Monthly*, Feb 1977)
Daisies Deceive (*Alfred Hitchcock's Mystery Magazine*, July 1962)
The Delicate Murderer (*Ellery Queen's Mystery Magazine*, Nov 1959)
The Disappearance of Mrs. Standwick (*Ellery Queen's Mystery Magazine*,
  July 1968)
The Do-It-Yourself Solution (*Ed McBain's 87th Precinct Mystery Magazine*,
  May 1975)
The Dower Chest (*Ellery Queen's Mystery Magazine*, Nov 1977)
Fear (*Alfred Hitchcock's Mystery Magazine*, Nov 1977)
A Friendly Murder (*Ellery Queen's Mystery Magazine*, Aug 1961)
The Gentle Miss Bluebeard (*Alfred Hitchcock's Mystery Magazine*, Nov 1959)
In the Fiction Alcove (*Ellery Queen's Mystery Magazine*, Sept 1967)
Killed by Kindness (*Alfred Hitchcock's Mystery Magazine*, July 1963)

The Lady Dared (*Love Fiction Monthly*, Feb 1943)
Last Call for Romance (*Love Fiction Monthly*, Apr 1943)
Laughter Before Dying (*Ellery Queen's Mystery Magazine*, May 1975)
Locks Won't Keep You Out (*Ellery Queen's Mystery Magazine*, Feb 1973)
The More the Deadlier (*Alfred Hitchcock's Mystery Magazine*, Oct 1978)
Mr. Smith and Myrtle (*Red Wine First*, Simon & Schuster 1947; *Ellery Queen's Mystery Magazine*, June 17 1981)
Mrs. Sloan's Predicament (*The Man from U.N.C.L.E. Magazine*, Sept 1967)
Murder at the Poe Shrine (*Ellery Queen's Mystery Magazine*, Sept 1955)
Murder Between Friends (*Alfred Hitchcock's Mystery Magazine*, Aug 1963)
The Murder Game (*Ellery Queen's Mystery Magazine*, Feb 1970)
A Murder Is Arranged (*Alfred Hitchcock's Mystery Magazine*, Mar 1975)
A Neighborly Murder (*Mike Shayne Mystery Magazine*, Mar 1964)
A Nice Place to Stay (*Ellery Queen's Mystery Magazine*, June 1970)
The Night Runner (*Ellery Queen's Mystery Magazine*, Dec 1979)
On Little Cat Feet (*Ellery Queen's Mystery Magazine*, Feb 1976)
The Perfect Jewel (*Ellery Queen's Mystery Magazine*, June 1979)
Priority on Romance (*Love Fiction Monthly*, Mar 1943)
Recipe for a Happy Marriage (*Ellery Queen's Mystery Magazine*, Mar 1971)
Reflections on Murder (*Sleuth Mystery Magazine*, Dec 1958)
The Same as Murder (*Ellery Queen's Mystery Magazine*, Aug 18 1980)
The Stranger Who Came Knocking (*Ellery Queen's Mystery Magazine*, June 1972)
The Teddy Bear Crimes: One (*Ellery Queen's Anthology* #57, 1987)
The Teddy Bear Crimes: Two (*Ellery Queen's Anthology* #57, 1987)
They Shouldn't Uv Hung Willie (*Red Wine First*, Simon & Schuster 1947; *Ellery Queen's Mystery Magazine*, Jan 1 1982)
Tour de Couleur (*Ellery Queen's Mystery Magazine*, Aug 1956)
Typed for Murder (*The Diners Club Magazine*, 1966; *Alfred Hitchcock's Mystery Magazine*, Nov 1979)
The Web (*Mystery Monthly*, Oct 1976)
Wedding Anniversary Story (*Ladies Home Journal*, Oct 1947)
You Can't Trust Anyone (*Ellery Queen's Mystery Magazine*, June 1973)